By J.L. O'FAOLAIN

Published by DREAMSPINNER PRESS
http://www.dreamspinnerpress.com

SCRATCH & SNIFF

SNIFF

J.L. O'Faolain

Dreamspinner Press

Published by
Dreamspinner Press
5032 Capital Circle SW
Ste 2, PMB# 279
Tallahassee, FL 32305-7886
USA
http://www.dreamspinnerpress.com/

Cover Art by Shobana Appavu
bob@bob-artist.com

ISBN: 978-1-62380-295-0
Digital ISBN: 978-1-62380-296-7

Printed in the United States of America
First Edition
January 2013

To the two who brought me this far.

And to the one waiting for me further down.

PROLOGUE

THE arcade out on Route 9 was a place Wrath had never visited. Even before he'd arrived for the meeting with Sloth, he'd known it was the sort of place his mother would not have approved of.

The building was covered in aluminum siding and looked derelict. One solid gust of wind should have brought the place crashing down, yet it stood in defiance all the same. There were no other buildings or houses anywhere nearby. The place stood isolated from the rest of the community, which was all he needed to know. It was no accident this place was kept so far away. People wanted to pretend it didn't exist, at least during daylight hours.

Now, after dark, there were cars parked around it. A set of ancient gas pumps stood before the front doors. Despite being advertised as an arcade, this place was apparently also a service station. Through the double doors, a counter barred any further entry. Beyond it lay an open area lit by hanging lights that flickered constantly. Several pool tables crowded the center. Over by one wall lay a string of pinball machines. An air hockey table had been crammed in a far corner near a lit jukebox. Several other game machines that looked like something out of an eighties film were spaced along another wall unevenly.

The crowd looked rough, at least by the area's standards. Wrath surveyed the room for a moment as the man behind the counter watched him closely. His mustache twitched slightly as Wrath strode around him, but other than that, he gave no indication of wanting to stop him.

Several people eyed Wrath as he walked over to a Pac-Man game. None of them were Sloth, though. In fact, Sloth was nowhere to be seen, though that didn't worry him much. The man would show up eventually or not at all. In the meantime, though, Wrath could at least enjoy himself. He'd arrived early to case the place and to find out what he was getting himself into. Now, as the game kicked into play, he wondered if this wasn't a poor waste of a night's sleep.

Wrath kept his back to the room. No one made a move toward him. He could feel them staring, but the room as a whole gradually relaxed to his presence. As Wrath wiggled the malfunctioning joystick in frustration, he managed to lose his first game. While the machine announced his failure for the whole room to hear, he spotted movement out the corner of his eye and turned just in time to catch a glimpse of a figure disappearing through a door next to the jukebox.

"Hey," someone called out.

Wrath looked toward the pool tables. "You play?" a young man with ginger hair and freckles asked, pointing to the table next to him.

Wrath considered for a moment, then nodded. "A little," he said, walking over as the fellow dropped four quarters into the slot to release the balls.

"Name's Tony," the kid said as he began racking the balls up.

"Who asked you?" Wrath replied, picking up a stick and testing the weight of it.

Wrath placed the cue ball near the end of the table, took aim, and waited as Tony raised the rack. Once he was clear, Wrath took his shot and made the break.

"Nice," Tony noted as two solids sunk into opposite pockets. "Stripes go to me, I guess."

Wrath ignored him and continued, sinking two more balls before missing the third. "You're not much of a talker," said Tony, missing the corner pocket by a good foot. "What brings you here?"

"Meeting someone," Wrath said. "So far, they haven't shown up."

Tony watched Wrath out the corner of his eye as he broke for the corner, sinking another ball. "Man or woman?" he pressed.

Wrath said nothing and kept playing.

"If it was a guy, they may have gone to the back," Tony told him. "Did you check there yet?"

Wrath's eyes drifted toward the door. "What's back there?" he asked, taking aim again.

Nervousness radiated from the young man now. "Want me to show you?"

Wrath glanced his way, then went back to playing. As soon as he was done putting the eight ball in the side pocket, he set the cue stick down. "Let's go, then."

Tony smiled, perhaps a bit too eagerly. "Okay."

The area behind the door was dark. It took a second for Wrath's eyes to adjust. Before he could see anything, his other senses were already kicking in. The first thing that came to him was the distinct stench of urine. It smelled as though someone had taken a piss somewhere nearby, and recently. Even more overpowering than that, however, was the electric charge that hummed through the air. Wrath could hear the deep grunts, but it was the feeling of sex and heat sliding over his skin that clued him in to what sort of place this was.

Tony was standing behind him, eagerness rippling out of his small frame in waves. "Where do you want to go first?" he asked. "They have private rooms...."

Wrath sincerely doubted he would find Sloth there. Assuming, of course, this wasn't all some sort of a trap. Wrath couldn't imagine Sloth being caught dead in a place like this, not unless the servers on the opposite side of the carved holes he could faintly make out now were female.

"There's also a film room," Tony added, pointing off to the side. "If you want to check in there."

Wrath looked in the direction Tony was pointing and saw another door with the words "Film Area" marked on a piece of paper that had been taped to the panel of plywood. Eyes narrowed, he marched over and cracked the door.

There, sitting about halfway down a row of metal chairs, was Sloth. The albino African American was lounging in his seat in a position that looked uncomfortable, his eyes turned lazily up to the screen as a gay porno played.

"Is that him?" Tony asked, peeking around Wrath's frame as best he could.

"Get out of here," Wrath told Tony as he began closing the door behind him. "You don't want to be here right now." Wrath caught the hurt look on Tony's face. "Please," he whispered. "Just go. It'll be better for you if you leave."

Fear flickered in the young man's eyes in the second before Wrath shut the door the rest of the way. Turning around, the pyrokinetic walked down the right side of the room until he came to Sloth's row. Sloth still had his eyes fixed to the screen. Wrath eyed the film for a moment as a man who looked to be about Tony's age braced himself for the impact of having two cocks shoved up his ass.

"I can't believe you watch this shit," Sloth said casually.

"I don't," Wrath corrected, not looking over at the man. "I've been in jail for the past ten years. Haven't had much time to brush up on my classic films. Do you know the guy that's in this one or something?"

Sloth shot him a glare, then motioned for Wrath to take a seat. Wrath hesitated barely a second before edging down the narrow gap separating the rows of chairs. Coming to where Sloth sat, Wrath lowered himself, keeping a space of two chairs between them for good measure.

"I thought you might be more comfortable here," the albino explained once Wrath was settled. Sloth began to shift anxiously in his seat and adjusted himself while watching a hole on the wall as a pair of fingers brushed the lower half of the opening invitingly.

"Why would I be comfortable here?" Wrath looked away from the screen to watch as Sloth ran his tongue along his lower lip. "What's this about?"

Sloth didn't answer him right away. "You really had it coming in the woods earlier," he said with a thread of warning in his voice. "Lucky for you, I had other priorities."

Wrath wasn't about to play this pissing game with Sloth. He'd arrived expecting Sloth to be pissed about the beating Wrath had handed him in the woods yesterday morning. With the strange vibe he kept getting, Wrath almost thought Sloth was indifferent to their fight, which was completely out of character for the man.

Wrath still had trouble accepting it all. Less than twenty-four hours ago, he and his so-called teammates had uncovered something beyond belief. A puddle-jumper plane had crashed on the unsuspecting town of Shove Point, Arkansas, brought down by what they all assumed was a spacecraft. The relatively small ship had crash-landed in a lake out in the woods beyond town. Sloth had discovered it first, though, which had led to him and Wrath coming to blows.

Then the ship had exploded, ejecting some sort of pod into the air before reducing itself to shrapnel. Sloth had gotten away during the confusion, and now acted as if this were a regular day for them both.

The casual way he spoke was getting under Wrath's skin, even though he knew better than to let the man rile him.

"I think it's past time I left," Wrath said, getting up.

Sloth watched as Wrath headed for the door. "The fuck is with you?" he demanded. "Sit back down."

Wrath paused. "I don't take orders from you anymore, Sloth," he said, gripping the metal knob. "Don't give them out like you expect me to. You're just setting yourself up for a big disappointment."

The muscled man laughed. "You've grown some brass ones since we were working down in N'awlins. I expected jail time to make you soft, but you've toughened up nicely there."

Sloth gave Wrath an earnest smile, and the sight was enough to turn the pyrokinetic's stomach. "Sit back down," Sloth said, gesturing to the chair beside his. "We've got stuff to talk about. I really did think you might be more comfortable here, and there's almost no chance of somebody overhearing us. They're too busy turning each other crooked to care."

Wrath hesitated again, not moving away from the door. Someone tried to turn the knob, and, thinking it was Tony, he opened it. Two men in caps and overalls looked at Wrath, wearing irate expressions. Wrath flashed a handful of fire in their faces, running them off.

Sloth found this hilarious. "Nice one."

Two more figures were standing farther back in the shadows. Wrath shook his head at them before letting the door close. Furious now, he stomped back and took the seat next to Sloth.

"What do you want?" he insisted. "I know you well enough not to think you brought me all the way out here so we could bond over cheap porn."

Sloth's wide shoulders shook with laughter. "Don't you want to watch the rest of the movie before we talk business?"

Wrath started to get up again. "Fine," Sloth said, giving a long sigh. "If you really want to know, I've been working on a big project for a while. Until recently, a lot of the details hadn't been hammered out yet. That was why I sent you the message, telling you to stick it out in prison for the time being."

The words left a sinking feeling in the pit of Wrath's stomach. "Pride sent me that message," he cut back with adamantly.

"No, that was me," Sloth replied. "I had to make sure you didn't do anything dumber than getting your ass caught by a hick cop."

Sloth spoke like this was a personal insult against him.

"Where is Pride?" Wrath asked after a moment. "Do you know what happened to her?"

"Why?" Sloth cocked an eyebrow. "You still care for the cunt?"

Wrath raised his hand, alight with flames again, threateningly.

Sloth went rigid at first but then rolled his eyes toward the ceiling.

"Chill, kid," he said, using a less abrasive tone. "I didn't come here to wrestle. We've got to get our shit together if we want to find that pod."

Wrath lowered his hand slightly at this. "You mean the pod that ejected from the ship?" he wondered. "Why would you be looking for it?"

"My employers want it back," Sloth said before correcting himself. "Our employers, I should say. Something brought that ship down, and the jet along with it. This whole mess has been one huge clusterfuck from the start. I'd have packed my ass up and left a long time ago, but if what they're telling me holds up, we could all be back in business real quick."

Wrath let his eyes wander up to the screen as the next scene played. "What was in that ship?" he asked calmly.

"They wouldn't tell me," Sloth replied, watching him more closely now.

"That isn't what I asked," he countered. "I know you better than to think you'd take a job that vague. You know what landed in those woods."

"Yes," Sloth said unabashedly. "That doesn't mean you're going to find out anytime soon, though. I want some guarantees you haven't gone soft on me before I let you in on all the little details."

Sloth abruptly turned to the nearby hole, where a different pair of hands was rubbing the bottom half now.

"Do you want to try it?" he asked.

Wrath looked at him, then noticed where he was pointing. "Pass."

"Suit yourself."

To Wrath's great shock, Sloth stood up and calmly walked over to the hole, undoing his fly as he went. It might have been coincidence, but Sloth appeared to turn at an angle before eight or so inches of his thick, flaccid cock entered the hole, giving Wrath a clear view.

Sloth gave a loud grunt as the man on the other side began sucking. "It's like this," he said in a strained voice as his hips bucked back and forth. "Big things are coming, and I need to know who is going to be on the winning team. Those two shmucks you've been stuck with could've been killed. I don't know where your head is right now, but you need to get in the game before somebody takes you out permanently."

Sloth rocked his hips back and forth faster now. "So," he breathed out, giving Wrath a hard look. "You in or not?"

CHAPTER
ONE

"ARE we clear?"

Scratch stuck his head up and gave a quick look around. "Clear," he said. "Wait, there's a security camera up at the corner."

Push went perfectly still. "You're kidding, right?" he asked, anxious to get out from under the burlap covering them. "This place has a security cam?"

"Um, one sec," said Scratch, picking a small rock out of one of the metal grooves of the Pussy Wagon's bed. "I've got this."

It was getting harder to breathe underneath the burlap blanket as Push watched Scratch lift the side so he could take aim with the rock. Scratch gave the stone a hard flick with his thumb, sending it flying through the air off the lower fender of a car, the edge of a trash bin leaning heavily against the building's side, and finally upward toward the camera. The rock struck the camera's side, knocking it away from them.

"Done," Scratch told him. "And I don't see anyone else."

Push practically jumped out of the back of the truck. "I cannot believe he talked us into doing that," the telekinetic gasped. "I'll be tasting dirty burlap in my mouth for a week."

"It can't be any worse than the taste of cock," Scratch replied.

Push froze, his eyes wide enough to be saucers. "Dude," Scratch gently reassured when he saw the look on Push's face. "I was only kidding. Let's get inside before you have a heart attack."

Push had to order his feet to move a couple of times before they complied. The Route Nine Arcade, as a dimly glowing sign by the road named it, was covered in aluminum siding and looked ready to fall over. Cars were scattered haphazardly across the parking lot in what could hardly be considered a pattern. Only the front of the building was adequately lit. The duo made tracks for it, Push catching up to his partner before they reached the doors.

"You okay?" Scratch asked hesitantly.

"Yeah," replied Push stiffly. "Let's just go inside and get this over with."

A man was watching them from behind the counter directly in front of the door as they entered. Push spotted a wisp of long dark hair disappearing through a door on the other side of the room. Apparently, the meeting place with Sloth was in the back part of the building somewhere. As the front door swung shut on its own, Push wondered how much trouble they would have to cause to get back there.

However, Scratch beat him to it. "What's back there?" he asked the man at the counter, pointing to the door Wrath had gone through.

The man didn't bother turning around. "Not much," he said, giving Scratch an amused look. "Just a place for the locals to blow off steam."

"Is it a problem if we check it out?"

Discreetly, Scratch slid a fifty across the counter toward the guy, who eyed it a moment before palming it.

"Help yourselves," the man said, pocketing his prize.

"Thanks." Scratch gave the man a small nod as he and Push passed around the counter together. "Much appreciated."

"You're starting to go native," Push warned. "Next you'll be asking the Association accountants if there's room in the budget for a tractor."

Scratch snorted and rolled his eyes. "Let's see what our boy's gotten himself into."

Push did not have a good feeling about the place. The patrons were obviously locals, and each one of them watched him and Scratch like hawks as they crossed the room, dodging the obstacle course of pool tables.

"I'm surprised you don't want to play," Push noted.

"Later," Scratch said. "Something tells me these guys wouldn't react well to having an out-of-towner take all their cash."

Push caught the look of one rather large man in flannel watching them. "You're probably right," he said softly as they reached the door.

It was supposed to be a simple plan. Wrath had wanted to go first and meet with Sloth for a few minutes before they busted the former crime boss. Scratch and Push had opposed this at first, until Wrath pointed something out.

"I watched Sloth for years," he had told them as they sat together around the poker table. "I know how he thinks. It's one reason why we're all stuck here for now. The Association believes I'm the guy who knows him well enough to help you two bring him in."

Push and Scratch had shared a look while Wrath continued. "This isn't like Sloth," he'd insisted. "Sloth is careful. He plans things weeks, maybe months in advance. He doesn't get his hands dirty. He'll go out of his way to avoid doing the grunt work."

"Maybe he doesn't have a choice," Push offered. "If he doesn't have anyone else working for him, there's not many options left."

"He's still better than this," Wrath pressed. "This is some kind of setup. Whether it's me he's planning to set up or the two of you, I haven't quite figured out. Sloth will have some sort of plan when I meet with him. Make no mistake about that."

"Okay," Scratch had said. "So, um, what are you suggesting?"

In the end, they'd agreed. The plan was to wait and let Wrath conduct business with Sloth, then follow him back to his hideout. As Wrath had said, a place like the arcade was probably not the best location for super-powered battle anyway. They could find out where the man was located and maybe even get a little information out of him before moving in. All in all, it wasn't a terrible idea, except that Push was convinced something would go wrong.

The idea of leaving Wrath alone with a man like Sloth worried him, and not out of concern for Wrath's personal safety.

The door opened up into a cramped area that smelled like piss. One look around, and Push was certain he knew what sort of establishment the arcade served as a cover for.

"Maybe you ought to wait outside," he said nervously to Scratch.

"Um, what for?" Scratch gave him an odd look as a red-headed young man with freckles walked past them, looking slightly put out. "Since when do you get the itch to fly solo?"

Scratch took a quick glance around. The space was visible, thanks to the dim light coming from the actual arcade area behind them. His eyes landed on several holes in the wall across from them.

"You think I can't handle something like this?" he asked, giving Push a wry look.

Push wasn't sure what to say in answer. "Let's find Wrath," Scratch suggested. "We can talk after we're finished here."

It was a good thing they'd come in their civvies. Spandex would have made them stick out like sore thumbs. That, or be mistaken for employees.

Scratch walked over to a set of doors on their left. The first one was closed but not locked. Scratch took a quick look inside, moving back as the sounds of deep groaning spilled out into the hallway.

"Sorry," he apologized in a calm, amused voice. "Wrong room."

The second room, it turned out, was empty. The door to it had been left cracked open, so Scratch peeked through it as he moved past. Number three was locked, but whoever was on the other side clearly had no qualms about letting the world know what was going on inside. Scratch boldly knocked, cutting someone off in midgrunt. A minute or so later, the door opened, and two men emerged, looking irritated.

"Sorry," Scratch apologized, like he'd just interrupted their tea time. "Have you seen a guy with long black hair and creepy-looking eyes?"

The men looked at each other. "This ain't a hotel, son," one said in a thick accent.

"My bad," said Scratch, backing up.

"It's cool, kid," replied the other, moving out of the doorway. "We were about wrapped up anyway. Feel free to help yourself."

The two lovebirds left the door open and gave Push a friendly nod as they passed him in the narrow corridor. Looking back over his shoulder, Push saw them heading for a room marked "Film Area" by a sheet of paper taped to the door. The bigger of the two men fumbled with the door for a moment, shaking it like it was stuck. After a moment more of frustration, he managed to get it open. Standing in their way was Wrath, who glared at the two for a moment before flashing a handful of flames in their faces.

Push and Scratch watched the scene from further back. Wrath saw them as he closed the door, however, and shook his head discreetly.

"Well, now we know where they are," Push muttered.

"Right," Scratch said. "So, um, how do you want to play this? Wrath wanted some time alone to talk to Sloth, and we agreed not to fight here, anyway."

"I know." Admittedly, the narrow hall wasn't exactly ideal for moving around. "Maybe there's another way in," he suggested, unsure of what else to do. "Or a room that's connected to that one."

Push didn't say out loud he was thinking of more glory holes. Despite what had happened between them earlier, he was convinced Scratch was only holding his panic in. He didn't understand how his partner could be so calm in such a setting. Places like this made Push nervous. That, and the smell got worse the farther along they moved.

"This place feels almost like a maze," Scratch noted as they worked their way around.

"People come here for the anonymity," Push explained. "You can move in and out without running the risk of seeing someone you know. The whole idea is to hook up without ruining your reputation."

"Ah," was all Scratch said.

The corridor they were in split off in several directions, one after the other. Push led them in a C-shape back toward the film room, hoping they would end up in a place near it. All around them, sounds were coming from the rooms they passed. The more he overheard, the higher his anxiety grew. Scratch, on the other hand, simply tuned everything out and kept going.

Something caught Push's eye as they came near a sharp turn. A curtain hung up against the wall had been left open slightly, enough that Push got a glimpse of what was behind it. A second corridor split off from the first and branched down about twenty feet or so before dead-ending. Two young men were crouched down, sucking on an enormous fat cock that barely made it through the glory hole. One of the boys was licking away at it like he'd just been given the world's biggest ice cream cone.

More sounds, much louder than the others, wavered through the remaining holes dotted along the wall, and Push thought he recognized Wrath's voice coming from one.

"This is it," Push said, hesitating outside the entrance.

"Um, if that's Wrath," Scratch commented, "I'm going to feel really inadequate the next time we're in a room together."

Push rolled his eyes. "Like you have anything to be ashamed of."

That got him a smile. "Thanks," Scratch said. "Now's not really the time, but just so you know, neither do you."

Push felt a blush creep up his neck. This was most definitely not the right time or place for that. "Let's move in for a closer look," he said. "If you don't mind."

"When do I ever?"

Push saw neither of the guys near the end of the small hallway was paying them any attention. The two young men appeared to be focused solely on the task at hand.

"I'm almost done," a gruff voice said, muffled by the wall. "Sure you don't want your turn? He's not bad."

"What are you trying to accomplish?" Push heard Wrath demand over the porn flick playing in the background. "If this was some kind of plan to try and bond with me, I'm afraid you got the wrong idea."

Sloth snorted. "Don't play games," he told Wrath between grunts. "You've been into this sort of stuff since before the gang got started. Everybody knew about it, even Pride."

Wrath was silent for a moment. "I was the one who told Pride," he informed Sloth. "You, however, made your disdain loud and clear from the start."

"I had to," Sloth said before letting out a long, low groan. His load exploded from the head of his shaft, splattering over the face of the young man down from where Push and Scratch were crouched.

"It was N'awlins," he went on. "Nobody gets very far in our line of work unless they fuck straight and true."

"So, what?" It sounded as though Wrath didn't believe a word of it. "You're saying you were really more 'flexible' this whole time?"

Sloth was still cumming. "A cunt's a cunt," he said flippantly as the last few spurts of his load dribbled down onto the floor. "And I like gettin' my dick sucked. So what if the mouth on the other end of the wall has a pair. It's not like they're using 'em, and I'm not returning the favor, so what does it matter."

Through one of the glory holes, Push thought he saw Wrath shake his head. "You're not winning me over with this conversation," he said.

"I'm done, anyway," Sloth said calmly, pulling himself back out. "Let's get the fuck out of here, unless you've changed your mind."

Wrath looked toward the hole where Push was watching. "Go on," Sloth insisted. "Just stick your damn junk in and let the bitch do the work. Fuck, you've been in the can for the past ten years. Some good head from somebody other than the prison bitch would help you lose all that tension."

Push's eyes went wide as Wrath walked over to the hole, undoing the fly on his black jeans as he came closer.

"No fucking way in hell," Push whispered.

A hard tap on his shoulder made him turn around. The other young man, this one not wearing Sloth's load all over him, motioned for him to move as Wrath's cock slid through.

Push backed away without a word, letting the fellow go to work. Turning around, he saw the other one moving in closer to Scratch, who was very gently keeping him at bay.

"Um, thanks," Scratch whispered, his voice barely audible in the cramped space. "But I'm spoken for. Sorry."

Something fluttered in Push's chest. Motioning for Scratch to follow, he got up and moved toward the curtain as quietly as possible. Once they were back in the main hallway and a safe distance from being overheard, Push turned to face him.

"That was interesting," Scratch noted, unperturbed.

Whatever Push had been about to say left his mind as his train of thought derailed. "Sorry," he said, looking away awkwardly. "I didn't think that other guy was going to make a pass at you."

Scratch frowned a little. "No big deal," he said. "It's not like this was the first time I've been hit on by another dude."

Push opened his mouth. To say what exactly, he had no idea. Whatever had been about to come out of him was cut short by a guttural yell, followed almost immediately by the sound of something heavy impacting the wall of the film room. Both he and Scratch jerked their heads toward it at the same time.

Through the artificial moans of the film and the more realistic, throaty ones coming from the rooms all around, they heard Sloth laughing.

Wrath's voice followed, along with the sound of flames igniting. "Shit!" Push swore. "He'll burn the whole place down."

Scratch was already gone. "Move your ass!" he yelled at Push, racing down the hall the way they'd come.

The trip through the maze didn't take long, maybe thirty seconds at most. The thought of the whole building going up in flames helped motivate Push's feet, and he was up against Scratch's back by the time they reached the entrance corridor where the door to the film room was located. The fight between Wrath and Sloth had already spilled out there. Several heads peeked out from behind the room doors, lured by the sounds of violence, and ducked out of the way as Wrath unleashed a wave of flame at Sloth, blowing him out into the arcade area.

The fires swirled around the man, eagerly reaching for the plywood walls that formed the back room. As Wrath drew in a deep breath, the flames were dragged away from the fuel source into Wrath's waiting hands.

Push couldn't help but be impressed by the sight.

Crouching down, Wrath brought his open palms up and fired a slew of what Push could only describe as flaming rockets through the door into the main arcade area. Coming up behind him, Push and Scratch heard people shouting, saw them throwing whole tables to the ground to make a shield for themselves. Billiard balls scattered noisily across the floor as Push and Scratch stood by Wrath's side. As several straggling onlookers backed out of the way, Push hoped they didn't need to restrain the man.

Sloth was taking the heat but hadn't fallen. "I've waited years for this, Sloth," Wrath said. "Ordinarily, it would be satisfying enough to just burn you up, but as somebody pointed out to me, watching you rot away in a prison cell has a certain appeal."

"You never were tough enough to tangle man-on-man with the big boys," Sloth roared. "You always had to fall back on those second-rate parlor tricks."

"Maybe," Wrath admitted, unperturbed. "But I'm not the one running scared at the moment."

A ball of flame glowed in his left hand. "Let's see how those muscles of yours stand up to about three hundred degrees Fahrenheit."

Sloth didn't look enthused.

"If it doesn't burn your balls off," Wrath continued. "The whole room will at least know you had some."

Sloth's eyes darted behind him to where Push and Scratch were waiting.

"Don't mind them," Wrath assured him. "They're only here to make sure I don't kill you."

Push frowned, though that was true. "And to give you a hand," he added for good measure. "Though it looks like you have things wrapped up here."

The unmistakable sound of a gun being cocked rang out through the otherwise silent room. Push's head turned automatically toward the noise, and he saw the man behind the counter holding up a shotgun, with the barrel pointed directly toward Wrath's head.

Scratch was already on it. A rack lay against the wall, loaded with extra cue sticks. Scratch had one in his hand before Push could blink. One of the billiard balls had rolled near their feet, and with a quick stab to the floor, Scratch sent it flying. Push didn't think Scratch had taken more than a glance at the layout before making his shot, yet the ball bounced perfectly off a hanging light, the edge of an overturned table, another light, one of the old arcade games, and off the counter tender's head before slamming home against the barrel of the shotgun.

The gun fired, though horribly off-course, taking out a Galaga machine straight through the screen.

Sloth decided to capitalize on the confusion. Push saw him move before Wrath did. Wrath was still eying the wrecked game with disdain. Knowing it wouldn't stop Sloth, Push leaped sideways and thrust his palm out, sending a shock wave into the charging bull as hard as he could. The angle didn't help things, but the impact knocked Sloth back all the same, and that was all it took for Wrath to gain the upper hand.

Raising his arms, the pyrokinetic let loose a massive wave of fire that engulfed Sloth, blasting him backward through the air onto a table that caved under the man's weight. Keeping one hand raised, Wrath snapped his fingers, extinguishing the fire that had covered Sloth from head to toe.

"So tempting," he muttered, before looking toward the sparking arcade game. "And a waste of a perfectly good classic, to boot."

The extinguished flames left black marks all over Sloth's clothes. Patches where red-tinted pale flesh shined against what light there was. Smoke curled up off the burned fabric, but Sloth got to his feet anyway.

"Still want to do this?" Wrath asked him, staring the man down. "Because I can go all night, as one of your little girlfriends on the side could attest to back in the day."

Hate seeped out from Sloth's eyes, but he quickly looked away to assess the situation.

Wrath conjured flames to one hand again as Sloth pulled something from the back of his jeans. Both Scratch and Push frowned as Sloth held it up to the light, revealing a plastic bag full of what looked to be about a hundred grams of cocaine.

Sloth tossed it to the table. "Party's on me," he announced to the room's occupants, who, despite having taken cover, hadn't cleared out yet. "The prize goes to whoever takes these faggots out first."

Hesitation gripped the spectators for a moment as their eyes wandered from the bag of coke to where Wrath stood with Push and Scratch at his sides. Rolling his eyes, Sloth reached in and yanked out something else.

"And a thousand damn bucks," he added, throwing that down next to the bag. "Bunch of damn pussies."

The money was, apparently, enough to tip the scales. The shotgun wielder took aim first, forcing Push to blast him back. The gun went off a second time, blowing a hole straight through a nearby wall. The sound seemed to encourage everyone in attendance, and they all rushed at Push, Scratch, and Wrath like angry dogs.

"Give me a break," Wrath mumbled.

"No killing," Push reminded, whipping out the telescopic bo he'd brought with him. "Feel free to hurt them, though."

"I know I plan to," Scratch said, as the first wave struck.

Wrath strode forward as Push and Scratch stood with their backs pressed together. The horde closed in quickly, but then held back as one or two of the smaller ones swiped at them. They'd seen this sort of thing before.

The big dogs were sending the little ones to test the waters.

Push blasted one back into a wall. The redneck left behind a cracked impression of his body shape as he fell to the floor.

"Next?" he asked calmly.

Rather than deterring anyone, the shit hit the fan. Push and Scratch separated as the mob rushed at them, kicking and attacking with everything they had. Out the corner of his eye, Push caught Wrath striding over to the table where Sloth had left his prize. Someone had taken the smart route and waited for a clear shot at it. As the blond reached his hand out to snatch it up, Wrath let out a blast of fire, igniting both the drugs and the cash in one shot, leaving the culprit with singed fingers.

A handful of the hay-balers saw this and charged the pyrokinetic with arms swinging. There was too much going on for Push to stand around and watch. The distraction left him wide open, and he took two punches to the head. Angry now, Push let his fury boil up inside of him, unleashing it in a wide shot that gave him enough space to spin the bo around a couple of times, before tripping up the ones crowding Scratch.

"Where the fuck did Wrath go?" Scratch demanded as they came together back to back.

"Gone after Sloth," Push answered, catching one man up the side of the head with his bo.

"Oh," replied Scratch, sending a gas bomb out to clear a path for them. "Let's go, then. This is a waste of time."

"I agree."

Push took a deep breath and shut his eyes, holding on to Scratch's coat with one hand as they raced through the poisonous fog. The mob gasped in pain and clutched at their eyes as the pepper-laced knockout gas filled their side of the arcade.

Once they'd cleared the gas's range, Push let go of Scratch's coat and ran for the door, breathing hard as they passed through it together. Wrath was nowhere to be seen.

"There!" Scratch called out, pointing with the cue stick at the edge of the gravel-strewn parking lot.

The whole area where Wrath stood was aflame. Wrath was watching Sloth flip him the bird as he rode off across a field on an ATV.

"Wrath!" Push cried out, getting the pyrokinetic's attention. "Get in!"

Push pointed to the truck as he and Scratch ran for it. Wrath was climbing into the truck bed as Push turned the ignition.

"He's heading across Folsom's acres," Wrath said, after beating on the truck's rear window to get him to lower it. "There used to be this old dirt road that cut across it a little ways down."

Push nodded. "Hold on as best you can," he warned. "I'm gunning this thing!"

Despite the warning, Wrath was almost thrown forward as Push spun the wheels, kicking dirt and gravel up into the air as the truck turned backward into a curve before shifting gears and racing out of the lot. Push steered the Pussy Wagon down the road Wrath indicated, who was almost too busy holding on for dear life to look for the turn. When he spotted it, Push jerked the wheel hard and sent Wrath tumbling sideways.

The bumpy dirt road did not help things.

"Are you trying to kill me?" Wrath shouted through the window after getting to his feet.

"I said, hold on," Push reminded, keeping both hands firmly on the wheel.

Sloth's ATV was up ahead of them, cutting across the expanse of dry field and leaving behind a dust storm in its wake. Following him was all too easy. Keeping up in the truck without coughing themselves to death was another matter.

"Bring him down!" Push ordered Wrath.

Wrath placed himself behind the set of cat ears fixed to the truck's roof and took aim. With a sweep of his hand, he sent several fireballs out in an arc through the air. The bombs landed on either side of the ATV, kicking up a flume of fire each time. Sloth's ATV wavered slightly but didn't slow down.

"Again," Push ordered, even though he wasn't sure Wrath could hear him.

Another wave of fireballs sailed out in front of the truck, coming closer to Sloth this time. "He's not slowing down," Scratch warned. "And we can't keep up on this bumpy terrain inside the truck."

"Dammit," Push snarled. "I thought these things were supposed to handle all sorts of bad road."

"Commercials always lie," his partner replied.

Wrath continued to open up, but each shot fell short of its mark. The movement of the truck kept throwing his aim off. Push rolled his window down to take a shot, but missed seeing what must have been the world's biggest gopher hole. The telekinetic blast not only went wild, kicking up dirt near the Pussy Wagon's front wheel, but also caused Wrath to almost set himself on fire.

"Watch the damn holes!" he barked from the back.

"Sorry."

Sloth was losing them. Up ahead, a stretch of what looked like barbwire fencing blocked their path. Push smiled, knowing there was nowhere for Sloth to go now, even on that ATV of his. Sloth, however, did not slow down as he approached the fence. Push began to see why as the ATV revved straight up a sharp incline.

"Is he crazy?"

"Most likely," Scratch replied. "And going to get away."

Sloth's ATV bucked high into the air, a feat Push would have thought impossible considering the man's weight. The ATV came crashing down on the other side of the fence, missing the barbwire by inches, then roared off into the night.

Push hit the brakes and bashed his fist against the steering wheel. Wrath's frustration echoed off the top of the truck.

"Don't worry," Scratch assured him, keeping his eyes fixed on where Sloth's ATV had disappeared over a large hill. "We'll get him. He can't run forever."

CHAPTER
TWO

THE drive to the house was not a pleasant one. Try though he might, Push couldn't seem to avoid hitting every single bump and dip in the field as he worked the Pussy Wagon to the small path. Their mood did not improve upon reaching the main road. Push had stopped to let Wrath climb in the backseat after one of the bumps almost threw him out of the truck bed. Now, the pyrokinetic sat fuming quietly to himself. He was taking Sloth's escape harder than either of them.

Then again, it wasn't as though Push or Scratch felt happy about it.

"Tell us what he said to you," Push asked, after turning onto the main road. "I'd like to know what all of this was about, at least."

Wrath looked up at the gap between Push and Scratch. "He asked if I was with him or not."

Scratch's mouth turned up awkwardly as he glanced over at Push. "Are you?" he asked, looking back to where Wrath sat.

"Sure," Wrath replied sardonically. "I'm just dying to hitch my wagon to that guy's star all over again. It probably has something to do with why I just spent the last half hour getting thrown around in the back of a truck bed like a stoned hamster in a washing machine."

Push snorted. "That makes for an interesting mental picture," he noted.

"He kept hinting at having something really big in the works," Wrath went on. "And that the Deadly Seven might be coming back."

"Shit," Scratch hissed. "That's all we needed."

Push silently concurred as they drove out onto the main road.

"He wouldn't say what was in that pod," Wrath added after a moment. "Or who hired him to retrieve it. I didn't expect him to, honestly, but it still bothers me he was being so tight-lipped."

"Why?" Push asked when Wrath paused.

"Because Sloth used to love to brag," Wrath replied. "Tonight, he was different. I could sense a great change in him. He was, overall, the same guy, but something big has happened. He wasn't the same asshole I worked with ten years ago."

"And that's a problem?"

Wrath looked at Push via the rearview mirror. "Yes," he said. "Because predicting what Sloth will do next won't be easy now."

Scratch turned in his seat to look at Wrath. "Um, quick change of topic, but which of you was it getting the blowjob in that room?" he asked.

"Sloth," Wrath answered unabashedly, though his face twisted slightly in bemusement at the question. "He invited me to join. That's something that never would have happened before."

"What?" Scratch asked. "Getting a blowjob from a dude or asking you to join in?"

"Either," Wrath replied dryly.

"You said you could sense something in him," Push interrupted after giving Scratch a stern glare. "How does that work?"

Wrath looked at him again through the rearview mirror. "It just does," he said. "I've never been able to put it into words. For me, emotions have textures and tastes, just like more substantial things do for you two."

"So you really do feel the emotions of others around you?" The thread of doubt in Push's voice was evident even to himself. "Is it always like that?"

Wrath shifted on his seat. "Always," he replied darkly. "Especially with the more... unpleasant emotions people have."

Scratch saved Push from what he was about to ask next by turning around in his seat again. "You told us before that your flame powers are fueled by other people's rage," he stated, meeting Wrath's eyes this time. "How does that work?"

Wrath did not answer right away. "Imagine there are vents in your body," he explained, moving forward to sit closer to Scratch. "They breathe emotions in and out like the respiratory system takes in air. Think of the emotions of people as air, but color coded. Rage has a very black-and-red feel to it, like blood. It is everywhere, in every situation, however big or small. People are always walking around with something they're furious about because they're ultimately unsatisfied creatures."

"You're full of shit," Push declared, though not as unkindly as he'd expected.

"The fact that you said that proves I'm not," Wrath replied in a calm, knowing voice that made Push go rigid. "But whatever you think, people are unsatisfied creatures. They deny themselves things out of fear of what others will think, the possibility of rejection from their peers, or because they are simply unsure if what they want is best for them. In time, that fear and dissatisfaction turns to frustration, and from frustration to anger. From anger, the natural progression leads to hatred and, finally, rage."

Wrath leaned back again. "Everyone has something they're afraid of and are too afraid to act on, so they keep it buried inside of them. But I am an empath, and that hatred flows through my vents. From there, my power takes it and transforms that rage into fire."

"Um, you're like some sort of power convertor," Scratch summarized.

"Of a sort." Wrath nodded. "But I don't expect anyone to understand. Unless they've experienced it, this isn't something people are willing to take at face value."

"Whatever."

Push could feel Wrath staring at him at that comment. "How about your powers?" he asked as the truck ambled along. "What gives you the ability to focus force waves?"

"They're bubbles," Push corrected without thinking.

"Ah," Wrath replied, and it sounded as though he found that funny. "My mistake. What gives you the power to make bubbles, then?"

Scratch snorted. "It's probably not something you'd understand," Push countered, gripping the steering wheel. "But, I guess I just do it. I want to push something away, so it happens."

"What makes you want to?" Wrath pressed. "What makes you need to?"

Push suspected Wrath was enjoying himself. "I just," he tried, before hesitation took over. "I guess I don't think of it in the same terms as you. It's not like breathing for me. I have to consciously make it. I don't know why I think 'bubble'. That's just how it looks... how it feels."

Wrath moved forward until he was leaning slightly between the two front seats. They had gotten back to Shove Point's city limits, meaning home was not far.

"What triggered it?" Wrath asked quietly. "The first time."

Push's face went sour, but he answered regardless. "I was around seven or eight," he said. "Don't ask me when, exactly. I'd had problems learning to read from the start. The school sent me to different programs, but nothing stuck. One day, my teacher got pissed and told me I was faking it. She said I couldn't read like the other kids in class because I was lazy. I got so mad I wanted to kick her. When she turned around...."

Push went quiet for a moment. "She was walking up the aisle, and something made me raise my hand slightly. I don't remember what possessed me to do that, but I felt something go flying out of my hand. No one else seemed to notice it, but to me, it looked kind of like a clear bubble. I used to blow bubbles out on the patio when I was a kid, and this one looked about the same."

"What happened?"

Push swallowed as he steered the truck down their street. "It hit her in the back," he answered. "Right between the shoulder blades. I must have given it everything I had at that point, but it didn't do more than knock her off her feet. Everyone else thought she had tripped, but I was scared shitless."

Wrath shifted in his seat as the truck came to a stop in the driveway. "I see," he said. "That must have been scary at the time."

"Yeah," Push said, killing the engine. "It was."

Wrath waited as Scratch opened the passenger door, climbing out after him. "So what about you?" he asked, once Scratch shut the door behind him. "When did you first discover your power?"

Scratch looked at him. "I don't have one," he said, as though it were obvious.

"Scratch is just really good at pool," Push explained, stifling a yawn.

"Right," Wrath responded, giving Push a look from the opposite side of the truck. "Because ordinary people can make solid objects fly across the room in geometric patterns with a flick of the wrist."

Push watched as Wrath headed for the door. "Whatever," he said, before turning to face his partner. "I'm going to bed. We'll probably have to be up in a couple of hours."

Scratch stood there, not moving, giving Push an odd sort of look. "Um, okay then," he said quietly. "I guess we can talk later, then."

Push refused to analyze what that statement meant. Ignoring it outright, he marched across the threshold of the front door, then made tracks to the back where his bedroom, sleep, and sanctuary from the rest of the world lay. It was late enough, or early enough, depending on one's viewpoint, that Push didn't bother dressing for bed. His civvies were left in a pile on the floor. He could always shower after he woke.

Again, though, sleep eluded him. It seemed to take forever before his eyes closed and the darkness came to claim his thoughts. Several times, he could have sworn he heard footsteps in the smaller hallway beyond his bedroom door. Nothing could have made him get up to check, though.

Well, almost nothing, but Push was sure Scratch was passed out in his room on the other side of the house by now. The man could sleep like the dead most nights.

WHEN Push finally awoke, it felt like a fog had settled in over his brain. Several minutes passed before the previous night's events came back to him. Still groggy, he wiped the sleep from his eyes and kicked back the covers to expose himself. In his dazed state, he'd forgotten all about going to bed nude the night before. Apparently, during the night, he'd sweated almost a bucket, so the sheets were soaked with his moisture. He needed a shower now more than ever.

Even with this in mind, Push didn't move. For some reason, it was hard for him to collect his thoughts. Looking down, Push saw to his embarrassment that he'd woken up with an erection. His shaft was swollen to its full length, bending at the slight curve near the base so that the head stared up at him like some contrary cat waiting to be fed.

Push considered ignoring it, but the stubborn thing jerked of its own volition, as if urging him on. Finally, after a moment's hesitation where he watched his open door closely, Push cautiously snaked a hand down to his groin and gripped the head.

He should have covered up first, but the moist bed sheets discouraged the idea. Also, after sweating all night, the cool air in his room felt nice. Push found himself getting even more aroused as his damp flesh tingled with each feather-light brush of the air. As he smiled to himself, though he couldn't think clearly of what was making him so chipper, his hand began a slow, languid stroke up and down. The head was caught tightly between his thumb and forefinger, coaxing drop after drop of precum out to form a small puddle just below his navel.

Push couldn't remember the last time he'd let himself lie in bed. Each morning had been routine for so long: get up, get dressed, go on patrol. He and Scratch were usually out the door after breakfast, if not before. As his breathing quickened slightly, he shoved aside the list of things undoubtedly waiting for him in favor of the chance to enjoy himself.

Leaning back against his pillow, Push increased his pace and felt the sensations build inside his gut. His hand seemed to move all on its own now, needing no encouragement from him. The need to get out of bed soon still lurked somewhere in the back of his head, but Push herded himself forward, out of the sudden need for release more than anything.

With his free hand, he cupped his boys and gave them a swift tug, hoping to prolong things. A flood of prejizz flowed out in answer, but at the same time, the orgasm that had been building staved off. It was an old trick, one he'd learned as a kid. If he held himself back, the release in the end was much bigger.

The need to climax returned much faster than expected. Push gave his nuts another hard tug to hold off again before moving the hand up to pinch his nipples. Combined with the increased pace, this was enough to send him over the edge after just a few more minutes. This time, Push didn't hold back. Biting his lower lip, he nevertheless emitted a long, soft grunt as a torrent of cum exploded in ropes over his tight abs. Push counted a total of eight before his balls exhausted themselves. The head of his cock belched out one last glob before lying to the side, defeated and deflating.

"Wow."

Push jumped and jerked his head toward the door, expecting to find Wrath there. Instead, Scratch stood watching him with smoldering eyes while one arm leaned heavily against the doorframe. A noticeable bulge was sticking out below the man's waist, and by the look in his best friend's eyes, he knew Push had seen.

"You should have waited," Scratch told him. "I would have joined you."

Before Push could answer or move far enough away, Scratch crossed the threshold, walked over to his bed, and knelt down. With one hand, like he'd already expected Push to bolt, Scratch held him in place. Push watched with wide eyes as Scratch ran his tongue down the crevice in Push's abs. He licked greedily at the seed that had gathered there, eating it up like a cat. Push felt his breath catch as he watched in horror while his best friend, straight as the week was long, lapped up every last drop. Push tried to fight him off, ordered his arms to lift and shove Scratch back, but something had happened. His body was outright refusing to cooperate.

Push's breath quickened to the point he felt he would hyperventilate. His stomach was glistening now, not with sweat but with the saliva from Scratch's tongue. Knowing it was there got him hot all over again, despite his resistance. Push's cock was at full mast again. Scratch saw this and gripped the shaft in his fist.

"Don't!" Push cried out. "I can't... we shouldn't... Scratch, don't! I'm going to...."

Scratch bobbed his hand up and down as he gathered up the last drop. Giving Push a hooded stare, he then shifted himself to where his mouth was positioned directly above his buddy's erection. With a single lurch forward, Scratch inhaled half of Push's cock into his throat, stopping short of gagging to breathe.

Push's eyes were as big as saucers. Again, he tried to raise his arms so they could move Scratch away, but his hands had somehow gotten tangled in the sheets. That was what he said to himself before all thought vanished entirely, anyway. Scratch was using his tongue to roll Push's cock around in his mouth, and the result sent Push over the edge all over again. Unrepentant now, Push bucked his hips as another load rocketed out of his cock to paint the back of Scratch's throat white.

Push didn't have enough breath to warn the man, but just as before, Scratch gulped the load down hungrily, as though he were meant to have it. Each blast made Push raise his hips higher, urging more of his cock down his friend's throat as he emptied his balls again.

By the time his second orgasm had subsided, he had arched his ass up at least a foot off the bed.

As his strength left him, Push fell back down, his cock popping out of Scratch's mouth in the process.

"Not bad," Scratch said, licking away a drop or two around his mouth. "I was worried I wouldn't get used to the taste of it, but yours is a little bit like mine. Kinda saltier, but still has that sweet undertaste to it."

Push looked down at Scratch like he'd never seen the man before. "I've…," he stammered, rolling out of bed away from his friend. "I've got to shower."

Push didn't bother covering up as he dashed for the bathroom. It would have been pointless and taken up more time. He was at the bathroom door when Scratch called out to him, freezing him in his tracks.

"Do you want me to join you?"

To his own incredulous shock, Push felt his face burn. "I'll be out in just a minute," he mumbled, before closing the door tightly behind him.

Push jumped into the shower and turned the hot water all the way to the left. As steam filled the room, he tried to force away all the images racing through his mind. The sting of the water didn't provide nearly enough of a distraction. In defeat, Push added some cold to the mix to even out the temperature and stepped back so he could catch his breath.

He was being panicky and hated it. There was something going on, and he was running from the problem. Coldly, clinically, Push rewound his brain to yesterday morning. He recalled word for word everything Scratch had told him.

Scratch loved him.

Scratch wanted them to be lovers.

And, evidently, Scratch had no problem crossing serious boundaries Push had set up for himself in order to do that.

"He's straight," Push told himself, unwilling to believe this was typical behavior. "Scratch has been straight since the day we met. People do not magically swap orientations overnight for someone."

Push stayed under the water until it ran cold. Despite his methodical approach, remembering the events of yesterday morning with Scratch had given him yet another erection. And again, in spite of his efforts, Push thought back to what Scratch had said before.

Had his best friend been in love with him this whole time? The thought made Push snort with derisive laughter, which in turn sent water right up his nostrils. Once he was done coughing, Push turned the shower off. He had known Scratch for years, and they were roommates, for crying out loud. If Scratch had nursed any sort of deeper feelings for him, Push of all people would have known.

"Good fucking grief," he swore, staring angrily down at his unruly dick. "You weren't this enthusiastic when I was with Jeremy, and he could be a raging sex fiend."

Scratch was either going through some kind of belated experimental phase, or being around Wrath had messed up his emotions. Wrath had admitted his presence made people act irrationally sometimes, and this was about as irrational as Push thought he'd ever seen Scratch get. Ignoring his hard-on, Push dried himself off in a rush, defiantly keeping his theory in the forefront of his mind. If the latter was the case, he was going to have a few choice words with Wrath. Just thinking about it made him furious, and being angry filled him with a sense of purpose as he cautiously exited the bathroom to retrieve some clothes from his closet.

Thankfully, Scratch had vacated the place. Letting out a sigh of relief as he dressed himself, Push clutched his anger tightly to his chest like a child with a small toy. When he was ready, he checked his reflection in the mirror, careful to avoid his eyes, then headed out into the kitchen.

Scratch was standing there sipping coffee. Just the sight of him made Push feel weak in the knees. Scratch met his eyes over the top of the cup in his hands, and something in the telekinetic melted.

In that moment, he wanted to go over to where Scratch stood and put his arms around him, then never let go. The feeling was so intense it terrified Push to his core.

Thankfully, Wrath picked that exact moment to enter the room.

"You're up," he said plainly, reaching for a plate on the counter that had been wrapped up in plastic. "I saved you some breakfast. Hungry?"

Push wasn't exactly, but he accepted it regardless, forgetting for the moment he'd been ready to murder Wrath with his bare hands for attempting to screw with Scratch's mind. Underneath the clear covering was an omelet made from egg whites. What looked like a mixture of cheese, salsa, dried basil, and bacon bits had been added for garnish. Push busied himself with removing the wrap while Scratch retrieved a fork for him.

The first bite set off an explosion of taste in his mouth. "Good, huh?" Scratch offered, smiling. "I think we're going to have to forfeit a few chores in exchange for getting him to take over all cooking duties."

"I don't do lawns," Wrath stated flatly. "Or dishes, unless that entails putting them in a dishwasher."

Push actually laughed, despite still feeling a twinge of annoyance. "So," Wrath asked, as Push polished off his morning meal. "What is the Association's standard protocol for dealing with alien threats?"

The fork in Push's hand froze in midmotion. "We don't know," Scratch told him when Push refused to answer. "This… hasn't happened to us before."

"Seriously?"

Wrath wasn't trying to hide his skepticism. "We don't deal with terrorists, invasions, or world-conquering megalomaniacs," Push explained.

"It's a common misconception," Scratch added, amused.

Wrath looked from one to the other. "Neither of you seem especially worried about it," he noted. "What's your secret?"

"It just hasn't sunk in," Scratch replied calmly.

"That," Push went on, finishing his omelet. "Plus, this could turn out to be a hoax. Just because we don't deal with the sort of stuff that comes up in comic books doesn't mean we haven't seen our share of weirdness before."

"People are always doing crazy stuff," Scratch elaborated, moving away from the sink so Push could set his plate down. "People have tried to fake this stuff before. It wouldn't be the first time the Association has had to come in and deal with a hoax."

Wrath nodded. "I see," he said. "Have any of these hoaxes involved actual laser weaponry, or people that explode if you punch them too hard?"

Push's mouth turned upward, glancing toward Scratch automatically before the memory of what had happened in his bedroom hit him like a ton of bricks.

"No," he said quickly, looking away again. "That was new."

"Well, I was just wondering," Wrath replied, sounding nonchalant as always. "Has the Association responded to your report yet?"

"I haven't checked," Push admitted. "I'll go do that now."

Scratch followed him step for step. Push wanted to protest but couldn't come up with an excuse for him not to fast enough. Worse yet, Wrath decided to come along. Ignoring them, Push sat down at the desk that had come with the house. The delivery company that had brought their stuff had been nice enough to hook his computer up for him, thankfully. Bringing up the website, he keyed in his personal password and hit enter. Wrath was standing by the door, looking away the whole time, as if understanding Push hadn't wanted him to see.

Then again, being an empath, the man undoubtedly had sensed that. Push made a mental note to monitor his emotions more carefully, a feat that made him cringe inwardly, as the window loaded.

"I don't believe this," said Push, leaning forward slightly.

"What?"

Push looked to Scratch first, who had taken up a spot behind him, before answering Wrath's question. "There's nothing here," he said. "They don't say anything about the aliens, or whatever they were. All the Association wants is for us to keep looking for Sloth."

"That's suspiciously vague," Wrath commented.

"Um, no shit," Scratch agreed.

"There's also a note at the bottom about the Cape Cabinet voicing suspicions about the Pranksta Gayngsta's death," he added, moving the mouse around. "They think he faked his death in order to make skipping town easier."

"The Cabinet still considers him a priority?" It sounded as though Wrath didn't believe that. "Even after everything else you told them?"

"I guess," Push said, growing aggravated. "What the hell is going on?"

No one seemed to have an answer at first. The members of the Cape Cabinet were the founders of the Real-Life Superhero Association, the first costumed volunteers to band together for a greater cause. Ever since the Association had branched out, the Cabinet had looked for ways to continue proving themselves. This was just the sort of thing they would be all over, generally. The fact that no one was taking it seriously worried Push.

"This isn't like them," Push resumed, sweeping the web page once more in case he'd missed something. "The Association doesn't just ignore a problem. Even for them, this feels wrong."

"Maybe they know something," Wrath offered from his position in the doorway. "Maybe they're being ordered to keep quiet on it for now."

Push almost fired off a scathing remark before Wrath's words sunk in. "Maybe," he admitted. "You could be on to something there."

"Um, so what do we do?" Scratch asked.

"We find Sloth," Push said, getting up. "And maybe the Pranksta Gayngsta while we're at it, assuming he hasn't fled the state. We haven't gotten any new reports of him being sighted outside the area. The body in that alley could have just been a coincidence."

"I doubt it," Wrath objected quietly. "That looked like a professional job to me."

Scratch gave him a look, though not unkindly. "I guess we'll find out sooner or later."

"And in the meantime," Push finished. "If we see any more aliens, we'll handle the situation as best we can. At least, until the Association gets up off its ass."

Push was avoiding looking at Scratch. Each time he met his friend's eyes directly or spent too much time staring at him, his head got fuzzy. He was acting like a freshman in high school with a crush on the football quarterback.

Sweat was running out of his pores underneath his clothes. Being this close to Scratch was making his heart race. Push felt like the self-control he'd perfected over the years had flown south on him. He'd been better at keeping his emotions in check. Now, the more he struggled to control himself, the worse it got. If anything, he was going to send things flying around the room if this didn't stop.

The doorbell rang.

Push wanted to give thanks to whatever god hadn't forsaken him, but he was already past Wrath, out the bedroom door, and headed for the front of the house. In such a rush, it took a moment for his brain to catch up with him once he opened the door. There was no one there, but Push thought to look down a second after he heard a high-pitched sound.

The little girl standing on their doorstep was young, probably no more than six or seven. Her parents, undoubtedly, had dressed her up in a cute-as-the-dickens cream-colored dress with red lace woven into it and a large bow on the back that was visible from the front.

"Sorry to disturb you," she said in a sweet, polite tone. "My stepmom asked me to deliver a message to you."

Push backed up slightly so as not to crowd the girl. "Sorry," he said, caught off his guard by her manners. "Who is your mom?"

"Stepmom," she corrected automatically. "Sorry, sir. You met her before. She's Laura Thompson. You're renting the house from my dad."

"Oh, right."

"She wanted me to tell you Sheriff Black said to meet him in town where the jet crashed," the girl went on. "He needs to talk to you."

"Okay," Push said, remembering to smile so she didn't think he was being rude. "Thanks for delivering the message."

"You're welcome," she said before adding quickly, "My name's Sally, by the way. I should have introduced myself before."

"It's okay," he reassured her. "Tell her we'll be there shortly."

The girl called Sally was already turning around. Push closed the door as she left and did the same, finding Wrath and Scratch watching from the kitchen entrance.

"Is this normal?" he asked.

"Pretty much," Wrath replied, nodding. "Even though telephones are widespread, people here still occasionally forget it takes more time to send their kids several blocks down the street by themselves to deliver news."

"The aliens almost seem normal now," Scratch noted.

Push closed the door. "No kidding."

"Are we going in uniform?" Wrath asked as Push walked back across the room. "Or as civilians?"

"The sheriff is the one who called," Push reminded. "And he wanted us to meet him by the crash site. I'm taking that to mean this is official business, so we go as the Association."

"Right," Wrath said, turning around. "Let me get my long coat, then."

It took Push a second to realize Wrath was all but dressed and ready to go. "Give us a few more minutes," Scratch said, following after him as they headed for their rooms. "We weren't expecting to be on call today."

"Take your time, ladies," Wrath teased, his voice sounding uncharacteristically mirthful all of a sudden. "I'd hate for either of you to go out in public without your faces on."

"Fuck you, Wrath," Push shot back before storming off to his room.

CHAPTER
THREE

THE three of them arrived in the Pussy Wagon less than twenty minutes later. Sheriff Black was waiting for them in the damaged street next to his two cronies, Deputies McGee and Fortenberry. The minute Black spotted their vehicle, his face began to show strain. Even from as far back as they parked, Push could see the blood vessels popping on his forehead.

Wrath got out last, climbing out of the backseat behind Scratch. Several bystanders, who had gathered to help load up debris, stopped what they were doing to stare. Some were giving them appreciative, if slightly wary, looks. Others, however, wore faces that would have soured milk in a heartbeat.

"Ignore them," Push advised, even though Wrath appeared to be doing that very thing already.

"Not the most grateful crowd," Scratch said, eying the locals discreetly. "It's a good thing we don't do this for the applause."

"Get used to it," Wrath advised as they made their way up the street toward the sheriff. "This town isn't known for its compassion or welcoming of strangers."

"Can you hear their thoughts?" Push asked, slowing his pace ever so slightly.

"I'm not telepathic," Wrath said, frowning. "My powers don't work that way. What I can tell you, though, is that a lot of the people here would just as soon crucify us. I can't be absolutely sure, but it seems they consider this to be our fault."

Scratch scowled. "Why?"

Wrath shrugged in answer. "Three strangers show up out of the blue," he said, "dressed like circus freaks. Then, the next day, a plane crashes on the town. It's a lot like those old superstitions about newcomers and meteor showers being bad omens. People here are cowardly and paranoid. They'll blame misfortune on the first thing that crops up."

Scratch seemed to find this entertaining. "You're saying we should watch our backs?" he asked, chuckling. "Um, will they run over us with tractors?"

"Possibly," Wrath replied, utterly serious.

"Stay on your guard," Push advised. "But don't do anything to get us in trouble. Just keep your heads up and eyes open. If it looks like your life is in danger, feel free to defend it, but things will go much smoother if we don't do anything to turn the whole town against us."

They were close enough to Black and his men that someone might overhear them, so Push fell silent.

"Fellas," Black greeted.

Up close, the sheriff didn't look half as pissed off as he had before. "Something wrong with the phones?" Push asked after giving Black a nod.

"Half the lines are down," he replied, gesturing all around them at the damage. "The Thompson woman said she knew your number."

"She sent her daughter down," Push replied. "What's up?"

Black's expression went grim. "Nothing much," he said stiffly. "Just clearin' stuff away. This shit's not gonna move itself, and until we get some contractors down here to survey the damage, Shove Point's pretty much shut down."

Scratch bit his lower lip as his gaze swept through the skeletal remains of downtown. "Um, it looks like a good stiff wind would collapse half the street," he noted.

"Probably," Black agreed sadly. "We've told people to keep clear of this whole area for right now. Most won't likely listen, though."

Black's eyes fell on Wrath. "I saw what you were doing the other day," he said. "You helped out a hell of a lotta people with that... whatever you call it."

"Pyrokinesis."

Deputy Fortenberry chuckled at the word, as though it were beneath him somehow. Push recalled seeing Wrath use his powers immediately after the plane crash to snuff out fires before they could spread. Black had been impressed with Wrath's work, and it was good to see the feeling hadn't ebbed away quickly.

Black seemed to be waiting for Wrath to elaborate, but the former supervillain stayed quiet. Just as Push thought he was going to have to smack the man, Wrath spoke to the sheriff again.

"Sheriff Black," Wrath spoke, his voice rife with tension. "Would it be a problem if I had a word with you in private later?"

Behind the sheriff, McGee and Fortenberry frowned hard. Black hesitated a moment but ultimately nodded. "We'll see," he said. "First, though, I'd like to show you three something. We were digging through a few of the smaller buildings earlier, and somebody found something mighty peculiar."

Push's eyes went wide, but he and the others followed after as the sheriff led them uphill to a familiar-looking spot.

"Busted," Scratch said under his breath.

"We'll see," Push replied. "Remember, we're supposed to be here."

"Let's see if they feel that way," Wrath quietly threw in, warningly.

The sheriff and his deputies had stopped in front of a cracked and broken shop with shattered windows. Police tape had been spread out over the entrances. Black swatted at it, carelessly knocking the obstruction aside as he stepped through. Fortenberry, the shorter and wider of the two, sent a nasty look their way before motioning the three to follow.

"In here," Black called out, standing behind a shelf near the center of the room. "Somebody found it while making sure the place was unoccupied."

All three came to the shelf where the sheriff and his men were standing in a semi-circle. There, at the sheriff and deputies' feet, was a large stain of dried fluid. There wasn't as much of it as Push recalled from when he and Scratch had fought the creatures before. A lot of it looked smeared.

"There's more of it all over the place," Black added, pointing. "Over yonder. Any idea what this shit is?"

Push frowned. "Can't say," he replied. "What made you think any of us would know?"

Black gave Push a hard stare in response. "You boys are the spandex club, right?" he asked, like it should have been obvious. "Don't you deal in weird shit like this?"

Scratch knelt down. "It could be anything," he said. "But, um, if you'd like, we can take some of it with us and get a professional to have a look."

"You got professionals in that screwy organization that deal in blue shit?" McGee asked sarcastically.

"There's a whole team of them," Scratch replied seriously. "Not to mention a department that specializes in forensics."

That shut McGee up. "The things people will throw their money away on," Fortenberry said, disgusted.

"A friend of ours is on vacation," Push explained to Black directly. "But if I ask, he might be willing to fly down. Would that be a problem for you?"

"Hell, I don't know what this shit is," Black replied, looking down at the goop worriedly. "Some kind of experimental rocket fuel or something illegal? I just don't want it screwing up anything in my town like stuff happens on TV."

Scratch gave Push and Wrath a look. "We'll go call him right now," he said, getting to his feet. "Um, does anyone around here have something we can carry a sample of this back in?"

There was no forensic team on site, but a volunteer helping to clear the debris had an empty mayonnaise jar he was willing to part with. Push didn't bother asking why someone would just happen to be carrying one around with them, much less one that looked like it had been thoroughly rinsed clean recently.

"You probably shouldn't ask," Wrath advised, catching the curious expression on Push's face.

Push accepted the advice graciously. There was nothing to scoop the sample up with or any gloves to put on, so he wound up scraping what he could with the lid. Once he felt there was enough, Push sealed the jar, then went straight to the Pussy Wagon.

"We'll be back later to help out," he told Black, who had opted to follow them for whatever reason. "If that's all right?"

Black nodded. "Dress casually," he advised. "Not everyone here is used to your fashion statements."

"It's just as well," Scratch told him as he climbed inside the truck. "Spandex chafes if you spend too much time sweating in the sun."

"Which is one reason why you won't catch me in it," Wrath stated, not climbing aboard. "You guys go on ahead. Since I don't need to change, there's no reason for me to head back with you. I can get started on some of the stuff that can be burned away."

Push looked at Sheriff Black for a moment but didn't object. "We'll be back soon," he said, giving Wrath his blessing. "Stay out of trouble."

"Yes, Dad."

Black actually seemed to find that funny. He was still snickering as Push pulled out of the parking space into the street.

"What do you suppose Wrath wanted with the sheriff?" Scratch asked, once they were on their way.

"No clue," Push replied. "Why don't you ask him when we get back?"

"Um, why me?"

Push felt himself getting angry again, though he couldn't explain why. "You two seem to be getting along fine," he said, gripping the steering wheel. "He wasn't the one sucking on my dick the other night, after all."

"Oh." Scratch looked uncomfortable suddenly. "Do you want to ask me about that?"

"No," Push answered flatly. "I don't."

Push didn't want to talk about it, much less think about it, but the image stayed stuck in his mind. Scratch swore it had meant nothing, that Wrath had gotten him to wager a blowjob during a late-night poker game while Scratch was drunk. Push had walked in on them while Wrath was going to town on Scratch's cock.

That had happened before Scratch confessed being in love with Push, and before they'd hooked up. Push couldn't explain why, but remembering it made him furious. Even if Scratch was just going through an experimental phase, the fact remained Wrath had gotten to his best friend first.

It sounded petty, and Push realized with a heavy sinking feeling that he was being a complete asshole to the man he'd secretly loved for years.

"I'm sorry," he said quietly as they reached their street.

Scratch said nothing.

Once again, Push thought to himself, *you manage to cosmically screw up a good thing. Nice going, hero.*

THE line was busy when Push called, so he switched to text message. When that didn't go through, he tried sending a message through Twitter.

The call came back a few minutes later. "'Sup, Gar?"

"You are not an easy man to get hold of. You know that, Trix?"

Professor Trixter snorted on the other end of the line. "Bitch, I'm on vacation. What is it you need from me this time, Barnes?"

Push frowned, trying to think of an excuse. "I just called to say hi," he tried, knowing Trix would call him out on it but enjoying the bullshit game all the same. "And to see how your vacation is going."

"You're lying," Trixter said, completely unconvinced. "You want me to come to whatever godforsaken rathole the Cape Cabinet sent you and your boy to so I can bail you both out of trouble. Am I right?"

Push rolled his eyes toward the ceiling. "You and your black powers, huh?"

"Me and my awesome black powers," Trix affirmed, the grin on his face audible through the connection. "What seems to be the problem this time?"

Push opted to forgo subtlety. "Aliens."

The other end of the line was silent. For a moment, it seemed as though Professor Trixter had stopped breathing.

"You still there, Trix?"

"Aliens," Trix repeated suspiciously. "You'd better not be jerking me off on this."

"That's kind of why I need you down here," Push admitted. "These things looked like aliens, but we're all trying to keep up a level of skepticism until a professional can confirm it. Scratch has a sample of the goo these things left behind. I was wondering if you'd mind—"

"You're in Arkansas, right?" Trix interrupted. "What town was it, again?"

It sounded like Trix was punching some keys in the background. "Shove Point," Push said. "I don't think there's an airport, though."

"There's a landing strip about ten miles from where you are," Trix replied. "Big enough for a small private plane to land on."

Push hesitated. "You're not going to bring that flying machine you built last year, are you?" he asked, feeling slightly sick at the memory. "Not after what happened last time, right?"

"I've made improvements," Trix said dismissively, making Push's insides writhe. "There should be no problems."

"Trix," Push insisted. "This town just had a commercial jet crash-land on top of it. The last thing the locals need is more post-traumatic stress."

"Let me run home so I can pick up some equipment," Trix was saying, ignoring Push completely now. "I can be there in a day or so. Is that good?"

Push sighed. "It's cool," he said. "Just try not to land on anything narrower than a two-lane road. The local sheriff hasn't warmed to us being here much, and you pulling up in the Albatross won't help smooth things over."

Professor Trixter had already hung up on him. Push tucked his phone away before joining Scratch in the living room. He'd changed out of his spandex into some lightweight, breathable clothing. Scratch was waiting by the door, having lost his long brown coat and guard accessories.

"He's coming," Push informed him. "Where'd you leave the sample?"

"In the refrigerator.

"What?" Scratch wondered at the look on Push's face. "Where else should I have left it? Besides, I sealed the jar inside one of those airtight plastic bags."

"Still…." Push decided not to argue with him. "Okay, just don't set anything we might want to eat near it."

Push waited while Scratch went back to the kitchen to make some rearrangements. Once he was done, the two made tracks in the Pussy Wagon for the middle of town.

It was more of the same routine as before. Scratch and he split off, helping where they could and clearing away rubble. The day was much more hopeful, however. The townspeople of Shove Point seemed more determined. There was a sense of unity in the crowd, a coming-together Push could appreciate despite it not extending all the way over to him.

The locals appeared to relax some in his presence, though. Both he and Scratch were having an easier time getting people to communicate with them now they were wearing street clothes. Apparently, in this town, clothes really did make the man.

It also helped that the injured were already being treated. Every so often, someone would come across a dead body in need of identification. Occasionally, one of the people in the crowd would be able to positively ID the deceased, though not without a few tears. It was an awful situation, but there was nothing more Push could do. Everything that could be done was being done, so he hunched his shoulders and kept on.

Several times, someone called for a break to pass out food and drink. Whenever this occurred, Push automatically found Scratch and Wrath, and the three would convene at a spot in the shade away from the crowd. During these times, they were the subject of speculation from the rest of the group. Push hadn't needed Wrath to fill him in on that. At this point, no one was bothering to hide the glances thrown their way or the whispers slipping out through the air.

"Um, they are kind of paranoid," Scratch noted, speaking to Wrath now. "I kept thinking some of them would warm up to us after a while."

"Paranoid and superstitious," Wrath reminded. "Don't expect much."

Push's mouth turned upward slightly as he picked over the last of his sandwich. "I'm starting to see why you wanted out so badly."

"This bothered me less than what I dealt with at home," Wrath said, taking a sip of soda. "It hurt more knowing people knew what was happening and didn't care. I was born here the same as them, but I was also different, so it didn't matter."

"You could go over there now," Scratch suggested. "The sheriff was singing your praises earlier. That's got to count for something."

"Pass," Wrath replied at once. "They're only putting me up on a pedestal so they'll have something to knock over later. Still, if you two wanted some privacy, all you had to do was ask for it. Suggesting I throw myself to the rabid coyotes wasn't necessary."

With that statement, Wrath walked down the road toward the area he'd been working before, tossing his can in a bin along the way.

"I didn't—" Scratch started.

"Forget it," Push said, cutting him off. "If he wants to be moody, he can go somewhere else."

Scratch cocked an eyebrow at Push upon hearing this. "That's funny coming from you," he stated dryly. "Being moody, I mean. You've been that way since this morning."

Push felt himself tense up again. "I'd rather not talk about it."

"Why?" Scratch tossed his own can too hard toward a much closer bin, and it bounced out into a spot of grass on the other side. "What's the matter with you today?"

Push wanted to answer that question, but the words wouldn't come. "Just forget it," he insisted, panic slowly filling him. "Nothing's wrong. We can all just pretend the last few days didn't happen and go back to the way things were."

Scratch's face twisted into a wounded expression. "What made you think I ever wanted things to be the way they were before?" he asked quietly.

Push's hands gripped the plastic plate he was holding. "Don't you?" he demanded, looking his friend in the eye now, only to have what he was going to say next stop short as a lump formed in his throat.

Scratch had never looked so devastated. His eyes were dry, yet something told Push the tears weren't far away.

"Why do you want this?" he heard himself ask.

Scratch blinked and looked away slightly. "I'm still not sure," he confessed. "I've felt this way for a while, longer really, if I were honest with myself. I just didn't know what to do. I wasn't sure if you felt the same way about me. I thought, if I threw that card game with Wrath on purpose, I could find out what it was like. If I could push my limits even a little bit, then maybe I could give you what you needed."

Again, Push was floored by this.

"I was going to work up the nerve to ask you," Scratch continued, heedless of the effect he was having on Push. "I wanted it to be you, but I was scared. If something went wrong, it would be my fault because I couldn't cope."

"How do you know all of this isn't because of Wrath?" Push demanded, even as he felt his resolve slip a little. "He said it himself. Sometimes people have problems controlling their emotions around him. He could be making you feel this way."

"He isn't," Scratch replied flatly.

Still, Push wouldn't let it die. "You have that much faith in him?"

"No," Scratch said. "Well, it's not really that. I know he isn't making me feel this way, by accident or otherwise, because I knew I was in love with you a whole year ago."

That statement made Push snap back. "When?"

"Haven't you noticed?" Scratch cocked his head to the side when Push didn't answer. "Um, how many girls have I brought home this year?"

Push had to think for a minute. "I don't know," he said, wishing Scratch had thought of some other way of settling this now. "I stopped paying attention."

"Three," Scratch stated. "Since Wiccan Witch and I split, I've been with a total of three women this year. Does that sound at all like me?"

Push frowned hard. "Are you sure?"

"Positive," Scratch said. "Honestly, I think she already knew. We both agreed it just wasn't working out, and on the night we called it quits, she hinted she'd known I was in love with somebody else. It took me a while, but I started to think about what she really meant by that."

A moment passed before Push could fully absorb this. "Wiccan Witch knew?" he marveled. "She never said anything!"

"I know," Scratch said, rolling his eyes. "It annoyed me too, a little."

A breeze drifted between them. "What about those other three girls?" Push asked once it died down some. "If you knew, why them?"

Scratch actually looked a little embarrassed. "Fuck, man. Everybody's got needs, and I was still trying to work out what I was going to do about all this."

"Are you bi?"

Both men froze as the crowd of townspeople broke apart and began moving up the street toward them.

"No," Scratch said in a much quieter voice. "I don't think so. Other guys don't really do it for me like that. You're different."

"Why?" Push was getting more confused by the second and more frustrated as a consequence. "What's so special about me?"

Scratch glared. "I already told you, idiot," he growled. "I love you."

Push didn't say anything. "Why is that so hard for you to accept?" Scratch demanded, forgoing any attempt to keep their conversation private. "I just said I love you, not that I was planning to run over your dog!"

"Because you're straight," Push shot back, though in a slightly lower octave. "And you just said you don't believe you're bi."

"I'm not," Scratch affirmed. "But I fell in love with you. I want you because of who you are, not because you're a guy or a girl."

"Why?" Push insisted, balling his hands into fists. "What made you fall for me?"

Scratch smiled then. "I think maybe I was always supposed to," he said. "I know, that sounds like a lame come-on, but it was easy for me to like you. You're fun to be around. We've been best friends for years. You've had my back since we started at the Association. If I needed help with something, you were the first one who offered. We like the same stuff, and you have a great sense of humor. You're what drives me to try and do more for others."

Scratch slowly let out a deep breath. "And, I guess, after a while, it just crept up on me. I didn't plan for any of this to happen. The more I was around you, the better I felt about myself. Everything I felt about you got stronger and stronger the longer we knew one another. After I thought about what Wiccan Witch said, it started to add up."

Scratch met Push's eyes and refused to look away. "What about you? What made you feel that way about me?" he asked.

Push gulped. "Do we have to do this here?" he asked, looking around at the people nearby who had already gone back to work.

"We don't," Scratch said. "But if we stop now, I'm worried you'll panic on me again and try to dodge the subject."

Off in the distance, someone shouted as another corpse was uncovered. "I deserve that," Push acknowledged. "The same things, I guess. You are one of the best friends I've ever had, and I don't think I've ever met someone who wasn't gay that didn't feel at least a little uncomfortable with the whole idea. The fact that you honestly didn't care was kind of a relief. When it first started, I thought it was just lust."

Scratch smiled.

"Don't look too smug," Push warned, making light of the situation. "But yes, you are a hot piece of Sicilian stud."

Scratch's smile got wider. "I wasn't expecting it to matter more when you said it," he confessed. "But I'm glad it does."

Push looked away, blushing. "I was afraid you'd be freaked out, and what we had would change," he continued. "I didn't want that."

"I do," Scratch said softly.

Push's eyes widened. "What?"

Looking around first to make sure the coast was clear, Scratch took Push's hand in his. "I don't want things the way they were," he said, leaning in closer to Push's face. "I don't want us to just be friends. I want what we did this morning and yesterday morning. I wasn't freaked out by it then, and I'm not now."

Scratch gave Push's hand a squeeze. "I want to love you like that," he whispered as he nudged Push backward into one of the dilapidated buildings. "I want us to be lovers, like I said before. I've wanted this for a long time, and I'm not about to give it up now that I know you feel the same way."

As they moved into the shadows, Scratch lowered his head until their brows pressed tightly together.

"Kiss me," Scratch insisted, pulling Push closer to him.

"Here?"

Scratch nodded. "I'm tired of waiting," he said. "And worrying. Kiss me."

There were a thousand more things for Push to say and a thousand more worries for him to give voice to. All of that faded away as his mouth connected with Scratch's.

"Stay," Scratch said breathlessly when they disconnected. "Don't run. Stay with me now."

At some point, Push had no idea when, their arms wrapped around each other. Push savored the strength he felt in Scratch's slightly bigger frame.

Someone cleared their throat sharply, and Push was unsurprised to find Wrath watching them near the gaping hole that served as the entrance.

"Not eavesdropping," Wrath reminded before Push could utter a word. "Not my fault you two pick lousy places to make out, either."

"This is a great place to make out," Scratch countered, in surprisingly good spirits. "No one else was here until you showed up."

"And there are great big holes in the walls for that very thing to happen," Wrath pointed out, turning. "You might want to save it for later, though. Some of the locals are starting to wonder what's keeping you, and we still have work to do."

"Fair enough." Scratch released Push from his grip and took hold of his hand for a moment to give it one final squeeze. "We can finish this later."

"I'm sure you will," they heard Wrath mutter as he left.

"Count on it," Scratch told Push, giving him a heated glance before letting go of his hand. "But don't think I'll be finished with you anytime soon."

A tug of war began between Push's head and heart, with his cock jumping in immediately. Try as he might, he couldn't stop worrying over whether this wasn't a huge mistake.

Then his eyes landed on Scratch's ass as the man marched out into the street ahead of him, looking absolutely thrilled with the world. It took a moment for Push to realize he was the cause of the spring in his best friend's step, and a minute longer before it occurred to him he didn't need to worry about Scratch getting pissed over his staring.

Worrying could wait until later.

CHAPTER
FOUR

EVEN in his civvies, it was hot working outdoors. Sweat had saturated his shirt and jeans by the time the denizens of Shove Point were ready to call it a day. Push raised the shirt's hem to wipe his face off, flashing his abs at a nearby group of middle-aged housewives in the process, who all simultaneously blushed. Each one's eyes were on him as he moved farther up the street to see what Scratch and Wrath were up to.

Both were waiting for him near a power pole that had survived the onslaught. Lines were scattered around them, but Push had already been informed the electricity for this region was dead, so he stepped over them deftly.

"I'm exhausted," he said in a flat tone. "And I stink. Let's run home so we can all shower, then grab something to eat."

"We were just talking about Sloth," Wrath said, watching Push carefully.

"Yeah." Scratch nodded. "Um, Wrath thinks the guy might have gone underground. We were trying to work out where his hideout would be."

"Tell me on the way back to the truck," Push said before moving past them.

Scratch obliged by offering to drive. Push opened the door so Wrath could climb in the back, then got aboard himself as Scratch cranked the engine.

"I have a theory," Wrath said as Push fiddled with the AC controls, turning it up full blast.

"I can't get over how much warmer it is down here," Push interjected, throwing his head back against the seat. "How do people stand it?"

"It's the humidity," Wrath replied, not bothered by Push cutting him off. "You should drink more water. Dehydration is common for people who aren't used to the climate here."

"That explains the headache," Push mused, pressing a hand to his temple. "Sorry I interrupted you. What were you saying?"

"The pod," Wrath resumed, leaning back in his seat as Scratch steered toward their rented home. "Whatever was ejected from that ship, Sloth obviously wants it. Nothing else would keep him in this place for so long."

Push thought back to the ship they'd found on the shore of the lake deep in the woods. The aliens, though Push still hadn't gotten used to calling them that, had been heading out of town toward the forest border. Push had followed behind while Scratch had gone for reinforcements. With Wrath as their guide, they'd traversed a path leading to what Push suspected was the reason for the aliens being there in the first place.

It sounded ludicrous to him even now, like thinking back on the plot of a second-rate film. The aliens had shown up and attacked, forcing them to retreat farther into the woods. Once they'd dealt with that problem, however, Sloth had shown up to cause more trouble. In the end, the damaged ship had ejected some kind of pod from its insides before self-destructing.

"If we find the pod," Wrath was saying now, "we'll either locate Sloth or lure him out from whatever rock he's been camping under."

"The problem is," Scratch replied, "we don't have a clue where the thing landed."

"Or if it landed at all," Push added.

"So we check the area," said Wrath, undeterred. "It was launched from the lake. Anything like that would stand out in a place like Shove Point."

"So why hasn't Sloth found it?"

Push sighed at Scratch's question. "It's not a bad idea, though," he admitted. "And I'd be lying if I said I wasn't curious about what was inside that thing or why Sloth was so keen on finding it."

"He just wants to get paid," Wrath said. "A better question would be who is he working for and why do they want it."

"Okay," said Scratch as they pulled into the driveway. "Where do we start?"

"Town records," Wrath declared, getting out after Push. "If that pod was only propelled a short distance, it probably landed somewhere in the woods. Let's check the local reports and see if someone saw something unusual."

Scratch thought hard as they headed for the door together. "But Sloth is still looking for it, right? If he found the crashed ship that fast, hunting the pod wouldn't have taken much longer."

"Exactly."

Push frowned, not following. "The pod was rocket propelled," Wrath explained as Scratch unlocked the door. "It must have been a secondary ship, something to take its cargo farther away if the main ship was damaged."

"Sounds like a bad cop-out from a cheesy sci-fi novel to me," Push derided, nudging the door open.

"Then how come nobody has found it?" Scratch asked pointedly.

Push sighed again. "No, you're right," he acknowledged, walking through the kitchen for his room and the shower he so desperately needed. "I'm just pissed because I'm tired, hungry, and covered in shit."

"We all are," Wrath reminded, closing the door behind him. "I wasn't suggesting we forgo dinner in favor of hunting aliens."

"You don't have to convince us," Scratch said, giving Wrath a smile as he followed Push out of the room. "We'll get cleaned up, chill for a minute while we eat, then go looking for spaceships."

"Sounds like a plan," Wrath said, crossing the living room with broad strides. "See you two when you're finished."

Push was far enough away that he almost didn't hear. The statement made him stop short, however, which caused Scratch to bump into him.

"Sorry," Push said. "Did you want something?"

"Yeah." The smile Scratch gave him was bashful yet impish at the same time. "Can we shower together?"

Push stepped back slightly at the request. Scratch was watching him now, as though afraid of how Push was going to respond. The man was holding his heart out to him, thinking Push might stomp all over it at any given moment. Push had spent most of the day not thinking about it. The truth was, as much as he'd wanted this for so long, having Scratch return his feelings threw him for a loop.

A hurt look began to take shape on Scratch's face.

"Sure," Push said, a little too fast. "Sorry, I'm just tired. I don't think I'll be good company for you, is all."

"We don't have to do anything," Scratch replied, looking hopeful again. "I could just scrub your back, if you don't mind returning the favor. I feel like I've got three different layers of dirt covering me right now."

Push smiled slightly. "I feel the same way."

Push was aware of every step Scratch took. His feet hit the carpet in time with Push's, making the shorter man's heart speed up. They were standing outside the bathroom door when Push heard something rustle behind him and realized Scratch had already started undressing.

They had changed in front of one another before. Once in a great while, circumstances didn't allow for modesty. During those moments, Push had always kept his eyes defiantly away as his friend stripped down. Mind you, those times, neither of them had undressed all the way.

Scratch was slowly sliding his T-shirt over his head. His head appeared to have gotten caught on the hem, so it was with a loud gasp that he finally freed himself. Push felt his throat go dry, and he swallowed hard as it dawned on him he didn't have to pretend not to notice anymore.

Sweat, dirt, and grime clung to the rich brown expanse of Italian skin stretched tight over Scratch's chest and abs. It made him look even darker, though unevenly. Scratch hadn't been kidding when he said there was filth covering him three layers deep. Push didn't want to think about how much worse he looked, so instead, he focused on the remaining droplets of sweat rolling slowly down the contours of Scratch's body, picking up speed as they neared the brief treasure trail near the waistline of his jeans.

Scratch tossed the shirt unceremoniously off to the side, then saw how Push was staring. "See something you like?" he asked coyly.

Push turned away sharply.

"Don't," Scratch insisted, almost pleadingly, before seizing him gently by the forearm. "Keep looking."

Hesitantly, Push turned back. Scratch was watching him closely now, smiling as their eyes met. "Go on," he encouraged. "I want to see something I like too."

Push swallowed again as the hairs along his forearm where Scratch held him tightly began waving excitedly, as though thrilled by the very prospect of Scratch's skin making contact with his. Letting out a deep breath he hadn't realized he was holding, Push reached up with one hand to yank his shirt off. Scratch realized the problem and released him. Push thought that would be it, and went rigid a second later as he felt Scratch's hands seize the shirt and yank it off the rest of the way.

Half-naked, he stood before his friend, feeling exposed and vulnerable. Scratch's eyes were wandering over him slowly, giving Push warm goose bumps.

"Did I ever tell you how much I envy those abs?" Scratch asked, his gaze lingering at the chiseled six-pack.

"Yours aren't anything to sneeze at," he pointed out.

Scratch let a hand drift down over the surface of his stomach, trailing through the hairs there and smearing some of the grime. Push should have been disgusted by it, but the sight was making him salivate. He wondered how the salty taste of Scratch's sweat would feel rolling around on the back of his tongue. They both stank from the hard day's labor, yet Push couldn't recall ever being this aroused in his life.

To his shock, Push realized he had been on the verge of reaching out to feel for himself. Scratch locked eyes with him, though, and nodded, encouraging Push with his gaze to keep going. The moment Push's fingers pressed against Scratch's flesh, the tips dipped into the grooves where a great deal of dirt had settled. Push brushed it aside, ignoring it for the moment as he explored with his fingertips the dips and contours there. Scratch watched him like a hawk perched in a tree the whole time, his gaze never wavering. Their breathing had quickened at the same time. For Push, it felt like the heat radiating from Scratch's body was passing up his arm and drifting down to some cold, dark part of himself he hadn't been aware of before.

Scratch grabbed Push's arm suddenly and pressed the hand flat against the hard edges of his abdomen for a moment. Slowly, he led Push's hand upward, guiding him to the valley between his pecs. At the same time, Scratch's own hand drifted down the length of Push's arm until it cupped the hard bicep near the shoulder.

"Damn," Scratch breathed out. "Your arms have gotten huge."

Push couldn't help but smile. "You told me you'd been working on building your chest up more," he said breathlessly. "It's paid off."

Scratch's chest rose and fell as Push explored this area of his body. Gradually, though, the man became more impatient and seized the hand there again.

"Do it," Scratch ordered, as he worked the hand back down to the waistband of his jeans. "I want you to."

Push gulped. Even under two thick layers of clothing, there was no mistaking that Scratch was in a very good mood. Nevertheless, he managed to tune out the loud doubts screaming obscenities near the back of his mind. With both hands, Push undid the first button, exposing the outline of a pair of white briefs that were saturated with sweat.

Against all reservations, Push brushed each thumb across the elastic band there, feeling the moisture the fabric had soaked up. A thought flashed through his mind, and Push had to force himself to remain calm as a vision of him sucking the sweat right out of the drawers while Scratch was still in them made his knees go weak. Desperate to get his mind off that, Push worked on the next button in the row, exposing more of the swollen package buried behind the strained fabric. When Scratch's fly was all the way open, his cock jutted out like some angry, pulsating beast trying to escape from its prison.

The air around them burned as Scratch stared down into Push's face. His own was contorted into a lustful snarl that reminded Push of a wild animal gone too long without food. Scratch moved forward, brushing the head of his still-restrained tool against Push's skin.

"My turn," Scratch all but growled out.

Scratch did not waste as much time. Taking the waistline of Push's pants in both hands, he quickly undid the top button before yanking down the zipper. Looping his fingers over the boxers Push wore underneath, Scratch jerked both down in a single stroke, exposing Push's painfully hard cock to the open air.

Push stood with his cock at full mast, waving happily at Scratch, whose eyes remained locked on the thick shaft.

"You're pretty thick," Scratch noted, still breathless. "I keep forgetting."

"So are you," said Push, remaining perfectly still.

Scratch shoved his jeans and briefs all the way down, stepping out of them as Push did the same, albeit more slowly.

"Um, I wanna do something," Scratch said quickly, looking very nervous now. "It may seem a little weird, though."

Push cocked an eyebrow. "Weirder than this?" he blurted, unable to stop himself.

Scratch chuckled, then reached up to grasp Push by his shoulders. "What's weird about this?" he asked, leaning forward.

Push expected Scratch to kiss him and felt his heartbeat spike in response. Scratch lowered his head to the side, past Push's mouth, however, leaning into the crook formed by his collarbone. Once there, Scratch placed a chaste kiss before inhaling deeply.

"You smell so good," Scratch hissed, breathing Push in again. "I almost don't want you to get in the shower."

"I stink," Push insisted, trying to hold Scratch back as he buried his head deeper.

"You smell great," Scratch stated fiercely, holding Push to him tightly. "It's making me horny. I never knew a man could smell so good."

A nightmarish war exploded inside Push, as one half howled across the recesses of his mind that Scratch was just experimenting, while the other sang praises that Scratch was actually turned on by him.

"You're really sure about this?" he heard himself say.

Scratch gave Push a squeeze in response, took one last deep breath of him, then raised his head upright. "Let's go take that shower," he said, his eyes darkening with need. "And I'll prove it to you. Again!"

Scratch didn't wait for Push to protest. The telekinetic found himself being forced backward through the doorframe against the lavatory. Scratch cradled Push's face in his hands, pressing their mouths together for a brief but lightning-intense kiss.

"I've never kissed a woman the way I just kissed you," Scratch whispered in his ear. "No girl ever made me feel the way you do. Do you believe me?"

Push tried to answer, but the words froze in his throat. Scratch kissed him again, forcing Push's mouth open so their tongues could lick playfully at each other.

"Come on," Scratch said, taking Push by the hand.

Neither of them had bothered turning the overhead light on. Scratch led Push into the shower first before turning around to hit the light switch. The sudden change made Push blink for a moment, but then Scratch stepped over into the tub with him, and his brain flew south.

They were actually going to do this.

The shower wasn't large, but Push found if he inched back slightly, both he and Scratch could stand in the tub together without touching.

"Turn the water on," Scratch said after drawing the shower curtain closed. "You're closer to it than me."

Scratch's dick was standing at attention and aimed at Push the whole time he said this. Stiffly, Push turned around to grasp the hot and cold taps, careful the whole time not to move back even slightly. As the water from the faucet poured down the drain, slowly getting hot, he felt Scratch's hand brush lightly across his back, up and down, tracing a wide path along his spine.

Push heard himself groan.

"Stand up," Scratch ordered.

Push felt himself rise as Scratch bent forward, turning the shower head on. As the icy spray turned hot and filled the shower with steam, Scratch rose, kissing a trail across Push's shoulder blades. Both hands drifted across Push's chest and shoulders as Scratch turned him around so they were facing each other.

"You first," he said, the words breathing over Push as the water splashed off their bodies.

The soap was on a shelf built into the wall. Scratch's arm brushed across Push's wet skin as he reached for it, sending shivers through the telekinetic. Lathering up both his hands, Scratch turned Push around so his back was resting against Scratch's chest.

"Let me do you first," Scratch said, before running his soap-covered hands up through the crack between their bodies.

Push's breath came in quick gasps as Scratch kneaded out the knots. The soap spread across his skin, washing away the day's work like magic. Between the flowery smell and thick clouds of steam building up, to say nothing of the way Scratch's fingers danced circles around the sore spots, Push felt light-headed.

Scratch's hands drifted downward, stopping at Push's waist so he could grab hold and bring the two of them closer together. Push stumbled slightly as he felt the gap between their bodies close. He could feel Scratch's erection now, still as hard as ever. The difference in their height meant the head was rubbing up through the crack between Push's ass cheeks, making quick jabs at the curve of his spine.

Whatever resistance left inside Push was fading rapidly. With one arm, he reached up and around to grasp Scratch by the back of the head. Water splashed everywhere as their lips met in a warm, wet kiss that left Push weak in the knees all over again. Scratch brought his hands up, soaping Push's stomach and chest as water poured down on them, washing the soap away. Push turned, keeping his arm locked around Scratch's neck even as his shoulder protested against the awkward angle. When they were facing each other, Push pulled his buddy down for another kiss.

Their bodies rubbed against one another, smearing the soap between them. Scratch raked his fingers down Push's back, spreading them so he could cup Push's ass. Push groaned as he felt Scratch bring them even closer together. The steam was so thick now neither one could see clearly.

Scratch moved them until the jets from the shower were battering him on top of his head. Water cascaded down into Push's face as he grasped Scratch's lower lip with his teeth, tugging playfully as their cocks rubbed hard against each other. Finally, Push released Scratch so he could soap up the rest of his body.

Once this was done, Scratch pressed their foreheads together. "Now you do me," he said, gasping for air.

The water was starting to get cold now. With Wrath showering on the other end of the house at the same time, there wasn't much hot water. At that moment, Push could have stayed there until his body shriveled up and blew away. Even with the jets pounding cold water against his back, he wasn't willing to let go of Scratch just yet. The fear that this could all end in the blink of an eye was still alive and screaming in the back of his mind. Each one of his senses was on high alert as he ran his hands over Scratch, meticulously committing the miniscule details to memory.

When Scratch had been soaped up all over, save one spot, Push turned them around to where the water could wash him off.

"It's cold," he warned.

"I know," Scratch replied, his voice still deep with need. "I don't mind. Don't stop touching me."

Something in his voice left no doubt in Push's mind as to what Scratch meant. There was a small gap between them again. Both their erections had gone down slightly, a combination of the cold water plus neither of them paying their swollen organs much attention. Push reached over like he was about to touch a hot pan and made a fist around Scratch's cock. The shaft sprang to life again in mere seconds, hard and painfully erect. A hiss escaped through Scratch's teeth as Push's soapy hand moved back and forth.

"I can't," Scratch gasped. "Sorry! Can't last... long."

Push didn't stop. In a moment, the first thick rope of cum flew through the air, splattering Push's arm, chest, and bicep. The shower water washed the evidence away almost immediately, but not before four more shots joined it. Scratch started to pitch forward and grabbed Push with both arms to steady himself.

"Christ!" Scratch howled. "That was amazing."

Push heard himself giggle as Scratch nuzzled his ear. It tickled.

"Your turn," said Scratch, rising. "I still haven't gotten you off."

Push started to protest, feeling guilty for things he couldn't quite put into words, but Scratch didn't give him leave to speak. Push had expected his buddy to jerk him off as he had, but Scratch surprised him yet again by getting down on his knees.

"I need the practice," Scratch reminded, stroking Push's balls so his cock leaked precum. "Remember?"

Push didn't answer. Scratch had taken almost half the length of him into his mouth before he could form words. Everything after that became a blur. Push's body moved of its own volition now. His hips rocked, urging more and more of his cock down Scratch's throat. Scratch accepted it all too eagerly, moaning each time the thick head brushed over his tongue. Both of his hands, still covered in soapsuds, seized the back of Scratch's head to force him the rest of the way down. Scratch gagged, slowing his pace ever so slightly, but otherwise did nothing to stop the rough treatment.

All too soon, Push was feeling his balls draw up, signifying he was about to fall over the edge himself. With one last buck of his hips, he unloaded his seed down Scratch's throat. Scratch took all of it, only missing a few drops, which spilled down the sides of his mouth.

"God," Push groaned, breathing like he'd run a marathon.

Scratch stood up, grinning. "Was that better?"

Push gave him a look. "You didn't hear me complaining the first time, did you?"

Each took turns standing under the cold water to wash off any traces of soap. Once this was done, the water was cut off, and they climbed out onto the mat.

"Here," Push said, getting a towel for each of them.

"Thanks," Scratch replied.

It wasn't as awkward as Push had been expecting. Neither said a word, but it wasn't an uncomfortable silence either. When Scratch finished drying himself, he folded the towel in half and left it to dry on the rack behind him.

"I'll dry your back," he offered, holding a hand out to take the towel from Push.

"I'm done," Push replied, putting his towel next to Scratch's.

Scratch grabbed Push by the arm and yanked him in close. Their mouths came together for a long, deep kiss that set warning bells firing inside Push's head all over again.

"I know you still don't think I'm serious," Scratch said fiercely, once they'd separated. "I don't know what I can do right now to make you believe me, but I'm not giving up. I've thought about this, and you're the one I want to be with."

Again, Push felt the words he wanted to say jumble up inside him.

"In pool," Scratch said, letting go of Push abruptly, "you have to consider the whole table. It's not enough to have one shot lined up perfectly, because each shot affects how the rest of the table is played."

The sudden change of topic made Push's head spin. "Okay?"

"What I'm trying to say," Scratch tried, swallowing, "Is that you don't take your shot until you are absolutely sure. I spent a long time thinking this over. I'm taking my shot now."

Having said this, Scratch went for the door. "It's your move," he told Push before leaving him to stand alone in the bathroom, naked and still wet.

CHAPTER
FIVE

THE Pussy Wagon was on its way soon after. Despite having plenty of food, each had agreed it would be faster to pick something up. After stopping at a local Chinese place, Push made a call to Sheriff Black and, with a bit of coercing, got them access to the town records. All three of them had left the house in their uniforms. The trio showed up with their food in hand as the fat deputy was squeezing out of his car. Fortenberry was shooting daggers their way the whole time but let them in without a word, slamming the door hard behind them.

"He's as charming as ever," Wrath noted dryly.

Push and Scratch laughed. "Um, any clue as to where we start?" Scratch asked.

The town records were located inside the courthouse building in the basement. Fortenberry had let them in through the entrance down the flight of stairs outside. Clearly, security was not something the place took into consideration. The lock had rattled as the deputy turned the key in it.

The records room looked like some kind of very small library. A computer sat on top of a tiny desk that didn't appear stable enough to hold its weight. Someone had shut the machine down.

"I've got the maps," Wrath said, passing one to each of them. "They've been marked already with spots where that thing might have come down. Why don't we each just grab a corner and start looking for any of these places?"

Scratch took the printout from Wrath and shrugged. "Couldn't hurt," he replied.

Push took a seat at the computer and booted the machine up. It was an antique, hardly any RAM to it, and looked old enough to be framed. Someone had password protected the thing, but luckily, he remembered a couple of tricks some of the more tech-savvy heroes in the Association had passed on to him. Within minutes, he had access.

Unfortunately, this turned out to be a waste of effort. Several minutes of fruitless searching through the ancient hard drive yielded little more than what he would have learned digging through files with the others. Whoever had backed up everything clearly had no experience in cataloging. Following another ten or so frustrating minutes, Push gave up and stood.

The trip was turning out to be one big snipe hunt. "I hope one of you has had better luck," he grumbled, stretching.

"We would if I knew what we were looking for," Scratch replied. "Most of these records are just town genealogy charts and tax files for property. I think we're wasting our time trying to find a spot where a spaceship would crash in this dump."

"Same here," Push agreed.

Wrath said nothing, meticulously flipping through the file in his hands. His face was screwed up in concentration, as though intent on locating something. Push felt like admiring the guy for his dedication, but something made him think twice about it.

"Wrath," he called out. "We're calling it quits. There's nothing in this place for us to work with."

Wrath frowned but placed the file back in the cabinet he'd taken it out of. "It was a good idea," Scratch offered.

"No worries," Wrath said, crossing the short space to where they were waiting for him. "Where do we go next?"

"Maybe just have a look around," Scratch said.

"This is out of our range," Push pointed out, reaching for the door. "When Professor Trixter gets here, we'll see if he can't work out which way—" Push stopped short, his hand gripping the doorknob.

"Don't tell me it's stuck," Scratch groaned.

"It isn't stuck," replied Push, getting angry. "It's locked!"

Wrath didn't appear the least bit surprised, but Scratch's eyes went wide. "What?"

"We're locked in," Push stated flatly. "That fat bastard locked us in here."

Wrath stayed where he was as Scratch marched over to jostle the doorknob. Despite the lock rattling earlier, it stayed defiantly in place.

"Blow it down," Wrath suggested. "Unless you two would rather spend the night waiting for someone to come and find us."

Neither Push nor Scratch enjoyed that prospect. "I'd do it myself," Wrath went on. "But there's a chance the two of you would get flash burned because of how small this room is."

"Thanks for the concern," Push jibed, moving Scratch aside so he could take his shot.

"I'm fairly sure giving your probation officers third-degree sunburns is still frowned upon," Wrath managed to get in before Push launched a telekinetic blast.

The door went flying off the hinges and crashed to a stop at the foot of the steps. "I was trying not to hit it too hard," Push mumbled, seeing the damage.

"Nice shot," Wrath commented. "Can we get out of here now and go strangle the pig that locked us in?"

Push called the sheriff and left a message on his voice mail as they climbed the stairs. He felt awful about destroying public property, but chances were, there was nothing inside that records hall worth stealing. Following that, he gave Professor Trixter's phone a ring as they made their way toward the Pussy Wagon.

"No answer," he said out loud. "He must still be in the air."

Lights flooded the street from farther up ahead. All three men stopped short as they heard a familiar engine rev itself up.

"The hell?" Scratch wondered.

"That's the truck," Wrath said, cautiously taking a step back. The truck inched forward threateningly. "I think someone's just jacked our wheels."

Push lowered his goggles. "Afraid not," he said, zeroing in on the driver's seat. "There's nobody inside the thing."

The Pussy Wagon roared to life and peeled out of the parallel parking space into the street, heading at them. Scratch shoved Push to the side and landed on top of him in a roll while Wrath dove in the opposite direction. The Pussy Wagon seemed to consider Wrath the bigger threat of the three and veered off in his direction. Wrath managed to maneuver himself backward onto his feet and out of the way just in time to avoid having his head squashed under the road machine's wheel.

"Wrath!" Push heard himself cry out.

Wrath was working his way toward them as the Pussy Wagon spun sideways into a stop. "I'm all right," he said. "Thanks for asking."

"It's coming back, guys," Scratch warned as he and Push got up. "And I don't think it's finished with us."

The truck was inching back now, as though preparing for a charge. Tires squealed into the night as the Pussy Wagon bore down on them.

"Ideas?" Wrath asked.

"Run!"

All three dove out of the way toward the sidewalk as the truck raced past them again. "Take the wheels out," Scratch told Wrath urgently. "That'll stop it from trying to run us over, at least."

"The Association is going to kill us," Push moaned. "But do it."

Wrath waited until the truck was facing them. As the Pussy Wagon roared down the street, its tires halfway up on the curb this time, he raised both palms up, launching a barrage of fireballs at the ground. The flames caught the rubber and burned holes straight through, causing the tires in front to explode. The Pussy Wagon shook, and Push winced as the sound of metal scraping on concrete filled the air.

"Nice," Scratch said, stepping forward. "My turn."

Scratch tossed a maroon-striped ball into the air as he brought the two halves of his cue stick together. With a spin, he screwed them into place, taking aim for a spot on the ground not far from them. As the ball came down, he launched it through the air at the spot, hitting the mark perfectly. The ball split into two pieces, unloading a set of tiny road spikes. The noise from the rear tires exploding seemed even louder. The loss of all four tires proved too much for the Pussy Wagon, and it swerved hard, straight through the display window of a used appliance store.

"Break," Scratch said confidently. "Side spin."

"I can't take either of you anywhere," Push shot at them, though he was smiling the whole time he spoke.

"It stopped, didn't it?" Wrath countered.

In reality, the Pussy Wagon was still alive, but not going anywhere. The front of the store had caved when the truck hit it, leaving glass and debris scattered everywhere. The truck gave a feeble sputter before its lights began to flicker. Another moment passed, and it fell silent.

"So," Wrath said, looking between the two of them. "Who's going to explain this one?"

IT TOOK about a half hour before the sheriff, his men, and a tow truck arrived on the scene. The owner of the appliance store was conspicuously absent. Apparently, no one thought the owner needed to see something like this. It was just them, the sheriff, and his goon squad of deputies.

Sheriff Black was less than happy.

"You three are magnets for disaster," he said in a low tone that contrasted with the rage threatening to boil over on his face.

"It's their truck," Wrath reminded him, jerking a finger toward Push and Scratch, who each scowled at him.

"Tell me again," Black asked, keeping all three of them in his sights as he took a step backward. "How did this happen exactly?"

"Someone tried to run us over in our truck," Push said, deciding it would be best to leave out the part where the truck was driving itself.

"Right." Black nodded. "Where are they?"

"We don't know," Scratch said, his face guarded. "The Pussy Wagon was empty when we checked it. There was no one inside."

Black looked the three of them over a moment more, then sighed. "There's not going to be much of a town left if this shit keeps happening," he muttered. "At what point during all of this did the door to the town records room get blown off?"

"That happened before," Push said reluctantly. "Your deputy locked us in there, so I had to blow the door off."

Black's face was unreadable. "Did he, now?"

Push did not like where this was going. Thankfully, someone over near the truck let out a horrifying scream. Push had never been so happy to hear a cry for help in his life. Both he and Scratch snapped into position at once like a well-oiled machine, with Wrath bringing up the rear, not far behind.

"What's happening?" Push asked as they approached one of the men who had been hooking the Pussy Wagon up to the tow truck.

The stranger didn't have time to answer. Inside the appliance store, there came a horrible crash, like a body being tossed across the room. More people were inside the darkened structure, if the pleas for help were any indication. Two bodies, each bleeding badly, went flying out the broken window, landing in front of them.

Push lowered his goggles. "Don't enter the place until I can get some idea of what we're dealing with," he ordered. "Wrath, check those men and make sure they're alive."

"Nobody's going anywhere," Black yelled, coming up behind them. "What in land sake's is all that racket?"

There was a strange noise, like metal being put through a paper shredder, mixed in with what Push could only describe as a thousand electronic crickets chirping angrily. It was simultaneously the most confusing and chilling noise he'd ever encountered. The lens of his goggles flickered with static for a brief instant.

Wrath had gone around, and was kneeling in front of Push outside his range of sight. "They're alive," he confirmed.

Push gave the man a nod. "I'm switching to night vision," he told his teammates, hitting the zoom function. "It looks like…."

It looked like the room was full of cables, even though the rational part of Push's brain insisted this couldn't be the case. The cables were writhing around through the air like flying snakes, twisting and coiling with fury. The sound from before, of shredded metal and angry crickets, came again, causing the cables to withdraw from sight.

Push backed away. "What is it?" Scratch asked.

"Get back," he warned. "I don't know what it is, but it's coming out, and it sounds mad."

Push raised his bo staff and extended it. Flames erupted from Wrath's hands as he bent down slightly into a defensive fighting stance. Scratch had his cue stick out with the infamous eight ball clutched in one hand. For once, Push wasn't going to protest.

Black wasn't arguing with them either. The sheriff had drawn his gun and was taking aim on Scratch's right, keeping the gun leveled at the broken window. Everyone else had vacated the place once the noise got to be too much, those that hadn't been thrown through the air, anyway. The shifting figure lurking inside the appliance store shuffled toward the window, moving as though it were a baby taking those first tentative steps. As it stepped gingerly around the Pussy Wagon and came into the light, Black let out a very light gasp. For Push, the shock numbed him to the core.

"Um, guys?" Scratch said, backing away. "We may need to think of a strategy."

The flames in Wrath's hands flared. "I can take it," he insisted.

"It" was a good summation. Push had never seen anything like "it" before, outside of a film, at least. The monster was walking on two legs. It had arms, a body of some kind, and a head of sorts with bright red eyes. That was the best Push could come up with in comparison to a human being, though. Everything else about the creature screamed unnatural.

"Aliens were bad enough," Scratch muttered.

The monster was like something out of a nightmare. It looked as though someone had taken all of the mechanical appliances inside the store, pureed them in a blender, and then molded whatever remained into a mockery of humankind. The giant-sized result lumbered into view underneath the security light and looked around. Push could see pieces of a washing machine, several refrigerators, one or three microwaves, and a couple of television sets. An ice machine had been set on top as a makeshift head, and it glanced around for a moment before settling on the four of them.

Sheriff Black swallowed the lump in his throat and managed to keep his gun level. "I remember when this was such a peaceful little town."

"I don't," Wrath said flatly.

Scratch shot Wrath a glare. "Get ready," he warned, holding up the eight ball. "I think it's gearing up to attack."

The monster considered the four of them a moment longer, then turned to the crashed truck. Raising both appendages high, it released another high-pitched scream that caused Push to cringe inwardly. As the horrible sound echoed up and down the town street, the monstrosity of assembled parts collapsed in a scattered heap on top of their truck.

None of them moved. "Now what?" Wrath wondered, still crouched in his position. "Was that it?"

"Um," Scratch replied, dragging the sound out. "I don't know."

Push waited, and was rewarded for his patience a second later. One of the broken appliances began to vibrate, signifying it was still alive. Others followed, and as the noise grew worse, the lights on both trucks flickered. The tow truck moved first, though the Pussy Wagon was backing away in conjunction with it perfectly. Both vehicles rolled out into the street together, still connected by the tow truck's tether. The lights on the front of each one flashed angrily at them.

"My God," Black whispered. "The hell is happening here?"

"If I hit the fuel tanks, it might take them both out," Wrath said, looking toward Push momentarily. "What do you say, boss man?"

"There's no one driving," Black yelled, both hands shaking as they gripped his gun. "Jesus, fuck! What the hell is going on?"

The bone-chilling noise started up again. Push withdrew from it automatically. Scratch moved slightly to his left, keeping Push covered the whole time, while Wrath took a couple of tentative steps backward. The man's gait was lethal, like watching a panther move. Up ahead, the two trucks had begun falling apart in pieces. The metal coverings peeled away like chunks of flesh, exposing the frame and inner workings underneath.

The pieces that fell away scurried all over the ground under their own power, like ants. The sight made Push feel sick to his stomach. Once every last bit had been dismantled, the mountainous pile of wreckage moved in unison, each piece pulsating in time with each other like the rhythm of a heartbeat. Shaking, moving like a reanimated corpse, the wreckage formed a new body for itself, rising once more to stand on two legs.

Black was heard praying behind them. "Heaven help us," the man whispered fearfully. "The devil has come to Shove Point."

Scratch narrowed his eyes in answer. Three billiard balls were airborne before Push had time to see them clearly. Scratch launched each one through the air in a straight line, embedding them into the inner workings of the creature. The monstrosity let out a hissing version of the same sound as before while Scratch's balls sank deeper into it.

Just when it looked like his friend's effort had been in vain, each bomb detonated, splattering acid all over the inside and outside surfaces of the monster. The creature roared, as if somehow in pain, focusing the headlights that served as eyes on Scratch as the damage registered.

Wrath raised both fists and unleashed a torrent of fire. "Acid's flammable," Push heard him say. "Let's see if I can't turn things up a bit more."

A violent explosion rocked the air and sent the monster stumbling backward the moment the red tongues of heat touched the acidic liquid. Wrath backed away.

"Any idea as to what this thing is?" he asked.

Push swallowed his fear along with the lump that had been blocking his throat. Even the aliens from the other night had not been this horrifying.

"No clue," he said, before steeling his nerves. "Get ready to move."

Scratch glanced at him. "We're running?"

"For now," Push replied, motioning for Wrath to follow them. "We don't know what this thing is, and we don't know where it came from. On top of that...."

Push never finished. The pain the creature was feeling, assuming it had felt pain at all, had given way to what he was sure was white-hot anger. The monster roared again, that screeching wail of torn metal and insect chirps, then dove forward with its gnarled, gangly arms bent as if meaning to scoop them up.

"Scatter!" Push shouted, before unloading a burst of telekinetic energy into what passed for the monster's face.

The blast made it flinch but did little else. Push tried again, standing his ground bravely even as the monster closed in on him. His knees felt weak as the mechanical nightmare loomed over him menacingly. Push's telekinetic force bubbles rattled the monster but otherwise had no effect whatsoever. Just as he was sure the thing was about to close those spindly, cold metal fingers around him, a wave of fire smashed into its backside near the shoulder area.

The creature turned. "Move!" Wrath shouted, before launching a wave of fireballs through the air.

Push flipped backward out of the line of fire. Gunshots rang out, and he looked around instinctively for their source. Sheriff Black had taken cover behind a squad car and was emptying his clip into the thing. The bullets bounced harmlessly off the monster's surface, but Black refused to let up. Push spotted Scratch nearby, taking aim with his eight ball. The dark sphere went flying, smashing through the left lens serving as the creature's eye.

Several seconds passed. The monster looked around curiously, as though confused by what had just happened. This allowed the last second on the delayed charge to tick to zero. Shrapnel flew as the plastique bomb blew the monster's head into a thousand fiery pieces.

Wrath was still laying it on thick with the fire. His flames danced artfully through the air, as though moving to some high-speed waltz that was silent to everyone else. The fires moved around the beast's metal form, lashing out and striking each time it tried to move. Bringing both arms down, Wrath slammed into the monster with the full force of his powers, setting it ablaze.

The monster roared this time, clearly feeling the agony of being burned alive.

Something about the sound it made caused Push to wince in sympathy. "That's enough, Wrath," he called out as the flames covering the creature intensified. "Stop it! I said that was enough."

Wrath watched him for a moment, then slowly lowered his arms. The flames licking at the monster's body eased off a bit, though the creature was still flailing about in tortured pain. Push could feel Scratch's eyes on him as his best friend approached.

"Do you have one of your foam bombs on you?" he asked quietly.

"One," Scratch replied. "Why?"

Push didn't answer but nodded at the creature. "Please," he added.

Scratch nodded in reply and fired the ball into the monster's center. The white mess of foam spread over the creature in moments, blanketing it in the asphyxiating substance and snuffing out the remainder of the flames.

Wrath joined them a moment later, watching Push the whole time with a curious expression. Black did not emerge from behind the squad car until the monster fell to the ground and stopped moving.

Slowly, looking as though his entire world had been shattered in but a few minutes, the sheriff turned toward Push.

"What next?" he asked, his voice trembling.

This wasn't information he'd intended to share with Sheriff Black. Now, though, keeping secrets didn't seem as important.

"We have proof," Push said, feeling more determined now that the ordeal was over. "Hopefully, the Association will believe us."

"You're thinking it came from the same place?" Wrath asked.

Push frowned. "What are the odds it didn't?" he pointed out. "This is bigger than anything we've ever had to deal with."

"No shit," Scratch replied, letting out a deep breath.

"We need to find that pod," Wrath said, looking the smoking wreck over. "And Sloth. The man has to know what this is about. Finding one means finding the other."

"Agreed," Push said. "But in the meantime, what are we supposed to do about this?"

None of them had considered the fact that Black was standing just a few feet off to the side. His face had gone from scared shitless to bemusement before settling on suspicion.

"What the hell are you bunch not telling me?" he demanded.

The heap in front of them gave a twitch. "Not now," Push replied, backing away along with the others. "We should try to communicate with this thing. See if we can get it to tell us what it wants."

Sheriff Black glared at Push like he'd lost his mind, but the older man was cut off from saying anything as the monster lumbered up off the ground, headless but not out of the fight yet. It seemed what it had fixed upon its shoulders was purely aesthetic, because after a moment's confusion, it zeroed in on the three of them and brought a large metal fist down.

"Um, it looks busy right now," said Scratch, bringing his cue stick up in front of him. "Maybe we should leave a message?"

Wrath waved his hands through the air, sending out a blast of fire that struck the monster across the chest. The flames made the beast stagger back but not far enough. Push hit it with another barrage of telekinetic force blasts, but felt himself tiring. It was too large for them to take on toe to toe. Push's mind raced while the sheriff reloaded his gun and opened fire on it again. They were getting nowhere fast, and their efforts just made the thing even madder. They needed to come up with a plan.

That was what Push was thinking as a silver disk sailed over his head and stuck to the front of the monster. Two more joined it almost immediately, and as Push turned to see where they had come from, the three disks detonated simultaneously.

The shock wave made his ears hum. Sparks were flying as pieces of the creature blew off the main body to the ground. The beast howled now, but that didn't deter the figure in bright red racing past with her sword held high. Push felt his jaw drop as Scarlet Queen swung upward, brandishing the rapier she usually kept sheathed at her back, before cutting through one of the monster's hands.

"What's she doing here?" Push heard Scratch ask.

"Who is she?" Wrath wondered, watching as the dark-haired woman defiantly maneuvered around the monster's attacks. Deftly, Scarlet Queen ducked as it swung its wounded appendage at her in vain.

"That's Scarlet Queen," Push explained. "But how did she get here?"

"Unlike you, Push," came another confident voice from behind them, "women love riding with me."

Professor Trixter stood with his head held high as an unexpected wind whipped at his white lab coat. Next to him, the white-cloaked Wiccan Witch smiled, flashing her teeth at Scratch and sending a jolt of unanticipated jealousy through Push.

"Hey, guys!" Wiccan Witch called out as she walked over, unfazed by the creature attacking Scarlet Queen just a few feet away. "Who's your new friend? Is this the guy from prison?"

Wrath blinked before looking at the fight behind them. "Shouldn't someone help her?" he asked.

"Professor Trixter hit it with some new EMP pulse grenades he invented," she said. "It should go down any second. Scarlet Queen was mad because she wasn't getting to fight it first. Just let her have her fun."

Scarlet Queen was backing away from the monster, watching it carefully as it closed in on her. Wrath started to move toward her, but Push remained in his spot, seeing that the creature's movements were sluggish now. Professor Trixter's weapons had done their work well, as per usual. A few seconds later, it sputtered and let off several more sparks before falling forward to the ground. Scarlet Queen moved out of the way as several of the pieces breaking off it came flying near her.

Wrath stopped dead in his tracks. "Never mind, I guess," Push overheard him mutter.

"I hope we weren't interrupting," Wiccan Witch went on, like nothing unusual had happened. "Scarlet Queen and I heard Professor Trixter was coming down for a visit, and we had a little vacation time coming, so we thought we'd stop by and see how things were going. Plus, it has been such a long time since any of us worked together as a real team."

"No, no," Push quickly assured her, feeling embarrassed over just how close he'd come to dying a few minutes before. "In fact, your timing is perfect."

"Was this what you wanted me to look at?" Professor Trixter asked, eying the lump of metal not far away.

Push turned around. "Actually, no," he said, suddenly aware the sheriff was still lurking nearby and listening closely. "What we wanted to show you is back at the house."

"Don't get him wrong," Scratch added, smiling now. "We're really glad to see you, especially seeing as you managed to do all the hard work for us."

Professor Trixter shook his head, laughing. "You white people make everything harder than it needs to be. Just about anything that's mechanical can be taken out with a simple EMP pulse." Professor Trixter paused. "That," he added, "or some really big magnets, which I probably should have brought with me from the hovercraft."

"Guys?" Scarlet Queen called out from over near Wrath.

Push suddenly remembered Wrath was a former criminal, and he'd just turned his back on the man, leaving him alone with Scarlet Queen. Not that she was incapable of defending herself. It embarrassed Push further to think he'd neglected to keep one of his friends' safety in mind, though.

Then again, there hadn't been anything in Wrath's file that suggested he was a rapist.

The more Push thought on it, the more uncomfortable and confused he became, which was why he didn't hear what Scarlet Queen said next.

"I said, there's something you should see," she repeated, giving him a hard look. "This stuff that came off that thing?"

"What about it?" Wiccan Witch asked, looking around curiously.

Scarlet Queen pointed to a piece near her foot. "It's moving."

CHAPTER
SIX

SHERIFF BLACK left in his squad car after calling for a flatbed truck to come out and haul the mechanized corpse out of the road. Having his world shattered with the arrival of a monstrosity that may or may not be extraterrestrial would have been more than enough. Knowing there were three more members of the spandex club, which Push overheard him referring to them as, was the final straw. Something told Push this wasn't the end of it.

As it was, he should have been at least moderately freaked out. Just seeing the thing lying there was unsettling. The six of them had opted to wait and make sure nothing bad happened until the flatbed got there. Professor Trixter was fairly confident the EMP grenades had done their job but didn't take offense to the group wanting to make sure. It was having his friends so close that made the whole thing okay, even laughable. By the time the truck arrived to drag the hunk of junk away, they were joking about it.

Well, most of them were. Wrath lurked off to the side while the rest of them stood around talking. Though he wasn't sure, the few times he'd bothered to look over there, Wrath had given Push the impression he was not entirely thrilled with the others' timely arrival. When Push checked again less than a minute later, Wrath was looking down at a broken piece of street asphalt forlornly. It actually made him feel sorry for the guy. Luckily, he was spared from having to deal with the issue, thanks to Wiccan Witch.

"Hi," she greeted unflinchingly, after marching right over to his side. "You must be the new guy. They call me Wiccan Witch, but if it's too much of a tongue twister, just call me Megan. You'd be surprised at how many people stumble over those two words when they're put together."

Wrath stared at her for several moments in complete silence. Push caught himself watching the scene unfold but didn't turn away. A separate silence was beginning to creep over the group now as their eyes veered in Megan's general direction.

"Something wrong?" Wiccan Witch asked after a moment.

Wrath nodded toward Push and the others standing around him. "I think your friends are a little worried I might try something less than honorable with you."

Wiccan Witch snorted. "I have a black belt in judo," she informed him, laughter peppering her words. "Among other things. If you did try something, I would have to break your spine in three different places."

"I wouldn't blame you for doing so," Wrath replied calmly.

Wiccan Witch smiled at him before looping her arm through his. "Come on over," she said, leading a very reluctant Wrath toward the others. "We were all going to take a ride in the Professor's new hovercraft back to your place."

Push turned to Trixter upon hearing this. "What?" the big black man asked defensively. "I'm on vacation, and the hotels in this place are shit!"

"He isn't kidding," Scarlet Queen revealed, as they began making their way farther down the road, where Professor Trixter had apparently left his shiny new hovercraft double-parked. Wiccan Witch had her arm looped through Wrath's the whole time.

"We checked one of those hotel websites," Scarlet Queen was saying. "Would you believe someone actually gave the one hotel this town has a negative rating?"

"We were there for one night," Scratch told her, sticking close to Push as they walked side by side. "It wasn't that bad."

"I'd rather not risk it," Scarlet Queen replied, as Push felt Scratch's hand brush against his own, making his heart pound like a drum. "Any chance we could just crash with you while we're here?"

"Sure," both he and Scratch said at the same time.

Push swallowed, hoping his nervousness didn't show. He had no idea what they were going to do now that several of his friends had dropped out of the sky to stay the night. A part of him silently hoped, in the far recesses of his mind, that he would work up the nerve to let Scratch sleep with him. The saner, rational side, however, the one that had the largest deciding vote, was rejoicing that the opportunity was blown. He was sure there was no way the two of them would do anything with the others there.

That was what Push was telling himself as he felt Scratch brush his hand once more up against him. There was no doubt in Push's mind it was deliberate, and the sensation left him short of breath for a moment. Furthermore, all the blood in his body rushed south of the border to crush his dick painfully into his spandex pants. It was a very good thing darkness had already come, because the last thing he needed was for the group to see him getting boned up over his best friend lightly touching him.

Wiccan Witch's voice came sharply out of nowhere, and her words almost made Push jump out of his skin.

"There's something different about you two," she stated, watching them with a sharp eye as both she and Wrath wandered past.

"Yeah," Scarlet Queen agreed, looking back over her shoulder. "I noticed it too."

Scratch smiled slightly, but Push felt himself go pale. "We'll tell you later," Scratch assured her. "If that's all right."

"Sure," Wiccan Witch replied, shrugging. "It wasn't really any of my business anyway. Sorry if I was prying."

Scratch shook his head, then lightly brushed his fingers over the top of Push's hand as they reached the hovercraft.

"No problem."

Professor Trixter pressed a button on the cuff of his lab coat. The doors of the hovercraft unfolded upward like wings. Push was reminded of the DeLorean from *Back to the Future* as the others began climbing aboard. Scarlet Queen rode shotgun while Wiccan Witch took a seat beside Wrath, whom she was still holding on to. Scratch took the seat in front of them, then patted the spot next to him, giving Push a discreet, hopeful smile.

Like there was room anywhere else, really.

Professor Trixter was holding up the sample he'd collected from Scarlet Queen, the fragmented piece of the monster she'd spotted moving around on the street.

"What are you going to do with that?" Push asked as he climbed in, grateful for something to take his mind off the man next to him.

"Study it," the Professor replied, as if that had been clear from the beginning. "How many chances am I going to get to look at something straight out of a comic book?"

Push didn't answer as the doors whooshed shut. Scratch had chosen that moment to playfully rub his thumb over the back of Push's. Push felt his heart leap into his throat, and the feeling was in no way connected to the fact that Professor Trixter had just started up the hovercraft.

Scratch smiled, sensing Push's reaction, as the hovercraft began to glide down the hill into the backstreets of Shove Point. The man was becoming incorrigible.

"HOME sweet home," Scarlet Queen commented, giving the place a once-over as she climbed out of the front of the hovercraft. "Nice place they put you in."

Push thought she sounded suspicious. The others didn't notice, being too busy chattering among themselves. Wiccan Witch was firing question after question at Wrath. The man was clearly becoming uncomfortable with the amount of prying, yet even Push could see he didn't want to be rude. It made him laugh, but at the same time, he felt a twinge of pity for the guy.

"I've never seen anything like this before," Wrath said, nodding at the deflating bag of air that held the vehicle up in an attempt to shift the focus off himself. "Isn't it illegal to drive one of these things on a public road?"

Professor Trixter turned around. "Arrest me," he fired back.

The remark caught Wrath off-guard. "I was just asking," he replied.

It actually sounded like the man's feelings had been hurt. The result floored everyone so badly that, for a moment, nobody said a word.

"Let's go inside," Wiccan Witch suggested before giving Wrath's arm a tender squeeze. "I hope they left us some booze."

"Hell yes!" Scarlet Queen shouted. "We just had our first actual comic-book-villain fight ever. This is a time to be celebrating!"

A resounding cheer went up. "I hope there's enough liquor left," Scratch mumbled, though he looked happy as his key fit into the door lock. "Um, everyone, just make yourselves at home. I'll see what we have."

Professor Trixter made several additional trips out to his hovercraft for equipment while everyone else made tracks for the living room. Within minutes, Scratch was pouring from a bottle of wine that had somehow been overlooked. The Professor accepted a glass graciously, then promptly ignored it. The breakfast table on the other side of the counter had been commandeered as a makeshift lab, and the muscular black man was far too engrossed in the sample he'd taken to do more than mutter every other minute or so.

Push, however, was quite used to this treatment, and so was everyone else except Wrath, who didn't appear to care. He and Wiccan Witch were on one side of the three-corner couch. Scratch and Push had claimed the middle, while Scarlet Queen lounged regally near the end all by herself, looking tired but extremely satisfied.

"Let us know what that thing is once you've figured it out," she called as everyone settled down. "Damn, that thing we fought in the street was amazing! I can't believe I almost blew off this trip to watch reruns of *Walking Dead* online."

"Aw." Scratch pouted over his wine glass. "You mean you were just going to let us rot out here in the sticks without seeing you?"

Push chuckled, his laughter punctuated with nervous tension. Both Wiccan Witch and Scarlet Queen had noticed something between him and Scratch. Sitting on the couch together side by side, his brain kept coming up with more and more ridiculous scenarios about how blatantly obvious they were being. Scratch wasn't even touching him. There was a good foot and a half of space between their bodies, yet alarms blared each time Push thought he saw someone glance their way.

Thankfully, Scarlet Queen could always be counted on. "I cannot wait to rub this into Flexigirl's face at the next Association conference," she blurted out. "She's always bragging to anyone who'll listen about how she fought in the big brawl down in New Orleans."

Everyone froze at the same time. Scarlet Queen went rigid a second afterward and quickly darted her eyes toward Wrath.

"No offense," she added very quickly.

"None taken," he said, completely unfazed by her remark. "I'm surprised you were willing to talk about it. As I understand, it's something of a sore subject in the Association."

Scarlet Queen shrugged a little sheepishly. "I was in high school when I caught the news broadcast on TV," she said before taking a sip of her wine. "Watching it was what made me want to become a hero in the first place. My dad finally relented when I promised to graduate from college first."

Scarlet Queen chuckled to herself. "My mother has rued the day she nagged me to keep up with current events ever since. Twice a week now she calls, asking when I plan on getting a real job, and reminds me of how expensive student loan payments are."

No one else was taking the conversation so casually. "Let's talk about something else," Push suggested.

"Please," Wiccan Witch added, giving her friend across the couch a hard stare.

Scarlet Queen frowned. "Why?"

"Because," Wrath said in a thick voice. "The odds are good I killed someone during the New Orleans battle that one of you knew or, at the very least, admired."

Scarlet Queen looked like she'd been hit with a ton of bricks. "Sorry," she said to the room. "I never got into the Association until…."

"We know," Push said, feeling more at ease now. "And most of us are used to you being blunt."

Scratch snorted. "That's putting it mildly," he teased.

"I think everyone here has a 'How I Joined the Association' story," Scarlet Queen added, hoping to break some of the tension. "Most of us have shared ours."

"I think explaining mine would be redundant," Wrath told her, smiling slightly.

"True," she acknowledged. "No point in going into that, I guess."

Wiccan Witch rolled her eyes in mock exasperation. "I guess it wouldn't hurt to share mine," she said, patting Wrath gently on the knee. "I don't think everyone here has heard it yet, and it'll keep the Queen over there from putting her foot in her mouth for a little while."

Scarlet Queen laughed. "Only for a little while."

"At least she admits it," Wiccan Witch retorted, gearing up for her story. "I was part of this paranormal research committee in college. We were doing this documentary film on local lore as part of a bid to get funding from the school for a student film. One of the places we checked out was a swamp near campus that was reputed to be haunted."

"Was it?" Scarlet Queen asked. "I can't remember whether you told me that part before or not."

"It was," Wiccan Witch replied earnestly. "But that wasn't the problem. It turned out a couple of chemistry professors had set up a meth lab in a shack out there. They caught us and were about to poison all four of us when Swamp Wraith and Ghost Girl showed up. Apparently, the Association had sent them to help the police track down where the new influx of drugs was coming from."

Wiccan Witch took a deep breath before continuing. "Some of the ghosts in the area were actually pretty nice. When I saw how bad the fight was going, I asked a few of them if they would mind giving everyone a hand."

Wrath cocked his head and gave her a wry grin. "You can talk to ghosts?"

"Since I was a little girl," she answered calmly. "I can also do tarot predictions."

"I'd stay away from that if I were you," Scarlet Queen warned abruptly. "I didn't believe her when she told me my last boyfriend was cheating on me. She still brings that up from time to time."

Wrath chuckled quietly alongside the others. "I knew a woman who did the same thing in New Orleans," he said quietly. "You see a lot of that kind of thing down there."

"Did she ever do a reading for you?" Wiccan Witch asked, interested.

"She nearly did," he admitted. "Once. We'd spoken several times before, and one day I agreed to let her tell me my future. We shook hands, and she went pale and jerked her arm back like she'd just been bitten by a snake. After that, she never would look at me."

Wrath looked up at the stunned room. "I must have been around thirteen," he added.

Wiccan Witch observed Wrath for a moment, along with the rest of the room. Reaching into a pouch that was attached to her belt, she pulled out a small deck of tarot cards.

"Do you know much about it?" she asked, holding them up so Wrath could see.

"A little," he answered.

Wrath set his half-full wine glass aside and stood up. Keeping his back to Wiccan Witch, he slowly drew his black T-shirt up over his shoulders, exposing the tattoo Push recalled seeing in his apartment kitchen back in Chicago. Wiccan Witch smiled at the sight of the circles imprinted on each shoulder blade, holding what looked like a pair of antlers on the left and a silhouetted chalice on the right. Between the spheres, a tree of some kind sprang up along his spine.

"I don't get it," Scarlet Queen said, giving Wiccan Witch a confused look. "What's he showing you?"

Wrath obliged by turning ninety degrees so that she and the rest of the room could see as well. "What do those mean?" Push wondered, not thinking.

"The sign on the left is the Consort's antlers," Wiccan Witch answered for him. "And the chalice on the right is the mark of the Goddess, Consort's lover, primal other half, and partner in all things. Their coupling stabilizes the balance the world needs for survival. The tree is the World Tree, which holds the universe together."

Wiccan Witch was smiling at Wrath as he lowered his shirt and sat down beside her. "I knew there was a reason I liked you," she said, taking his hand in hers. "It's good to meet you, brother."

Push felt as though he'd just missed something significant.

"So he's like you," Scarlet Queen affirmed. "I guess that makes sense."

"If I might ask," Wrath began tentatively, not looking at Wiccan Witch. "If you can predict future events with tarot and speak with spirits, why does the Association not have you on the front covers of magazines more often?"

"Because she's a girl," Scarlet Queen answered for her, ruefully.

"I'm pagan," she reminded Wrath. "And I'm polyamorous. The Association has a list of my skills, and both of those are listed there, but I think whoever is responsible for the magazine just hand-waved them as the ramblings of a kook. You know how some people are about these kinds of things."

Even Push had to smile along with Wrath at that statement. "Vaguely," he said. "I still have people walk up to me on the street and ask to see me knock something away, just so they can confirm I'm not a fraud."

Wiccan Witch laughed. "Push's powers are easy to confirm," she went on. "And tarot is by no means accurate in every given situation. The Association likes results more than anything."

"Which is why I'm happy to break things," Scarlet Queen joked, wildly waving her police club in the air.

"Please don't," Push moaned. "The last time you waved that thing around while drinking, I almost had to go to the hospital for a concussion."

Scarlet Queen let the hand holding the club fall to the couch at once. "Sorry!" she apologized.

"Is she trying to kill you with her stick again, Push?" Professor Trixter called from his makeshift lab in the kitchen.

"Not yet," Scratch called back. "We'll let you know if it happens, though."

"Great!"

Most of the room laughed, except for Push. "Who wants to go next?" Wiccan Witch asked, shuffling the cards in her hands. "Push?"

"Everyone already knows mine," Push replied dismissively. "And it's not something I really want to bring up right now."

"Fair enough. How about you, Scratch?" Wiccan Witch asked as the cards flew through her fingers. "I know your 'How I Joined the Association' story, but I'm not sure Scarlet Queen does, and we both know Wrath hasn't heard it yet."

"No," Scratch mused, sighing. "I can't remember if it ever came up when Scarlet and I were dating, though."

"It did," she told him, throwing in a knowing smirk for good measure. "You wouldn't answer at first, and I had to threaten you with temporary denied access to certain parts of my body before you'd cough up the truth."

Something inside Push bristled at hearing this. "But go ahead," Scarlet Queen went on, unaware of Push's sudden mood change. "I'd love to hear this story again."

Wrath was intrigued. "How bad is it?" he asked, looking to Wiccan Witch.

"He got busted for table hustling at a pool hall," Push answered in Scratch's place. "Scratch was seventeen at the time, and the guy who nabbed him was a Cape."

"Marine Stormtrooper," Scratch recalled, staring down at his empty glass. "He gave me this ten-minute Captain America pitch about living right before letting me go. I thought he was going to kick my ass and drag me down to the nearest police station."

Scratch brushed a thumb across the rim of his wineglass. "I was hustling tables to raise money to start my own comic book company," he said, once his glass was full again. "It was a stupid idea, but I'd always been great at pool. Some friends and I were going to band together and take down Marvel and DC both. In the end, I was the only one who actually went to art school. It took me about two years to figure out what a huge-ass mistake that was."

Scarlet Queen laughed, but Scratch didn't look offended. "Anyway, a little while after he busted me, Stormtrooper came to speak at our high school. He spotted me in the audience and, after assembly was over, came up to see how I was doing."

"He must have made an impression," Wiccan Witch mused, smirking herself.

"At first, I thought he was a dick," Scratch revealed, after swallowing a mouthful of wine. "He was so full of himself, it made me sick. Then he started coming around my place to check on me, making sure I was staying out of trouble. That was how my mom found out about the pool hustling."

Push snorted into his drink. "I bet she took it well," he snickered.

Scratch's face soured momentarily. "I thought he was there to get in her pants," he said. "So I called him out on it as he was leaving one day. The man just stood there out on our front lawn, listening to me rant for fifteen minutes, before informing me polite as you please that he was happily married with two sons and a daughter, all of whom were in college."

Scratch got quiet then, and Push knew why. He had heard this story before, more of it than anyone else in the room, most likely.

"After a while," Scratch said, his voice thicker now than earlier. "He just sort of grew on me. He came over a couple more times before being shipped...." Scratch jerked his head toward Wrath.

"...before being shipped down to New Orleans," Wrath finished. "He was one of the heroes I fought during the brawl."

Something passed through Scratch, and Push winced. Scratch's father had run out on his mother when he was seven, leaving her to raise him alone. Like a lot of boys who grew up never knowing their dad very well, Scratch had, by his own admission, collected father figures. Marine Stormtrooper had been one of them.

"Did you kill him?" Scratch asked stiffly.

"No," Wrath replied, unfazed. "But we did fight one another." Wrath let the statement settle into the room for a moment before finishing off with, "He kicked my ass."

Wiccan Witch laughed first, but the rest were not far behind. "Seriously?" Scratch asked, smiling as Wrath let out a long sigh.

"Very much so," Wrath said. "I was fighting off some cops when he came at me out of nowhere. The police were pretty simple to deal with. Even with their riot gear, I just had to raise the fire high enough all around us to get them to back off. Marine Stormtrooper walked right through, cool as a cucumber. I'm guessing his outfit must have been flame-retardant. He didn't bother trying to talk me down. We went at it, and I was thinking the whole time it would be easy."

Wrath took a long swallow from his glass. "Nothing I did scared him off, though," he said softly, his face lost in thought. "He wouldn't back off, even after I warned him. No matter what, the man kept coming for me. When he got close enough is when the fight got heated, if you'll excuse the pun. I could tell he was a pro."

"What happened?" Scratch pressed.

Wrath cocked his head to one side as he set his glass down on the floor.

"Dude," Push scolded. "Use a coaster or something."

"Sorry," Wrath said, passing the glass over to Wiccan Witch when she offered to take it. Push found himself taken aback again. He'd expected Wrath to put up a fight or blow him off.

"Anyway," the man resumed. "Once I realized things weren't going my way, I took off and went to find Pride."

"You ran?"

Wrath looked at Scarlet Queen. "The Deadly Seven were over," he explained, unperturbed by her incredulous tone. "No matter what Sloth told us, we had already lost. Most of us hadn't planned on fighting in the first place."

"You were going to surrender?" Wiccan Witch had stood up to refill everyone's glasses and frowned as she sat down closer to Wrath, handing him his glass in the process.

"We were going to leave," Wrath clarified. "Everyone thought fighting was a stupid idea, but for some reason, Sloth was adamant. When the cops and the heroes cornered us inside that safe house, the plan was to sneak out through the passage into the alley, then make for the garage where some of our vehicles were stored. Sloth vetoed that, giving us this rambling speech about everything we had built and how we would show them what we were made of. It was all I could do not to flash fry the guy."

The gears in Push's mind started to turn upon hearing this. Glancing around the room, he could see he wasn't the only one whose thoughts had begun moving along the same track.

"The Deadly Seven were going to run?" he asked, sure he had somehow misheard despite seeing the same expressions on the others' faces. "Are you bullshitting us?"

"We had lost," Wrath replied. "There was nothing keeping any of us in New Orleans, so the logical thing to do was leave and start somewhere else. Pride and I were planning on leaving anyway. We had talked about getting out of the organization and moving to Europe. Greed was going to come with us, at least for the beginning of the trip. Things breaking apart seemed like a great sign."

Scratch was dead-set on learning more. Push could hear it in his friend's voice when he spoke next. "What happened?"

Wrath thought back for a moment. "We pretty much told Sloth he could go fuck himself and headed for the secret exit. All of our major spots had one. Someone must have leaked the information, though, because the SWAT teams were there to ambush us. From there, it felt like we were herded out into the open. In the confusion, I lost track of Pride and Greed, and then the fight turned into a full-blown riot. I was blasting people back, hoping to catch sight of either one. After I got away from Marine Stormtrooper, I found Pride, and we went looking for a way out of the melee. Then the cops cornered us again, and she told me to run."

Wrath's voice thickened as he continued. "There was nothing I could do," he whispered. "I'd used so much of my powers that my body was straining pretty badly. She must have noticed that. I still wanted to stay, but she told me… if I didn't run, she would shoot me herself."

The last words out of Wrath's mouth were the roughest. "I promised her I would find her and then took off."

It was a moment before Wrath would look anyone in the face. When he finally did, it was Scratch whose eyes he met.

"I don't know what happened to the Marine Stormtrooper," he said plainly. "Or who killed him, but it wasn't me."

Push watched as Scratch nodded toward Wrath. "Sure," he said. "Thanks for telling me, though."

Push had his mouth open, intent on saying something. Whatever had been on his mind was lost as Professor Trixter's voice rang out from the kitchen.

"Excelsior!"

They all watched as Trixter slid into the room on his sock-covered feet. "It's alive!" he shouted in a madman's voice. "Alive, I tell you all! Alive!"

The sample he'd collected was being held captive inside a petri dish. Professor Trixter had it clutched from underneath in one hand as he waved it around the room excitedly, somehow not sending the stuff flying through the air. In all the confusion, Push didn't notice right away how the sample wasn't moving nearly as much as before.

"Look at this," he said, finally holding the dish still long enough so they could all lock their eyes on it. "The stuff actually is alive."

Scarlet Queen glanced toward Push. "Virgil," she said, clearly fearing the Professor had lost his mind. "It came off a robot."

"Not a robot," Professor Trixter declared, holding the dish up higher. "An artificial life-form made out of nanobots."

Push snickered. "Dude," he began, which earned him a glare from the muscled man. "Have you been reading that S.C.I. Spy trade again?"

"Come see for yourselves," Trixter replied haughtily.

Wrath was the first one to follow after him. Nobody else seemed to want to risk it at first. They were all thinking the same thing. Push could see it on each of his friends' faces.

"Nanobots aren't real," Wiccan Witch asked as they all stood together as one. "Right?"

"We'll see," Scarlet Queen replied, straightening her top. "Assuming he hasn't gone off the deep end, this will be really interesting."

Wrath was looking through a microscope that Trixter had set up in the middle of the table. "It's nanobots," he declared. "Just like the man said."

The pyrokinetic backed up, allowing room for each of them to see for themselves. "Micro-sized machines," Trixter stated as the line shrank. "Programmed to work as a colony like ants or bees."

"We know," Push reminded. "But stuff like this doesn't exist in real life yet."

"And don't you need an electron microscope to see things like this?" Wiccan Witch added as she peered through the lenses.

Scarlet Queen gave Professor Trixter an impressed look. "Did you invent a portable electron microscope?" she asked.

"These don't fit the nanoscale size," Trixter explained. "The robots are tiny, but not *that* small."

"Then why call them nanobots?" Wrath asked. "Why not microbots instead?"

Trixter's face soured at the question.

"He thinks 'nanobots' sounds cooler than 'microbots'," Wiccan Witch explained as she straightened back up, which earned her a silent glare from Trixter.

"It is cooler," Push said, taking Trixter's side. "But like I said, this kind of stuff doesn't exist yet."

"You and I thought the same thing about aliens less than a week ago," Scratch reminded as he moved aside to give Push his turn.

Wiccan Witch frowned. "Aliens?"

"The other day," Wrath explained, as Push glanced through the lenses at the strip of metal that, upon closer inspection, was covered in little machines that resembled some tiny insect creature. "Scratch and Push fought them first. They were looking through the wrecked part of town for something, then took off for the woods."

Wiccan Witch and Scarlet Queen stared at each other, each one's eyes getting bigger by the second. "You two fought aliens?" Wiccan Witch demanded.

"Three," Wrath reminded. "And yes, we did."

"I hate both of you right now," Scarlet Queen declared, looking furious.

"We weren't keeping it a secret," Push said defensively, rising up. "At least, not from any of you. A lot of stuff has been going on since we got here, and... I guess I was just waiting for the right time."

"Still," Scarlet Queen insisted. "You three got to fight aliens."

Scratch sighed. "It's not as much fun as you'd think," he warned. "These things exploded after a couple of hits. They weren't very durable."

"He's right," Wrath told her, backing him up.

"I still have to find a dry cleaner," Push muttered.

"Do the aliens have something to do with this?" Professor Trixter asked calmly, like they were discussing the weather or something.

Push gave the man a look for a moment. "Maybe," he said. "We still don't know whether those were real aliens, or why they were here."

"It has something to do with that ship," Wrath insisted, propping himself up against the kitchen doorframe. "I'm sure of it."

Scarlet Queen, Wiccan Witch, and Professor Trixter turned to face Push and Scratch.

"Ship?" Scarlet Queen demanded.

"There was a ship?" Wiccan Witch asked, stunned.

"An actual alien spaceship?" the Professor rounded off, and even he sounded put out at them. "With actual aliens inside?"

"We don't know what was inside," Push began, feeling a headache coming on. "The ship exploded after it ejected this pod. Sloth was looking for it along with those... whatever they were. We found the ship while investigating what the aliens were up to, and—"

Wiccan Witch cut in again. "Sloth?" she practically squeaked, before looking over her shoulder at Wrath. "Sloth? As in *the* Sloth? Sloth is here?"

Wrath nodded. "I guess there was a lot more happening here than I realized," Push said, looking over to Scratch for support. "Has it really been that busy since we got here?"

"Feels like it," his almost-lover replied.

"Sloth is here in Shove Point," Wiccan Witch mused, running everything she'd just learned over in her mind. "Aliens have landed looking for a pod ejected from a crashed spaceship that blew itself up, and we just took down a robot built from a garage sale powered by nanobots."

"That about covers it," said Wrath.

"That's an awful lot to throw at two Association members who were transferred here because of one small screw-up," Scarlet Queen said sharply. "Has anything else happened since you got here that you've forgotten to mention?"

Thankfully, Push didn't hear her question. "Screw-up?" he wondered. "What's that supposed to mean?"

"Who said we screwed up?" Scratch asked her, shifting his weight to his other side. "Push and I were put here to find Sloth and the Pranksta Gayngsta."

Nobody spoke. "S'not what I heard," Professor Trixter replied at last, before turning away from them to examine the sample again under the microscope.

"Me neither," said Scarlet Queen, folding her arms. "Word around the Association was you two got yourselves stuck out here babysitting him because of a screw-up."

Scarlet Queen jerked a thumb at Wrath as she spoke. "Trixter told us he was on his way here to give you a hand with something, so we thought we'd tag along. I just assumed you asking him to come down was because you guys were bored out of your minds with nothing to do and wanted company."

"We haven't had time for any of that," Push replied, getting angry. "When the Pranksta Gayngsta escaped, the Cape Cabinet ordered us to track him down personally. Since we got here, it's been one damn thing after another."

"Who said we were put here as punishment for something?" Scratch wondered.

Scarlet Queen glanced at Wiccan Witch first. "It was Rocket Grasshopper," she admitted, looking uncomfortable. "He told me in private that you two were being assigned here to train Wrath because you'd let the Pranksta Gayngsta get away."

CHAPTER
SEVEN

"WHAT?"

The question came out of both their mouths at the exact same time. Push's eyes met with Scratch's, and he had to force himself to look away so as not to gaze too long into them.

They were brown. His mind had fixated on that fact numerous times, but this time was different. Every fiber of his being was committed to recalling the smoky look he'd seen there that whispered how badly Scratch wanted him. It was a look he'd never dreamed of seeing before, and now it made Push realize just how far down the rabbit hole he'd fallen.

He had to get his thoughts back on track. "Who said what?" he tried. The question had started out much more eloquent before leaving his mouth, so Push tried again. "Rocket Grasshopper said we were here as punishment?"

"Just temporarily," Wiccan Witch said reassuringly. "The Cape Cabinet was afraid the Grand Rapids police would try and pin this on the Association, so they were going to make it look like you two were being punished by placing you here."

Push said nothing, his thoughts racing like mad to piece it all together. "I don't think that's it," Scratch said, summing everything up nicely. "Not really, anyway. Making us recapture the Pranksta Gayngsta makes sense, but we had nothing to do with him getting away. In fact, we were wondering if there had been any news about how he escaped in the first place."

"Nothing," Scarlet Queen told him sadly. "Everyone has been asking questions, but so far, it's like the man just walked through a wall like a ghost."

"Was he?" Wiccan Witch asked.

"No," Push told her, fighting the urge to smile. "The Pranksta Gayngsta is solid enough. Somebody helped him escape from the holding cell."

"Then he comes straight here," said Wrath, who had been quiet for several minutes. "Does anybody else find that strange?"

Scarlet Queen looked hard at him, as though sizing Wrath up. "A little," she admitted, before turning sharply back to Scratch and Push. "Do either of you know why he came here?"

"Not a fucking clue," Scratch replied, sighing.

"I'm still not sure what the deal with this whole reassignment story is," Push went on, going back to what Scarlet Queen had told him. "Putting us here with Wrath fits, but why would they leave capturing Sloth up to us if they didn't think we were going to be able to bring Pranksta Gayngsta back?"

"Maybe they needed you out of the way for a while?" Professor Trixter offered, looking up from his equipment.

That made everyone stop. "What makes you say that?" Scarlet Queen asked incredulously.

"No idea," Trixter replied. "But if you want someone out of your hair for a while because you're planning something big, the ideal solution is to put them somewhere nobody else wants to be."

No one said anything for a moment. "He's right," Wrath affirmed to the quiet room. "A lot of what has been going on doesn't make sense. Maybe the problem is that no one has been asking the right questions."

"I've got a question for you," Trixter cut back, turning his chair around to stare at Wrath directly. "What would a top-secret experiment belonging to the Association be doing in a hick town like Shove Point?"

Wrath's face remained completely motionless. "I don't follow," he said finally.

"Me either," Wiccan Witch added for his benefit. "What experiment?"

Professor Trixter pointed to the table. "This one," he replied. "The Association has all sorts of private funding for pet projects. They've got stuff tucked away in storage facilities that aren't due to be made public for years. All the patents are in the organization's name too, so they get all the windfall once the inventions go public."

"How does that work?" Wrath wondered.

"The Association has all kinds of scholarships and programs for people of high intelligence," Scarlet Witch told him. "One of the stipulations is that, assuming you agree to their terms, you have to spend so much time in the Association's workshops either inventing or helping to perfect their toys."

"I've been inside one of their warehouses," Trixter revealed. "It looks like a mad scientist's garage, and all of it essentially belongs to the Cape Cabinet. Over the next fifty years, the Real-Life Superhero Association is going to become ridiculously wealthy."

"But they're nonprofit," Push pointed out in protest. "How do they expect to make money and still maintain their status as a charity?"

"Bylaw," Trixter said at once, calmly. "Legal loopholes. The Association has been setting up subsidiary companies for the past twenty years. There's enough red tape in all of that to stop a herd of charging elephants. Assuming the government ever gets wise, by the time it happens, they'll be too late to do more than skim off the top."

"Okay, let's go back for just a minute," Wiccan Witch spoke out, interrupting. "How do those nanobots relate to any of this?"

"They're one of the Association's experiments," Trixter revealed dryly. "They've been testing these things for over a year now. No one is supposed to know. It'll be close to half a century before testing on humans is viable. For right now, it looks like the programming that prevents these little shits from disassembling organic matter is still in place. That's something to be thankful for, at least."

"How can you be sure these things are from the Association?" Push demanded, hoping they were all simply wrong. The alternative was too horrifying to consider.

"I've seen something like these before," Trixter told him, dead seriousness in his voice. "They were a different model, and I was not supposed to know about it, but a friend in the department at the time showed me close-up footage. I recognize the design in the sample. The differences are really only minor."

"So they came from the same source," Wrath concluded. "That would mean these were taken from the storehouse."

"And that is impossible," Trixter declared, frowning. "Unless...."

"Unless there's a mole somewhere in the organization," Scratch finished gravely. "We're dealing with a traitor in the group."

"And that traitor," Wrath added, "is most likely whomever Sloth is working for."

Scarlet Queen scowled slightly. "How do you figure that?" she asked.

"He did say something about us being on the same side when we fought him at the lake," Scratch pointed out. "Maybe that was what he meant?"

Push had no answer for him.

The rest of the night did not pass quickly or easily. The entire group was exhausted by the time Push suggested they hit the sack. Rather than having fun together, they'd spent the last several hours going around in circles over who the traitor could be and why Sloth was working for them. None of it made any sense, and as the team split up to find blankets and pillows for everyone, Push saw Professor Trixter sliding the petri dish into a wooden box.

"The wood ought to be organic enough to keep them from digging through," he explained.

"Thanks," Push said appreciatively. "Before I forget, the sample I called you about is in the back of the refrigerator, if you wouldn't mind taking a look tomorrow. The stuff was what was left of one of the aliens we fought."

Professor Trixter's eyes were widening as he glanced over at the refrigerator door. "Get some sleep first," Push advised before making his way to his room. "You'll be no good to us tomorrow if you stay up all night looking at alien splooge."

It was late, but Push wanted another shower before heading to bed. His body ached slightly in places as the hot water washed over him. Even in his exhausted state, his mind kept flashing back to earlier, when he had stood here next to Scratch. Push's cock rose up hopefully in response, making him moan in frustrated arousal. Seizing the hot water tap, he turned the water all the way off and winced as cold hammered against him.

The shower didn't last much longer. Push dried himself off as fast as he could, threw on a pair of boxers, and headed straight for bed. A few minutes after he closed his eyes, Push thought he heard footsteps headed his way.

The bedroom door crept open, and he automatically knew it was Scratch before his friend whispered his name.

"Everyone's asleep," Scratch said quietly as he closed the door behind him.

Push frowned. "Already?" he wondered, looking toward the clock.

"They're exhausted, I guess." The covers rose up, sending a chill over Push's skin as Scratch climbed in beside him. "I wanted to sleep with you. Is that all right?"

Push opened his mouth, slammed it tight before he could say something stupid, and swallowed the lump in his throat.

"I guess."

Scratch froze, his body inches from where Push lay. Push could feel the heat coming off Scratch, brushing along the soft, short hairs that formed the light down covering the small of his back. The hairs there waved happily at Scratch's presence.

"Do you want me to go?" Scratch asked him.

Before he could stop himself, Push turned over to face Scratch. "No," he whispered. "I don't."

Even in the dark and without his goggles, Scratch's grin was visible. "Aren't you worried one of the others might catch us?" he asked as Scratch reached out to bring him closer.

"Let them," Scratch replied dismissively. "I don't care. They'll need to know about us soon, anyway. Won't they?"

Push didn't answer. "Don't you want them to know?" Scratch pressed.

In reply, Push let his head rest against Scratch's chest. "Later, maybe," he said quietly, as exhaustion began washing over him in waves. "For right now, let's get some sleep."

PUSH wasn't sure how long he slept. It didn't feel long enough, but he was having too good of a dream to care. A mouth kept brushing up against his. Hot breath blew across his face as a strong pair of arms turned his body to a more accessible angle before kissing him full-on again. It felt so good Push didn't want to open his eyes. For a moment, he let himself believe he was kissing Scratch. It was a dream, after all, so this one time would be okay.

"Push?"

Scratch's voice caused his eyes to fly open. "Sorry," Scratch said, backing away slightly. "I thought you were awake."

"I thought I was dreaming." The words came out of his mouth before he could think twice about it. "I was dreaming about kissing you."

Scratch smiled, his white teeth flashing in the dark. "Does that make me the man of your dreams?"

Push gulped.

"I told you," Scratch said insistently as he brought their faces closer together with one arm. "I'm not giving up, and I'm not going away. I spent a good year trying to figure out what I wanted. I'm taking my shot now."

"You're straight."

Even to Push, the words didn't sound believable. Scratch narrowed his eyes in frustration and let out a long sigh. "Why do you keep bringing that up?"

"Because you are," Push insisted feebly, though even he could tell this was a losing argument on his end. "And you'll want to be with a woman someday, and get married, and have kids with her—"

"What makes you so sure?" Scratch demanded, cutting Push off.

Push watched as Scratch turned and lay flat on his back, staring up at the ceiling angrily. "Have I ever talked about kids before, or finding a girl to settle down with?" he demanded, not looking at Push now.

Push watched his friend for a moment as he lay on his side. "I assumed the reason you were plowing through most of the female half of the Association had something to do with that."

"I was looking for something," Scratch stated forcefully. "And no matter where I looked, I wasn't finding it. So I thought, maybe I just wasn't cut out for that sort of thing. And then I thought about you and about us together, and things started to click."

Scratch looked at him then, and his eyes showed a ton of hurt. "Did you honestly think I hadn't gone over all of this to myself already?" he demanded.

"I...."

Push stopped himself short before he could finish his sentence. Even in his baffled and half-asleep state, he knew not to put his train of thought into words carelessly. The last thing he needed was to let it slip he'd assumed Scratch was just looking to satisfy an itch.

"I hadn't thought about it," he confessed instead.

Scratch turned away again. "I had," he said, his voice warm with frustration. "I thought about it every day. I fell asleep with it running around in my mind. I needed to know first, though, if this was something I could handle before I told you how I felt."

Scratch paused and met Push's eyes. "That was why I was with Wrath."

Push's stomach churned. "You don't have to—" he said quickly, but Scratch was several steps ahead of him.

"Yes," he stated, leaving no room for debate. "You've wanted to know since that night, so here goes."

Scratch took a deep breath. "It wasn't some master plan," he began. "Not really. I was more playing it by ear than anything conclusive. I just... went with it when Wrath made that bet. At first, I thought he would want it right away, but he never came to my room that night. Afterward, I started thinking he had been joking. When he caught me coming out of the bathroom, I was still buzzing hard, and it seemed like the best chance I'd ever get."

"You wanted to know how it felt?" Push asked.

"I wanted to know whether I could handle being with another guy," Scratch clarified. "I needed to know if it was something I could deal with. If I could handle being with a stranger, being with you wouldn't be a problem. I wanted it to be you, but I was scared, and a part of me worried you would say no."

Push tried to think of something to say, but his emotions were a jumbled mess. What Scratch was saying sounded impossible.

"Please," said Scratch pleadingly. "Don't kick me out now. Not after I finally worked out what I want. I don't wanna lose you to...."

Push waited, but Scratch had fallen silent. "What?" he pressed.

"Nothing," Scratch said unconvincingly. "Nothing. I just...."

Their eyes met again, and Push found himself imagining what it would be like to wake up to those deep brown eyes every morning. Scratch leaned forward, his breath hot against Push's cheek. Push met him halfway, closing the gap between them as Scratch's warm, wet mouth ate away softly, tenderly at his lower lip.

"What?" Scratch asked between kisses. "What can I say to make you believe me?"

It felt like a dagger was inching its way through the center of his heart. "I'm sorry," Push apologized, breaking away as he got out of bed. "It isn't you. Not really. I just...."

Push inhaled and tried to steady himself. "Wrath was right," he said, more to himself than Scratch at that moment. "I should have kissed him."

"Who?" Scratch asked, his voice suddenly carrying a hint of jealousy.

"My best friend from high school," Push explained, turning around to find Scratch still on the bed but easing closer to him now. "The one who asked me to kiss him while we were drunk. I should have kissed him back then, because he would have broken my heart afterward, and I'd have gotten over him and moved on."

A vise was gripping Push's chest as he forced the next words out. "Instead of wondering what it might have been like for so long," he admitted, feeling shameful. "I loved him, even though I knew it was impossible. I wanted him so bad, and he was right there, but his asking terrified me. I was drunk and so was he, and knowing what he wanted shook me to my core. So I turned him down and swore I'd never let myself be vulnerable like that again. I never wanted to love anyone else I had no shot at."

Push gave Scratch a hard look, which he met without turning away. "Except I did," he finished, weakened and bruised on the inside. "I met you, and it started all over again. I can't keep losing my heart to someone who's never going to love me back the same way. I know you say you feel this way, and maybe you do, but what if it's only for right now, huh? What if you change your mind later or this gets to be too much for you. What am I supposed to do with myself when you walk away?"

Scratch eased off the bed, and Push backed away, hoping to avoid him. Scratch kept in step with him until Push was against the wall.

"Don't make me choose between keeping you as a friend and getting what I want," Push pleaded, looking down at the floor. "I'm just not strong enough. My heart couldn't take it if you left me as a lover and as a friend."

Scratch took another step forward, keeping enough distance so that Push didn't lose it altogether, but close enough for him to reach out and take him by the hand.

Scratch held Push's hand in both of his and placed a kiss on top of it. "Kiss me," he whispered, letting his words drift softly over the worn flesh of Push's inner palm, making them both tremble.

"I'm here now," Scratch told him, squeezing his hand tightly. "I'm sober, and I want to kiss you. I want to be the one who's kissing you from now on. Like I said before, I'm taking my shot at this. If I have to fight for you, I will. I know what it's like to let opportunity slip through your fingers, and that's why I want this. I won't lose you to someone else."

Push heard himself laugh. "Like there's a big line of people waiting to take me away from you," he pointed out.

Scratch let go with one hand and dragged Push into him by the back of the neck. "I want you," Scratch said between clenched teeth. "I want you so much it scares me to think you might turn me down, turn a chance at us down. I'm not letting this pass me by, so if you tell me to get out now, don't think for a second that will be the end of it. I'm not going to give up."

Yet again, something in his friend's voice made Push think he was missing a very obvious clue. "I don't get it," he said plainly. "You make it sound as though someone were planning to steal me away from you."

This time, Scratch turned away. "Wrath?" Push wondered, throwing the guess out there as a gap formed between their bodies, letting a cold draft in between them.

"You slept in the same bed as him," Scratch said, wearing a sour expression. "The night we were in the hotel together. I kept waking up, expecting to hear you two."

Push laughed at this, unable to hold back the fit of chuckles that had seized him, and he gently bumped his head against Scratch's chest.

"Wrath hates me," Push declared, brushing a hand across the skin above Scratch's erect nipple, which made him shudder. "I doubt we're going to leap into each other's arms anytime soon."

Scratch covered Push's hand with his own, putting a halt to his caresses. "He has a lot of respect for you," Scratch insisted. "And a guy like that isn't likely to respect just anyone. Plus, there's the way he looks at you every now and then when you aren't paying attention."

It was so funny, and yet so insane. Push let himself stop thinking about all the various impossibilities and enjoy the feeling of being next to Scratch's warm body.

"I could stay like this forever," he said, sighing.

Scratch wrapped both arms around Push and held him tightly against his body. "Stay," Scratch told him. "I want it to be you. Tonight and every other night. I want to fight bad guys with you at my back, then come home and fall asleep next to you after we've fucked each other until we can't move."

Push's eyes flew wide open. "You want to…?"

Scratch's arms prevented him from moving. "I said," Scratch repeated insistently. "I wanted to be with you. That includes doing everything with you."

Push felt his face grow slack as Scratch leaned in to kiss him. "Everything," Scratch said in a low, needful voice as their lips met.

Just as their mouths touched, a pounding at the bedroom door made them jerk back. "Goddammit!" Scratch swore. "Who the hell is that?"

"Shh!" Push warned. "They'll wonder what the hell you're doing in my room."

Scratch gave Push a look before setting his face into a resolved, stony expression. Marching over to the door as the pounding persisted, he flung the door open with an almost theatrical grace and leaned against the frame.

"Push and I were just about to have wild monkey sex," Scratch said flatly. "I'm madly in love with him and want him to be my boyfriend, so this better be important."

Wrath stood outside the doorframe, unfazed. "It's about time, I guess," he fired back in a dry tone. "Sorry for interrupting you two again, but there's been another message from Sheriff Black."

Push shook himself out of his shocked stupor upon hearing this. "What's happened this time?" he wondered, coming up behind Scratch now.

"He said there was some sort of disturbance down at the tow yard," Wrath explained. "There was a lot of noise going on in the background, and it sounded like some people were screaming. I don't know what the problem was, since the call got cut off, but the tow yard was where they took that walking pile of scrap that attacked us."

"Get dressed," Push said, turning around.

"I'm already dressed," Wrath pointed out, which he was.

"Then wake everyone else up while we get dressed," Scratch replied as he walked past Wrath into the kitchen, heading for his room.

"Since when are you and the sheriff such good buddies?" Push asked as he reached for yet another clean costume. "And how did he get your number?"

"He got it from me while we were talking in private," Wrath said. "And I think he'd already tried to call you. Something about your phone being off."

Frowning, Push reached for his cell phone and saw that it was indeed turned off. Deciding this was a mystery for later, he quickly changed as Wrath left to wake the others. Soon, they were all up and rubbing sleep out of their eyes as Professor Trixter started up the hovercraft. In the distance, the morning sun was beginning its climb over the horizon.

"Be prepared for anything," Push said, fighting back a yawn. "If that hunk of junk really has come back to life, we may have a real fight on our hands."

"At last," Scarlet Queen said gleefully, sounding truly awake now. "Just point me at it, and watch me work."

Push leaned into Scratch as Professor Trixter backed the hovercraft into the street. "Let me guess," he muttered softly under the vehicle's humming. "She liked to be on top."

Scratch smiled before giving Push's leg a quick, playful squeeze. "I was generally the one on top," he whispered back. "But then again, things do change."

THERE was screaming.

Through the hovercraft's thick siding, they could all hear people screaming. The tow yard was lit up like a stadium, and there was movement in the distance. Push couldn't get a good look through the window, but he did see the locked gate up ahead. Professor Trixter simply mashed a button on the dashboard and slammed down on the accelerator. Part of the hovercraft's hood popped up in response, forming what appeared to be a shield of some kind. The craft jolted slightly as it barreled through the metal gates, but otherwise, there didn't appear to be any damage.

"You've made improvements," Scarlet Queen noted, releasing her hold on the dashboard.

"I like to be prepared," Trixter replied, veering the hovercraft to the left sharply. "Plus, it was a dull Saturday afternoon."

"Saturday afternoons usually are boring unless you're working or out on patrol," Wiccan Witch countered in her seat next to Wrath. "By that time, all the good cartoon shows are over."

"I hope you've got weapons," Push said seriously. "From the sound of things, there's no way we're going toe to toe with that monster."

"No worries," Trixter replied in a cheeky voice. "This token black guy has mad skills."

Trixter flipped several multicolored switches on the panel overhead, causing the dashboard to light up. Punching in a series of codes, he then gripped the steering wheel as the hovercraft switched into battle mode.

"Up ahead," Scarlet Queen called out, pointing.

"I see it," Trixter assured her. "Watch what my baby can do."

Push leaned forward, hoping to get a glimpse of what Scarlet Queen was talking about, and felt his jaw drop. Up ahead, lumbering around on two legs, was a towering giant made out of car parts. Lights shined down on the ground from its chest, legs, and head as it swept the area, as though looking for ants. The thing had to be at least twenty feet tall. Push felt his blood run cold as Professor Trixter brought the hovercraft around it in a circle.

"Holy shit," Scratch swore, his eyes the size of dinner plates. "We're being invaded by Decepticons!"

Wiccan Witch snorted. "As long as no one lets Michael Bay out of his cage, I'm fine with it."

"Seconded," Scarlet Queen agreed.

The lights from the giant swept over the hovercraft and zeroed in on them as they rounded the open area where the monster had been standing.

"Hey, Push?" Trixter called out, hitting a button on the steering wheel. "Have you seen this one yet?"

The whole craft gave a hard lurch forward as the interior was filled with the sound of what Push guessed was turbines powering up. The hovercraft jumped out of the way as the giant brought its great mechanical foot down where they'd been, missing them by inches.

"I wonder how it got to be so big?" Wiccan Witch said in a surprisingly calm tone as the monster gave chase. "Those EMP grenades should have shut it off."

"Um, in the movies, nanomachines can rebuild themselves," Scratch remembered, looking at the back of Trixter's head. "Can these?"

Trixter's hands gripped the steering wheel until they paled. "A minor oversight," he finally said bitterly. "I've made a mental note."

"Forget about it for right now," Push replied dismissively. "We can't let it chase us in circles all night long. Shoot it with something."

"Technically, I'm not supposed to," Trixter revealed as the craft was almost crushed under the giant's foot again. "The Association has to give permission before I can launch anything major."

The hovercraft shook again, rattling their bones as the giant missed them by another close call. "Then again," said Trixter, flipping two more buttons on the overhead panel. "I won't tell if you won't."

"Do it, Virgil!" Wiccan Witch cheered.

Everyone grabbed hold of whatever they could as Trixter turned sharply, bringing the hovercraft into a spinning stop. Push felt Scratch's arms fold around him, and by pure instinct, he held on tightly as Professor Trixter unloaded a torrent of missiles from the unfolding slots in the craft's front. The rockets didn't have far to travel before achieving impact. The giant mechanical horror was thrown back hard as it charged headlong into the explosives.

"Now this," Push heard Trixter say.

Looking through Scratch's arms, he saw a pair of grappling hooks fly out and attach themselves to the heels of the creature's feet. Its momentum caused it to topple backward to the ground, shaking the craft and everyone inside it like a canister of peanuts.

Push felt the fillings in his wisdom teeth rattle as Scratch was thrown off him. "Are you all right?" he demanded, not caring for the moment if any of their friends suspected anything.

"Fine," Scratch said as, outside, the wires connecting to the grappling hooks were expelled from their slots in the craft.

"Don't want to risk those nanobots getting all up inside my baby and taking her apart piece by piece," Trixter muttered, hitting a few new switches. "Time for round two!"

Another wave of missiles unloaded from the front of the hovercraft. In the distance, the group watched the monster's body jerk as explosions rocked it.

"Allow me," Wrath offered, holding a hand out in front of him as he slid over the top of the seat between Push and Scratch.

The flames rising up from the giant machine warped and twisted in the air, then dove back down as though given new life. The fires ate away at the creature's interior while it continued thrashing about. Sweat broke out over Wrath's face as he forced the flames into the dark crevices, burning its insides up.

"Die." Wrath's voice scraped over Push's skin, and he felt himself shudder. "Just die."

Professor Trixter gave a nod of approval. "Cool," he said, turning toward Wrath. "You couldn't have done that earlier, though?"

Wrath gritted his teeth and hissed. "Harder to do while it was moving around," he spat out forcefully. "Easier to focus when I'm not moving."

The robotic beast had stopped moving now. "You can stop," Push told him gently, placing a hand on his arm. "It's okay now. Ease up."

"Breathe," Wiccan Witch told him, adding a hand to Wrath's shoulder.

Slowly, Wrath relaxed and fell back into his seat next to Wiccan Witch, who didn't remove her hand. "Does it always hurt like that?" Push heard her ask.

Wrath didn't answer right away. When he finally did, it was with a curt "Always."

"This was pretty fun," Scarlet Queen was saying, meanwhile. "I'm not looking forward to giving my side of the story, though."

"Nah," Trixter replied dismissively. "It'll be fun watching the Cape Cabinet try and work this one out."

"True," she said. "What do you think we should call this thing?"

Push blinked. "What?"

"We've got to call it something," she insisted, looking at him directly now. "The Cape Cabinet will want to hear from all of us, and I'd rather not be stuck with typing out 'really-big-walking-scrap-heap' over and over again."

It made a certain amount of sense, but Push wasn't up for making recommendations.

"Trash Titan," Wrath offered out of the blue. "It's giant-sized and made from the wrecked and compounded cars in this area."

"I was going to suggest Carmageddon," Wiccan Witch said. "Then again, that may be copyrighted."

"Trash Titan," Professor Trixter said thoughtfully. "I like it."

Something pounded on the side of the hovercraft, cutting Trixter off before he could say anything more. Keeping his hand up just in case, Push unlocked the door and threw it open. A man on the other side was backing away from the wingspan of the door, wide-eyed. Going by his expression, he appeared to be in terrible shock. Push thought the fellow looked familiar, and after a second or so of further study, remembered him as the guy who had towed the scrap heap to this yard in the first place.

"Sheriff sent me...," the man managed to gasp out. "Said you should...."

Push waited while the man struggled to catch his breath. "Try again," he offered, speaking very calmly for his benefit. "What did the sheriff say?"

"The rest," he tried again. "Already gone. They were going for the town. Please!"

It felt like a bomb went off in Push's brain. "The rest?" he asked, afraid he already knew the answer.

"There are more?" Scratch demanded, moving to Push's side so he could see the stranger properly.

"They just came outta nowhere," he said, babbling now. "All of a sudden, these things were tearing the place apart, making more, and… Jesus! What the fuck is going on?"

"Go inside," Push ordered him. "Listen to me now. Go inside your office and sit down. Drink some water, sit down, and cool off. As soon as you feel better, get to a hospital. Call someone to give you a ride. Right now, you're in shock."

The man was still stammering. "Hey!" Scratch barked loudly, getting his attention.

The man's head snapped up hard. "What's your name?" Scratch asked, using a more approachable tone now.

"Stone," he blurted out. "Stone Corben."

"Can you do that for us, Mr. Corben?" Scratch asked.

Corben nodded and backed away from the hovercraft automatically. "Remember what I told you," Push said firmly. "The minute you calm down enough, call someone to take you to a hospital. We're going after those things."

Corben gave them one last nod as the door shut. "Typical," Wrath grumbled. "We get rid of one, and ten more show up for the funeral."

"All in a day's work," Trixter said, grinning from ear to ear as the hovercraft took off in the direction Corben had indicated.

Wrath frowned as the craft picked up speed. "You guys are actually enjoying this, aren't you?"

Scarlet Queen laughed in answer. "Of course," she declared. "It's what we've been waiting for since we first joined the Association: our first real supervillain battle!"

"I want to fight aliens," Wiccan Witch insisted. "If there are any aliens this time, you guys have to promise to save me some."

Wrath rolled his eyes as the craft moved out of the tow yard down the trail of destruction. "You people are weird," he groaned. "And they said I needed to be locked away for the safety of others."

CHAPTER
EIGHT

THE path of destruction was impossible to miss. Despite his friends' enthusiasm, Push felt his stomach churn as the hovercraft raced through the gaping hole in the tow yard's fence. Beyond that was a long stretch of field leading back toward town. In the distance, they could see the row of towering figures walking in a line. They weren't far from the city now, but at the rate the Trash Titans were moving, it looked as though they were too late to stop them.

Somehow, with so many of them moving together, they looked even more imposing. The nanomachines had constructed at least ten of them, each roughly twenty feet high, from the scattered automobile remains. Some of their movements were jerky, like the nanomachines hadn't finished building them yet. Others had a fluid grace to their long steps that belied their size.

The climate inside the hovercraft had cooled considerably. "I think we're out of our league here," Scarlet Queen noted flatly.

"This'll take more than the five of us," Trixter added, looking grimly through the windshield.

"Six of us," Wiccan Witch cut in, pointing to Wrath.

"Six," Trixter amended at once. "Sorry."

"It's okay," Wrath said quietly, speaking to Wiccan Witch. "I don't mind."

Outside, the Trash Titans were nearly at the city border now. In mere moments, they would be crashing through one of the smaller residential districts, whose homes were just starting to light up.

"We need the military," Scratch stated, watching the Trash Titans retreat further. "Something like this is way too big for us, even with the hovercraft."

"I really should name this thing," Professor Trixter muttered.

"Later," Scarlet Queen said flatly. "What do we do about the Go-bot rejects getting ready to stomp all over Mayberry Godzilla-style, huh?"

No one said anything. The silence was suffocating, and Push could feel the sense of responsibility welling up inside of him. He'd felt this way ever since Jeremy's bloody corpse had been left in their apartment for him to find. If there was something Garfield Barnes could do to push back the senseless chaos that plagued the world, he would.

Push started to move. It hurt just to shift his legs, in part because Scratch was sitting next to him. His mind kept playing over what Scratch had said to him before they'd left the house. Now, more than ever, Push wanted to take Scratch by the hand and tell him he believed him, that they had a future together. As one of the Titans stopped to look behind it, as though sensing their presence but unsure of what it meant, Push knew he couldn't. Touching Scratch now would mean never letting go, and he had to be the one to go out that door.

"I'll go."

Push turned sharply at the sound of Wrath's voice. "What?" both he and Wiccan Witch said at the same time.

"Open the hatch," Wrath told Professor Trixter. "I'll see if I can't lead them away from town. The first one seemed more vulnerable to my powers. I'll at least have a chance."

Wiccan Witch looked ready to slap him. "Sit down," she ordered, seizing him by the arm. "You can't go out there by yourself."

Wrath shook his head. "I have to," he insisted, gently removing her hand. "If I don't, he's going to."

Push's eyes widened as Wrath pointed to him. "Empath, remember?" he reminded Push, smiling. "You've got a good reason for staying here."

Before Wiccan Witch could grab him, Wrath moved to the door. Professor Trixter hesitated a moment, then silently depressed the safety lock so he could open it.

"I'm coming with you," Wiccan Witch declared.

"I might as well go too," said Scarlet Queen, opening her door. "You'll need backup."

"Stay," Wrath insisted, as he tried briefly to hold Wiccan Witch back. "This is no time for anyone to be a hero."

Scarlet Queen glared at Wrath as he gave up in his attempt to make Wiccan Witch stay behind. "What do you call what you're doing, then?" she demanded, as both she and Wiccan Witch fired razor-sharp glares at his head.

"What I'm paid to do," Wrath replied before moving across the field. "Like always."

Push was dumbfounded. "He's not going to make it in time," Scratch pointed out. "Can you knock him down without killing him?"

Professor Trixter started to answer, but was cut off as Wrath stopped several feet ahead of the hovercraft. The Trash Titans had reached the row of trees that made up the city border. Raising both hands, he launched twin shots of flaming missiles through the air in a long arc. A rush of something that sounded like gas igniting filled the vehicle. Again and again, Wrath fired as his first shots slammed into the back of one of the monolithic robots.

The Trash Titan staggered ever so slightly, more stunned by the attack than in pain, it seemed, as others found themselves under the onslaught. Wrath started moving again, keeping his steps even as he unleashed another barrage. The flame missiles that didn't hit their mark landed at the Titans' feet, setting the grass ablaze. The machines glanced at each other as though communing silently, then promptly turned around. In seconds, they were trudging back across the field with the hovercraft in their sights.

"Get out of here," Wrath yelled, continuing to stride forward. "I'll hold them off."

"The hell you will!" Scarlet Queen shouted.

Push jumped out of his seat. "Can this thing take on all of them?" he asked Trixter, who was watching the scene unfold with a mixed expression of incredulous admiration and grim trepidation.

Trixter turned away. "Truth?" he asked, meeting Push's eyes. "Not a chance in hell. It took most of the missiles in this crate to bring down one of them. It just doesn't have the artillery to take on all of them. Chances are, they'll tear it apart and use the pieces to add more onto their own bodies."

"Well, we can't just leave him out there!"

Scratch gave Push a sharp look before turning away. "This is crazy," he muttered. "How did this shit even get started?"

"We'll worry about that later," Trixter replied, his mind racing. "I gotta think somehow…."

Push wracked his brain for a solution. "What about those EMP pulse things you used before?" he pressed. "Why can't they work?"

"Not enough of 'em," Trixter said sadly, indicating he'd already thought of it. "Plus, these are bigger, and if one could shake a blast like that off, the best we could hope for is…."

Trixter's jaw went slack. "What?" Push demanded. "You've thought of something, so what is it?"

"It might work," Trixter muttered softly, punching in a few keys on the dashboard. "The generator should have enough power, assuming I can broadcast at just the right frequency."

Push's eyes caught the scene playing out through the front window. The girls had gone after Wrath despite his protests, though Push couldn't say he was surprised. It looked like some sort of plan was in the works now, as Wrath unloaded a stream of fire into a Titan's chest. Scarlet Queen and Wiccan Witch were doing their best to avoid the mechanical giants' feet. Because of their size and broad metal bodies, the Titans were lumbering, rather than actually walking. This gave the girls plenty of space to dodge out of the way, leaving the Titans wide open for an attack by Wrath.

Push had to acknowledge the impressiveness of their teamwork.

"Um, anytime you wanna clue us in," Scratch yelled at Trixter, snapping Push out of it. "We're ready to hear it."

"I can broadcast a scrambling wave using the transmission equipment in the hovercraft," Trixter said rapidly as he hopped out of the vehicle. "Combined with a low-level EMP wave that's similar to the one I used on the first Titan, it should be enough to knock them all out."

Push and Scratch followed Professor Trixter to the back. "For a little while, at least," Trixter added, opening up the trunk part of the craft. "That should give us some time to prepare."

"Prepare for what?" Push wondered.

"It'll knock 'em out," Trixter explained, before shoving an armload of parts into Push's hands. "But it won't solve the problem with the nanobots. The cops can quarantine those things or ship them off to the military to be disassembled, but the nanobots will just move on and start over again."

Scratch was better prepared when Trixter began handing tools off to him one at a time. "We have to take this problem out at the source," he went on, slamming the trunk shut. "But to do that, I need time to study the sample at your place and see exactly how these things operate."

Trixter was climbing atop the hovercraft as he continued. "At most, I can shut those things down for a couple of hours. Chances are, that won't be enough time to work out how to turn the nanobots off permanently."

"So we're screwed no matter what we do?" Scratch wondered, passing one of the tools up to where Trixter was perched.

"Maybe," he said, distractedly. "But maybe not. Go help those three while I work this shit out. You'll be a lot better off there, and it doesn't look like they can hold out for much longer on their own."

Push didn't see how Trixter had noticed but wasn't going to argue. The Trash Titans weren't working so well together, especially in such close quarters. The girls had caught on to that and were using it to their full advantage. Both Scarlet Queen and Wiccan Witch were ducking around in a joined pattern, keeping the Titans on their toes and leading them along to crash against one another. Wrath was doing his part right alongside them. Whenever the girls tricked two of the mechanical klutzes into stumbling in each other's way, he was there to open up with another flame blast.

Even from as far back as they were, though, Push could tell they were getting winded. Especially Wrath, whose tired face looked drenched in sweat. It dawned on Push that being in prison for ten years must have left him without the space to hone his abilities. Using his powers so extensively was apparently taking its toll.

"Let's go," he said, steeling his nerves so he didn't wet himself. "They need us."

Scratch's face was stony and grim as he moved beside Push, but his steps never faltered, keeping in time as both marched toward their deaths.

"I love you," Scratch breathed out over the din of battle up ahead. "Whatever happens, I want you to know that."

Push heard and felt a load lift off him. "I love you too," he said, leaving his heart wide open for his friend to see. "I think I always have, from the day we first met."

"Good," Scratch said, drawing out the eight ball explosive. "Then you sure as hell better live through this, because I'm not letting you duck out on me after saying that."

"Back at you."

Push had expected that moment to assuage all of his fears, yet the thoughts persisted even as they moved toward the clashing giants. Something tugged at his heart as he brought out his bo and switched on his goggles. Later, perhaps, he would be ready to deal with thoughts about what had just happened, for something had indeed flickered to life between him and the man marching along at his side. Scratch's head was tossed back proudly, ready to face whatever was about to be thrown their way. Push squared his shoulders in response.

He could do this. So long as they were together, he knew they would get through this.

Pushing his fears aside for now, he focused on the task at hand. A little voice inside his head whispered they would be waiting for him when he and Scratch survived. Push knew this, and tried not to let the fear take over.

The giant robots were nothing. Thoughts of being with his best friend romantically made him want to turn around and run screaming in the other direction. This helped put things into perspective as they reached the battle ground.

It was yet another testament to how messed up Push's head was, and why no one in their right mind should want to be in a relationship with him.

Scarlet Queen was closest to them as they approached. One of the robots almost got lucky, missing her by a few feet when it brought its foot down hard on the ground. The shock was still strong enough to knock her down. Scratch didn't waste time. After flipping the eight ball into the air, he whipped out his cue stick pieces and assembled them in that trademark movement of his Push had always enjoyed watching. One quick thrust with it sent the ball flying. Scratch had aimed for the Titan's robotic thigh. The explosion threw it backward into the path of another, blowing off the left leg at the same time. The result was a chain reaction that brought two more to the ground in a noisy pile-up.

"I love this game," Scratch said coyly, giving his cue stick a quick kiss.

"Great," Push muttered. "Now you've got me envying your stick."

He hadn't meant to say it aloud, and heaven only knew what had possessed him to give voice to his feelings, but there was a twinkle of appreciation in Scratch's eyes as he drew out another trick ball.

"I'll be sure to kiss yours later," he promised, taking his second shot. "A lot."

Scratch fired an acid grenade through the air, which struck the chest plate of another Titan seconds before Wrath opened up on it with his flame powers. The flammable liquid ignited, causing the robot giant to stagger back. Wrath took the cue and opened up on the Titan's legs, applying pressure to the mechanical beast's knees with his flames until they gave out.

"Worked last time," said Scratch, lining up his next shot.

"Let me," Push said, stepping forward.

This should have been a dumb idea, but something in that moment was spurring Push onward. Scratch's words and his own declaration had dropped a white-hot sun down into his chest, fueling him. The warmth from it poured into his hands, filling them with strength. Push let it gather there quickly as Scarlet Queen recovered and went right back into the game.

When he launched the telekinetic bomb, it struck the upper half of the robot closest to the center of the melee. Wiccan Witch had gotten herself caught there, and Wrath had been trying to get to her. The moment the bomb struck, all seven remaining machines were blown back. Push straightened, feeling only slightly winded, and felt his jaw drop as the Titans went down like dominoes.

Scarlet Queen surveyed the damage a moment before facing Push with a dumbstruck expression. "Nice one," she complimented, giving him a thumbs-up. "Got another one of those in you?"

Some of the Titans were already getting to their feet. "This is going to feel anticlimactic after that," Scratch mused, tossing several balls up into the air. "Still...."

Taking aim, Scratch fired all four glue bombs into the tangled mess of robotic limbs. "That should make things a little more difficult," he said as the glue expanded over the struggling robots, sticking several of them together. "I hope Trixter finishes soon. I'm running out of stuff to use on these things."

"I've got at least one more TK bomb in me," Push said, reassuring him. "It looks like our firebug is getting winded, though."

Wrath was helping Wiccan Witch get away. Scarlet Queen spotted them and moved at once to help.

"I'm fine," Push heard Wiccan Witch insist as they drew closer to where he and Scratch stood. "It's not bad, I promise."

"You were nearly crushed back there," Wrath replied, dragging her along insistently. "At the very least, you should stay off that foot until we can have a look at it."

"I've got her," Scarlet Queen told him, taking his place. "You guys are the heavy hitters. At this point, we'll just get in the way."

Wiccan Witch did not look happy. "I wanted to help fight more robots," she grumbled. "When my grandchildren ask me about this day, I want to be able to tell them that I was very brave, not that I stopped fighting because my foot hurt."

"You can have my part," Wrath offered. "No one is going to ask me what today was like, so they're not likely to fact check."

"Besides," Scarlet Queen added. "We both know any grandkids you have will be too focused on whatever new version of the Xbox is out then to bother asking you about your glory days."

"This is a conversation for later," Push said sharply as the Titans in the distance got to their feet. "Our square-dancing partners are back for another round."

The Titans whose limbs had been sealed together were straining against the bonds. At first, it seemed like the glue would hold, but after a moment, the robots were tearing away from it, one after another. The machines looked beaten up, but only two had fallen and stayed down. The rest were getting up, and Push felt a sick sense of reality settling in over the team as they watched the giants gather themselves up. No matter which way he looked at it, they simply didn't have the firepower needed to take those things down for good.

That was what he told himself as the hovercraft behind them roared to life. Professor Trixter blew the horn at them, then barreled forward while the group moved out of the way. Bringing the craft into a wide arc, Trixter stopped roughly ten feet out of the Titans' reach. Something had been attached to the back of the hovercraft and was sticking out like a strange, cancerous thing. Push saw the Professor punch something on his dashboard, causing the equipment in the back to light up like the Fourth of July.

The robots froze. Sparks flew from the craft, but Trixter defied them by gunning the engine harder. More sparks flew, this time from the Titans themselves. One let out a painful roar, the mechanical sound of angry crickets and metal being shredded, followed by a second. Everyone covered their ears as best they could as the Titans began to convulse. One after another, they collapsed to the ground. Smoke was rising out of the hovercraft now, and as the engine gave a rather sorrowful, high-pitched whine, Push spotted the Professor rolling out the door onto the grass.

The craft sparked again, gave a pitiful cough, then went silent.

"I thought for certain it would at least catch fire," Wrath commented as Trixter stood up in the distance.

The others were already moving toward him. "Are you all right?" Push asked, careful not to get too close to the craft.

"Had to empty the tank to do that," Trixter mused sadly, looking the vehicle over. "I just hope none of the power cables are fried. It'll take a week at least to repair. I think it worked, though. The robots shouldn't be up and about for a while."

"Great," Scarlet Queen said, looking over at the collapsed piles of scrap. "So what are we supposed to do about them in the meantime?"

"Yeah," Wiccan Witch added. "Those nanobots will just wake up soon and start all over again."

"I can shut the nanobots off permanently," Trixter assured her. "With the sample back at the house, it shouldn't be too rough."

Push thought he spotted several trucks and police cars headed their way.

"Um, cavalry's arrived," Scratch informed them, pointing.

Wrath did not look happy at the sight of so many cop cars. "Better late than never, I suppose," he mumbled.

It was a mob scene. Push stood in front with Scratch still faithfully at his side, as if afraid to leave him alone for even a moment, while Sheriff Black's squad car rolled to a stop. Two large hauler trucks with tanks loaded with gas had come along for the ride, as well as what looked like every police officer Shove Point had to spare and two fire trucks. The sheriff looked ready to shit bricks as he took in the scene.

Push waited patiently for the man to start yelling.

"Spread out," Black called, giving orders to his men. "It may not do any good, but keep your guns aimed at those things all the time. Get those gas trucks ready now."

Black leveled his gaze at Push as his men moved to do as he'd told them. A long, heavy sigh rushed from the older man's lungs as he hung his head.

"How'd you do it?" he asked, once they were close enough to hear one another over the noise in the background.

"Professor Trixter," Push said. "We kept them off his back while he rigged his hovercraft to transmit a signal that would knock them out."

Black stared hard at Trixter for a good minute, but Trixter didn't flinch. "Right," the sheriff said finally. It sounded as though he were admitting defeat. "You kids had best get goin'. We're about to carpet bomb this whole acre."

"What for?" Scratch wondered.

Black cocked an eye at him in reply. "So we can burn those walkin' trash heaps clear up to the sky, is what for," he snapped. "I don't know what sort of trouble you bastards brought to my town, but it stops here. Nothin' like this past week ever happened before. The minute they send a bunch of circus clowns to my neck of the woods, all hell breaks loose."

"Burning them won't help," Trixter warned, though Push suspected his friend knew he was wasting his breath. Sheriff Black seemed to have already made up his mind about the matter.

"Say again?" Black demanded, openly hostile now.

Trixter was keeping his temper, though Push detected a trace of underlying malice in his words. "The surviving nanobots will just regroup and start over. This problem isn't going to go away, and we didn't bring it here."

Black seemed to calm down enough to register some of what Trixter told him. "You're tellin' me fire doesn't stop them?"

"Fire will stop them," Push clarified. "But not permanently."

A flicker of pure hatred flared in the older man's eyes for a brief instant. "That's just great," he hissed through his teeth.

"This is strictly off the record," Push injected, hoping he wasn't about to make a huge mistake. "But an experiment was stolen from one of the Association's workshops. Whoever did it let a bunch of nanomachines loose on Shove Point."

"Nanna-what?" Black wondered, wide-eyed with incredulity. "What for?"

"We're looking into that," Push assured him. "More than likely, they were trying to keep us distracted. You've got a federally wanted criminal running around in your town wreaking havoc, and an escaped felon who may or may not be dead. This—"

Push paused and gestured behind him for the full effect. "—is out of both our leagues," he finished, giving the man a look. "But we fought it anyway. I don't know what's going on any more than you do, but whoever is behind this clearly wants us out of the way. And if they can turn your department against us in the bargain, that will just make things easier."

"Believe it or not," Wrath added, startling Push. "Not everybody is happy to be here. The sooner we leave, the better we'll all feel."

Black scowled at Wrath. "You got something against my town, boy?"

"Always have," he replied curtly and without hesitation. "Since I was a kid."

This caught Black off-guard. "You still don't recognize me," Wrath said to him pointedly. "Do you?"

Silence fell over the scene as Wrath's words hit home with everyone. Push realized that, aside from him and Scratch, no one else knew that Shove Point had been Wrath's hometown. Scarlet Queen went wide-eyed as the knowledge sank in. Wiccan Witch's reaction was slightly more subtle, yet her eyes did not leave Wrath once as he stood rigidly against the full force of Black's scrutinizing stare. Professor Trixter was frowning now, as if this were being presented to him as a complicated math problem.

Black seemed to have regained his composure by the time Push turned to him. "You ever find whatever it was you've been snooping around for?"

"Not yet," Wrath replied flatly.

It was clear by his expression Wrath had not wanted anyone else to know about that. Filing this away for later, Push cleared his throat to get the sheriff's attention.

"What happens now, sheriff?" he asked, making sure the man met his eyes. "You can toss us out of town if you want, but the problems won't go away. I noticed earlier nobody from your department was out there with us on that field trying to stop those machines from stomping all over your neck of the woods."

Black did not look happy at this, yet his voice stayed even when he spoke. "Get out of here," he said warningly. "If any more shit from you people's yard ends up here, I'm personally going to string each and every one of you up in front of the damn courthouse, badge be damned!"

In unison, Wrath included, the six of them turned to walk in a line back to the hovercraft. The fire trucks had taken up position beside the trucks hauling the gas tanks, which had been hooked up with hoses to spray down each Titan thoroughly. Push saw Trixter glance behind them at the spot where the sheriff was standing, watching them go.

"I really hope there's enough power left in the hovercraft," he whispered out the corner of his mouth. "Otherwise, this dramatic exit is going to get embarrassing real quick."

THERE was, in fact, just enough power in the hovercraft to get them home. The signal Trixter had broadcast to knock the Titans out had drained most of the main batteries, leaving only auxiliary power. By shutting off a few of the unnecessary systems, Trixter was able to get them on their way before the fires started. Most of them turned in their seats to watch as the flames began engulfing the giant mechanical corpses.

"This was pointless," Wrath said, looking even more winded than before. "If my powers couldn't do more than hold those things back, burning them won't solve anything."

"We know that," Push said, though not unkindly. "And I suspect the sheriff believes it, even though he really doesn't want to. The problem is, he has to make it look as though his department is doing something."

Wrath looked past Push toward Professor Trixter, who had been keeping both eyes on the road. "How long before the nanobots wake up and start this whole mess over again?"

"Not long," Trixter said grimly. "I've been thinking about the problem, though, and how to deal with it."

Push was interested. "What's your plan?"

"Not much of what I'd call a plan," Trixter said, turning the craft sharply. "Just a few ideas for when the shit goes back to hitting the fan. As soon as we get this crate home, I'm gonna have a look at that sample you told me about, and that laser gun thing you took from the aliens."

"Don't forget the nanomachine sample," Scarlet Queen reminded. "You could figure out a way to shut them down with it, right?"

"Probably," the dark-skinned hero said as the hovercraft lumbered wearily down their street. "Just in case, though, I want to be prepared."

The craft was running on electric fumes as they slid down the home stretch. The lights began to fade on the dashboard about twenty-five feet or so from the driveway. Push was afraid they were going to have to get out and lend a hand with their arms and legs, but Trixter was able to squeeze the last bit of juice from the batteries to get them the rest of the way.

"Do you mind?" he asked, once they were all out of the vehicle. Push saw that Trixter had pulled some kind of cable out of the back and was holding it up for him to see. "Your electric bill is going to skyrocket, thanks to this, but having transportation when those things return will be a big help."

"Go to it," Push informed him, stepping off to the side so Trixter could reach a nearby wall socket in the garage. "The Association is footing the bill for this place, anyway."

The others waited as Scratch went ahead to unlock the door. Push studied his friends' faces, gauging their reactions. They had just come from fighting something unstoppable, something they'd never in a million years imagined themselves contending with. Each one's expression was a mix of weary exhaustion and pumped adrenaline. They were happy to be alive, proud of what they'd accomplished this morning, and completely drained from the experience.

All, that is, except for Wrath. Push noticed how the man was standing a little off to the side, not far from Wiccan Witch but nowhere near her personal space. He alone seemed contemplative, unsure of something. As Push continued to watch, he also found himself thinking about how everything from Wrath's posture to his body language suggested the man felt deeply and utterly alone.

Scratch held the door open, and Push watched as Wrath entered the building that had once been his home. This house, in the town of Shove Point, had been where he'd grown up and set in motion the events that led to him becoming the supervillain he had been until recently. Wrath's feet seemed to drag as he crossed the threshold. Push followed after, leaving Professor Trixter behind to fiddle with his hovercraft. His and Scratch's eyes met briefly as Push entered. Scratch gave the knob a tug, closing the door behind him. Everyone seemed to be heading for the couch in the living room.

Push considered saying something but decided against it in the end and walked past them through the kitchen to his bedroom. Leaving the door cracked, he undressed down to his boxers and lay back on the bed. The room had a rather impressive, if somewhat small, flat screen television. Wanting to hear something besides the silence, he reached for the remote on the bedside stand and pressed the power button. As the canned laughter from some old sitcom filled the room, the door swung open slightly, revealing Scratch.

Push watched as his friend entered, closing the door all the way behind him, then proceeded to strip down. Save for the few seconds where his face was blocked by his shirt, Scratch never took his eyes off Push. He seemed to be waiting for something, as though fearful Push would ask him to stop or leave. Push kept his mouth shut the whole time, biting his tongue once or twice when he felt the urge to object.

Once Scratch was nude, having removed his boxers, he stood at the side of the bed, looking like he was waiting for a signal. Push patted the surface of the bed next to him invitingly, letting his best friend know he was welcome. Scratch all but launched himself through the air in an effort to get there, shaking the bed hard enough to bang the headboard against the wall. Once they were both comfortable, with Scratch resting his head on Push's chest, Push cuddled in close and let the warmth of his friend and lover's presence wash over him.

The thought still terrified him, yet Push couldn't find the willpower to shove Scratch away again. It might have been the near-death experience they'd just shared.

"Or," Push thought out loud to himself, "maybe you're just sick of running away."

"Hm?" Scratch asked, rising slightly.

"Nothing," Push told him quickly, jerking at the sound of Scratch's voice. "I was just… talking to myself. Did I wake you up?"

"Wasn't asleep," Scratch replied, lying back down. "You're warm."

That made Push smile. "So are you," he pointed out. "I could get used to this."

He hadn't meant to say it, but Scratch's arms tightened around him before he had time to think about taking it back. "Me too," Scratch said. "After this morning, I could stay like this with you forever."

Push's mind started racing at the speed of a mile a minute. His body seemed hell-bent on absorbing every last tidbit of information it could from this experience. The surface of Scratch's flesh was a mixture of dry roughness and silk. The life they'd led had marked it to where it seemed slightly worn, yet none of it had lost the smooth feeling of youthfulness Push remembered from their first sexual encounter.

Beneath the skin was muscle and sinew. Scratch's body could nearly have passed for a marble statue. Each tiny movement echoed through Push's own body, reminding him of just how much strength lay there. With each deep breath Scratch drew in, the skin blanketing Push's stomach and chest tingled in response. The sensations were impossible to block out, and after several minutes of senseless resistance, Push felt himself surrender to them.

Scratch had been lightly tracing a circle not too far from Push's belly button. This, combined with everything else he was feeling, caused a reaction below the elastic band of Push's boxer shorts. He felt himself blush and started to pull away, but Scratch held him tightly.

"Don't," he protested fiercely. "Don't pull away from me. I like it."

Push swallowed as Scratch raked the tips of his fingers down the crevice formed by his six-pack. Push thought he would stop there, but Scratch brazenly kept going, not stopping until his hand cupped the painfully swollen mound flexing beneath the cotton fabric.

"I like it," Scratch repeated emphatically, stroking his hand back and forth until Push let out a deep moan. "I like knowing you feel that way about me. I like knowing I made it this way."

Push heard himself gasp as Scratch exposed his cock to the cool bedroom air through the opening in his fly. "Scratch," he managed to get out. "You shouldn't be doing this."

Defiantly, Scratch ran his tongue across the slippery head that had already begun oozing precum. Air hissed through Push's clenched teeth as Scratch gripped Push's dick at the base before forcing his tongue into the piss slit, lapping away at the delicious clear liquid there like a cat after cream.

"Stop it," Scratch insisted. "I'm sick to death of labels and hearing you talk like it matters. What I said on the field back there doesn't stop as soon as we're next to one another."

Seizing the waistband, Scratch forcefully shoved Push's boxers down, bending his lover's legs at the knees so he could work them the rest of the way off.

"I love you," Scratch said, stretching himself back down beside Push's body so their eyes could meet. "I spent a year knowing I loved you and scared to death I couldn't be with you like this, thinking you might find somebody new during that time. I know I can love you this way, so why won't you let me?"

Push didn't have an answer. Granted, what Scratch was doing with his hand was scrambling his brain.

"I can't think while you're doing that," Push grunted out as a spike of pleasure hit him, sending more precum flushing out of his cock.

"Good," Scratch replied, moving his hand faster. "Stop thinking about it. Stop worrying about what we are or what I'm not, and let me make love to you."

The words send a jolt through Push. Though he hadn't thought of what they'd done together before as mere sex, hearing Scratch say it now made his eyes pop open.

Scratch saw this and hooked his leg over Push's. There, in the sixty-nine position with his cock aimed at Push's face, he stared through the gap between their bodies.

"I need you," he said softly, as though the evidence wasn't looming at Push right then and there. "I'll never stop wanting you this way, so please, stop trying to force me into being something else."

Somehow, this time was different. Somehow, Push knew there would be no turning back after this. Here and now, he could gently force Scratch off him and walk away with his heart still somewhat intact. Their friendship might not survive, but his soul wouldn't be burdened with the responsibility of knowing he'd accepted Scratch's offer without a second thought.

That was what he'd been thinking as he felt Scratch engulf the length of his dick with his mouth. Any remaining doubts or concerns exploded out of his mind, leaving Push a writhing mass of nerve endings and pleasure points. Reaching up, he wrapped both arms around Scratch's body at the dip in his spine above the ass cheeks and forced the man's thick cock into his own mouth.

The taste of Scratch's cock, laced with sweat from being crammed into those tight jeans he always wore, lit up the inside of Push's warm, wet mouth. Arching up off the bed, Push let out a low, guttural moan as the rest slid expertly down his throat. The taste of his best-friend-turned-lover filled him, spreading across his tongue, down into his stomach, and to the rest of his body like liquid warmth. Push felt his whole body spark and tingle as he worked the dick in his mouth. Scratch was helping by moving his hips back and forth in a slow thrusting motion, but the effort wasn't necessary. Push would have gladly twisted his spine in half during that moment to get to the gift presented to him.

Scratch, meanwhile, was working more of Push's dick into his throat. He hadn't been joking before when he'd talked about practice. Scratch seemed to approach the challenge with fervor, forcing more of the length past his tonsils. Now, he was having an easier time of it, and to Push's great surprise, he felt Scratch bury his nose into his pubes.

Taking the cue, Push engulfed the length of the man on top of him again, breathing deeply as he buried his own nose in the soft, tender skin where Scratch's ball sack began. He could feel a climax building and wasn't ready for any of this to end. Forcing himself to let go, he leaned away from Scratch's thick, throbbing manhood, clearing his windpipe so he could speak.

"Stop," he called out. "I'm about to go."

Scratch rose to reply. "I can tell," he said. "Get going. I want to finish this with a bang."

Scratch was back on his cock before Push could say anything more. Letting go of what he'd been about to say, Push went back to pleasuring the man he'd loved for years. Taking the tip back into his mouth, he began running his thumb and forefinger along the length of the thick shaft, applying pressure to the underside near the base as he went. This earned Push a grunt of approval as he felt his balls draw up.

His cock went off like a rocket. Push's mind swam with a dozen different emotions and sensations, not the least of which was amazement at the feeling of Scratch taking his load into him. The miracle of this made his body convulse, which, in turn, caused him to tighten his grip on Scratch's dick. Before Push realized what he'd done, Scratch was firing his own load right into his face. Push's mouth was still wide open as he felt several ropes of cum splatter over the surface of his tongue. The taste of it rocked him all over again, making him spasm. Over and over again, he felt his body roll with pleasure like a skiff out on the high seas.

He was still feeling the effects when the bed shifted. Scratch turned himself around until he was lying at Push's side. The last of the pleasure waves rolled off as Push felt Scratch taking his hand, holding it between his.

"I really got you," Scratch noted, smiling impishly. "Sorry about that."

Feeling bold and wanting to know just how far his love's limits were willing to be stretched, Push rose on his elbows and brought his face toward Scratch's for a kiss. To his utter bemusement, Scratch met him halfway and licked a stream of cum that was hanging down by Push's chin. Push felt it enter his mouth next. The taste of Scratch's essence was shared between them as they kissed passionately, their arms twisting around until each was holding the other in their grip.

"That was just for starters," Scratch said teasingly once he'd managed to pull away. "I'm nowhere near finished with you yet."

Still grinning, Scratch shifted positions again until his body was straddling Push's. Push watched as Scratch crawled his way down, facing him the whole time. Scratch didn't stop until he was kneeling in

SCRATCH & SNIFF 141

the space between Push's legs, shoving them aside until Push was lying spread-eagled.

"What are you—" Push began but got cut off by the sight of Scratch's face disappearing from sight. The tip of Scratch's wet tongue brushed against the underside of his ball sack, making Push jump. Scratch gave a chuckle before going back to work, teasing there with light, playful licks. Push felt his cock thicken again at the stimulation and reached down to pump it with his fist. When Scratch saw this, however, he smacked the hand away hard.

"Not a chance," he said warningly, moving back just far enough to speak. "Just lay back and let me do it."

Push felt his eyes bulge as Scratch wrapped one hand around his dick and worked it up and down while his tongue continued the assault on his boys. Soon, he had Push's whole sack glistening with spittle. From there, Scratch continued down, licking his tongue over the taint lurking out of sight. Push felt his breath coming fast now, and the room swam from the feeling of having Scratch touch him there. A moment later, though, something pressed into the smooth crack of his ass, and Push nearly jumped off the bed.

"God!" he swore. "The hell are you doing?"

Scratch didn't answer. His tongue was too busy working its way past the tight pucker hidden away between the soft folds of skin. Pressing hard, Scratch let out a grunt of personal satisfaction as the tip pressed past the tight sphincter ring.

"You're...," Push tried, but words failed him. "You're...."

Scratch moved his tongue in a circle, sending shock waves through Push and rendering him speechless. "Be quiet," he commanded, rising.

Through his daze, Push couldn't help but notice the anger laced through Scratch's words. "Enough with all the labels. Haven't they caused enough grief between us? Just lay there and let me please you."

Scratch's hand hadn't stopped moving the whole time. Each time his tongue started off in a clockwork motion, his hand would stroke down hard, moving up again as the wet appendage completed the circle. The simultaneous attack left Push writhing and gasping. Unable to control himself, he felt his balls unload a second time. This time he shot off like a Roman candle, blasting cum straight up into the air, showering the both of them. Droplets fell into Scratch's hair, contrasting with the dark locks, as he rose, wearing a pleased smirk.

Their eyes met for a moment as Push tried to gain some semblance of control over himself. "I...," he tried, finding he could at last speak coherently. "I got you."

Scratch never lost his grin. "Turnabout's fair play," he said, moving back up until they were face to face. "You're a mess," Scratch noted, lapping at the spots of cum that were slowly drying on Push's face. "But I think I can do something about that."

CHAPTER
NINE

IT WAS quiet.

Push almost wanted to say "too quiet," but that statement felt like a request for more trouble. At the moment, everything felt right. The world was at peace.

Somehow, during all of their activity, the digital clock next to the bed had been knocked to the side, leaving it facing away from him. Push couldn't guess how long they'd lain in bed together. Scratch had been adamant about licking every last drop of his seed away. Push had resisted at first, more from it tickling than his remaining squeamishness, but the resistance caved all too quickly. Afterward, the two lay together in each other's arms, occasionally brushing their hands over the surface of the other's skin. Every so often, Scratch would touch him somewhere just right, eliciting a moan from him. Just having his friend so close, holding him the way that lovers did, felt so right. His mind still had trouble reconciling both facts.

Scratch was his best friend. Scratch was also his roommate and partner, but now, Scratch and he were lovers. Rather than feeling at odds, the two factoids seemed to be settling into one another slowly, gently. Push accepted this as a sign that he shouldn't rush things and went back to savoring the now.

"I want to tell them," Scratch said softly into Push's side.

The words startled him. Scratch had been still for several minutes, so Push had assumed he'd drifted off. "Tell who what?" he wondered, late to the train of thought his lover had jumped on.

"Everyone," Scratch stated, giving Push a squeeze. "I want them to know about us."

It finally dawned on Push what he meant. "There's no hurry," he replied, hoping he sounded reassuring. "If you need to take things slow, I understand. Believe me."

"No." Scratch rose and looked Push in the face. "I don't want you to feel like we're something to be ashamed of. And anyway, aren't they our friends?"

Push couldn't bring himself to argue that fact. "They are," he assured. "And I'm really not that worried about the way they'll react. Even if it does take a little time to adjust to, I don't expect they'll reject either one of us."

That wasn't completely true. Push felt bad for lying even a little, but Scarlet Queen and Wiccan Witch had both been with Scratch at one point. Of course, according to Scratch, Wiccan Witch had been suspicious about them for a while. Scarlet Queen and Scratch were a few years old and had remained friends despite the initial bit of discomfort around one another following their breakup. Wiccan Witch, however, might be holding a grudge, despite the more rational part of Push's brain insisting otherwise.

"You worry too much," Scratch muttered on cue, brushing his lips across the surface of Push's left pec near the nipple.

"I don't want you to think this is something we have to do," Push began. "There's really no need to—"

The door suddenly burst open, cutting him off. "Are you two going to watch TV all day in here by yourselves?" Wiccan Witch asked before her eyes settled on the bed. "I know it was...."

Push felt himself pale as her eyes settled on the two of them, naked and clinging to one another as though their lives depended on it. Scratch went still for a moment as Wiccan Witch's eyes doubled in size.

"Yes!"

Her scream reverberated off the walls loud enough to rattle a few picture frames. The computer chair over by the desk went flying as her leg kicked high off the ground.

"Scarlet Queen!" Wiccan Witch shouted gleefully down the small hallway. "Get in here!"

Any remaining blood in Push's face promptly left as he heard footsteps come their way over the tile floor. Scratch, however, had started laughing softly to himself.

"What?" the brunette wondered as she entered the room. "Are they watching the movie with us, or…."

Scarlet Queen's jaw nearly hit the floor as she saw the two of them on the bed. Wiccan Witch had gone from wide-eyed to grinning like a fool.

"I told you!" she practically cheered. "I told you so. Guess that means you're out fifty bucks. Time to pay the piper!"

Scarlet Queen was glaring now. "You two couldn't have waited until we left to hook up?" she yelled, looking defeated. "I'll be listening to her gloat for a month at least."

"Try four," Wiccan Witch shot back, still grinning from ear to ear as Scarlet Queen shook her head. "Come on. Let's give the two of them some privacy. Anyway, your wallet and I have a little business we need to conduct, and this really isn't the place for it."

"Yeah, yeah," she muttered, looking very put out as the two of them made tracks for the door.

"Listen," Wiccan Witch added on her way out. "Wrath is going to cook something for us, and we were about to start up a movie. Whenever you're done, feel free to come join us. You two look like you could use a break anyway. Just be sure to shower first."

Push almost jumped clear off the bed, forgetting for the moment that he was naked. "Wait a second," he called out, feeling indignant now. "What's this about winning fifty bucks?"

"What?" Scarlet Queen asked, sticking her head back in. "Oh, that. About two years ago, after Scratch and I broke up, she made a bet with me that the two of you would admit you had feelings for each other and become a couple. I was dumb enough to call the tarot reader out, saying neither of you would ever acknowledge it, so here we are with me fifty dollars poorer."

Something dawned on Scarlet Queen as Push tried to cover himself with both hands. "Unless this was just a one-time thing?" she asked hopefully. "If it was, that means it doesn't count. Are you guys still working out whether you want to be together?"

"I'm not," Scratch said confidently, while Push stared at her in bemusement. "And this started right after we got here, so it looks like you're out of luck. Sorry."

"Damn," she swore, moving back through the door again. "Oh well. I guess it serves me right."

Push watched her leave, feeling his face go from pale to flushed in seconds. "Did the whole Association know?" he wondered softly.

Scratch was snickering as he moved up behind Push to kiss him sweetly on the cheek. "Come on," he said, giving Push a hard smack on the shoulder. "Let's take that shower together. I want to see what's for dinner, or lunch, or whatever Wrath is calling it."

Push couldn't form words as he stood up and went for the bathroom behind Scratch, who stopped short of the doorway and turned to him, wearing a curious look.

"What movie do you think they were wanting to watch?"

WRATH was moving around the kitchen when Push and Scratch emerged. Push watched the man work for a moment, impressed by his skills. Scratch came up behind him, eliciting a light gasp from Push. They weren't even touching, but having Scratch's body so close to his made Push tingle all over. His next breath caught in his chest as Scratch laced their fingers together and squeezed. Push felt himself lean back slightly to rest against Scratch's chest.

It felt like he belonged there.

"What's for lunch?" Scratch asked. "Or whatever."

"Seasoned baked chicken with rice, sauce, and potatoes au gratin," Wrath answered as though he'd heard the question several times already.

"Sounds good," Push commented, noting the way the dark-haired man moved gracefully around the kitchen. "Where did you learn how to cook?"

Wrath didn't answer immediately, busying himself by adding butter to the potatoes in the pan. "My mother," he grunted out eventually. "She spent most of her time cooking, when she wasn't cleaning, anyway, and always wanted me where she could see me. I guess she was worried I would slip away and set fire to someone's property."

"Charming woman," Wiccan Witch said dryly as she came through the kitchen by way of the opposite entrance. "Where did you live then?"

Push expected Wrath to dodge the subject, but he answered right away. "Here," he said calmly, while keeping his eyes fixed on the stove. "This used to be my house before it was renovated and put up for rent."

Wiccan Witch looked surprised by this. "I guess being back here sucks," she said lightly. "Sorry, I guess that was insensitive. Being around Scarlet Queen has made me too blunt."

"I heard that," Scarlet shouted from the living room. "And we've settled on two choices for the movie. The first X-Men or the first Iron Man movie."

"*X-Men* has my vote," Wrath called back over the sizzling food. "I haven't watched that since I was locked up."

"The Iron Man movie is pretty good too," Wiccan Witch told him, watching him give the rice a few quick stirs. "We could watch that one afterward."

Wrath straightened back up. "Weren't there giant robots?" he asked, looking to where Scratch and Push were still standing together, holding hands. "You know, the ones we just finished fighting a few hours ago."

"Not much we can do right now," Push replied.

"And what about Sloth?" he pressed. "And the Pranksta Gayngsta? And, well, aliens? Shouldn't we be worried about all that?"

"Until Professor Trixter is done analyzing both of those samples and works out how the nanomachines can be shut off, the best we can do is enjoy the downtime," Push insisted, feeling the weight of the situation pressing down on him. "We can't go out and look for Sloth until the hovercraft has recharged, and hunting bad guys on an empty stomach is a bad idea anyway."

"Plus," Wiccan Witch added. "Professor Trixter might not want anyone else driving his baby around."

"Um, speaking of which, has anyone see Trixter?" Scratch wondered. "Because he should probably eat something soon. You know how he gets when he has a new project to work on."

Push chuckled. "Like when he first got it into his head that he could make those rocket-powered hover-skates work?"

Wiccan Witch snickered. "And then didn't sleep for two days," she finished, chortling. "I think the Silver Buzzard was the one who found him in the Association lab muttering about Marty McFly."

Wrath went back to cooking as the rest of them laughed. Scarlet Queen was heard snickering from the living room as well. After a moment, Wiccan Witch walked over to where Push was standing and threw her arms around his neck.

"I'm so happy for you two," she said, hugging Scratch next. "Be good to each other."

"I will," Scratch swore, smiling as he took Push's hand again.

"You too," Wiccan Witch warned Push next. "I know how you think, so don't expect me to go easy on you if I find out you're the one making things difficult."

Push frowned, unable to think of anything to say. "I'm serious," she warned, waving a finger in his face. "I'll send a bunch of poltergeists to haunt your apartment if you try any of your wishy-washy behavior with him."

Scratch laughed again. "It looks like she's trying to bully you out of your lunch money," he remarked.

Push wracked his brain for a smartass remark to throw back at her, but his mind had stalled. Scratch saved him, however, by pulling him into his arms and kissing him.

Hard.

Push could feel two pairs of eyes on them as Scratch all but bent him over backward in an effort to work his tongue all the way down Push's throat. It should have shocked him. Push felt he ought to be embarrassed for the few seconds he had left of rational thinking. After that, though, everything below the belt took over, and he was kissing Scratch back.

His best friend.

His boyfriend.

The man he'd pined for these many years and never expected to get.

Wiccan Witch was staring quite openly when they disconnected. "Wow," she breathed, keeping her eyes fixed on them as she swallowed hard. "I have to say, I'm just the tiniest bit envious. He never kissed me that way."

"Me either," Scarlet Queen added, standing in the door leading to the living room. "The movie's getting ready to start, assuming you guys don't need a minute or two alone together."

"Maybe later," Scratch said, holding Push tightly to him. "I think I wore him out a little while ago."

Push had a smart remark to fire back then, but lost it as he noticed Wrath watching them out of the corner of his eye. The pyrokinetic was leaning over the stove again, carefully observing the food as it cooked. And yet, his head had been turned ever so slightly toward him. For a brief moment, Push thought the man looked heartbroken.

"I think Wiccan Witch should turn over part of the fifty she won from Scarlet Queen," he said loudly, still not looking up. "After all, it was you two she made the bet on."

"I'm all for that," Scarlet Queen agreed, grinning at her. "Since it means you won't be keeping as much of it."

Wiccan Witch turned and pouted woefully at Wrath, who refused to look at her. "You're supposed to be on my side," she grumbled, crossing both arms over her chest. "What happened to solidarity?"

"Solidarity goes out the window pretty fast when money is involved," Wrath replied.

Everyone moved out of the way so Wrath could finish cooking. Push had suggested it, but couldn't take his mind off what he'd seen on Wrath's face. Being around him suddenly felt suffocating, so he'd brought up the idea of them waiting in the living room. Wrath didn't respond either way, except to inform them dinner would be ready in twenty minutes.

The previews on the DVD were over, and the movie was just getting started when Wrath gave the call for them to come and eat. Wiccan Witch fixed a plate for Professor Trixter, who had been holed up in the back room the whole time. Even the smell hadn't been enough to draw him out, though Push largely wasn't surprised. Everyone else loaded up their own plates, Wrath taking the time to make another for Wiccan Witch while she was gone, then headed to the living room. Wiccan Witch returned a moment later, collected her plate, and joined them on the couch next to Wrath.

Push had taken the seat next to Scratch. The two of them scooted toward each other at the same time, causing Scarlet Queen to shake her head and laugh as she sat in the corner perpendicular to them.

"What?" Push asked automatically.

"Nothing," she replied, before spearing a bite of potatoes. "I was just thinking it might have been worth the fifty."

Wiccan Witch moaned as she bit into a piece of chicken. "Good food," she praised, giving Wrath's leg a squeeze with her free hand. "Oh, and Trixter said he was too busy to join us right now. He's in the middle of some 'upgrades', whatever that means, but promised to eat along the way."

"Figures," Scratch said, nodding as he took a bite. "This is good."

It was, in fact, delicious. Push nodded his appreciation as he chowed down. Everyone settled into a comfortable silence as the movie played. Wrath seemed to get into it, though there were a couple of times he pointed out something implausible, sparking a debate between himself and Wiccan Witch that slowly led to the two coming up with even more outlandish uses for rocket boots.

"Give it a rest, will you?" Scarlet Queen barked after several minutes of this. "The rest of us want to enjoy the film. Besides, it is impractical to use rocket boots to play ice hockey because the floor would melt."

Wiccan Witch's face went blank. "Mm," she hummed, looking at Wrath. "She's got both of us there."

"I thought you had already seen this," Wrath said apologetically.

"I have," Scarlet Queen replied haughtily.

"Four times," Wiccan Witch whispered loudly over an explosion occurring on-screen. "We can finish this later."

Push watched the two of them rather than the movie for the most part. When everyone had finished, Wrath offered to take Wiccan Witch's plate and gathered up the others as well.

"Thank you," Scarlet Queen told him as he exited the room.

"Yes," Push said, before Wrath disappeared out of sight. "It was great."

The credits were beginning to roll as Push heard Wrath moving around in the kitchen, cleaning up the mess.

"Need one of us to give you a hand?" Wiccan Witch asked.

"Don't look at me," Scarlet Queen protested at once. "I don't like doing my own dishes."

"I've got it," Wrath replied, as a pounding on the front door echoed through the living room, followed by three frantic rings on the doorbell.

"Um, the hell?" Scratch wondered, turning around on the couch.

"Who could that be?" Scarlet Queen wondered aloud.

Wrath was already moving to answer it, so Push stayed in his seat. From his vantage point on the couch, he could see the front door down the small foyer. The minute Wrath turned the knob, a figure forced his way in, slamming it shut behind him.

"Ya gotta help me!" the figure screamed, seizing Wrath by the front of his shirt. "The fucker's trying to kill me. Please, take me back to jail or whatever the hell you want, but don't let them find me!"

Everyone stood up at once. Push thought the voice sounded familiar, and it was easy to see why a moment later. Wrath came through the living room, dragging the figure behind him.

It was the Pranksta Gayngsta, looking wide-eyed, sickly, and scared out of his wits.

"I guess this explains why you two are so successful with finding escaped convicts," Wrath said sarcastically to Push and Scratch as he held the Pranksta by the back of the neck. "They just show up on your doorstep begging to be taken in."

SCARLET QUEEN kept watch on the Pranksta Gayngsta while Wiccan Witch checked the man over. "Don't worry," she assured him in a soft tone when he flinched at her touch. "I work as an emergency medical technician in my civilian life. I'm just going to check your vitals."

The rest of them were watching from off to the side, just in case. "I'll go get Professor Trixter," Scratch offered after a moment, pausing as he walked past Wrath.

"If he moves," Scratch told him in a deadly tone. "If he so much as flinches the wrong way, don't hesitate."

Wrath held up a ball of flame in the palm of his hand. "I won't," he promised as the fire crackled dangerously. "You can count on that."

"Good."

Scratch nodded, then left to fetch Professor Trixter.

"It's probably best if Trixter looks this guy over," Wiccan Witch told them. "I'm not sure how much of a medical background Trixter has, but he's the only genius we've got on hand, and I don't recognize a lot of these symptoms."

Wrath was standing beside Push now, who was doing his best to ignore him. Instead, Push focused on the sores dotting the sick man's flesh and the sweat pouring down his face. The man's body was like a tightened coil, ready to spring at a moment's notice. His face contorted in pain as Wiccan Witch brushed his skin.

"Sorry," she whispered. "I'm not sure what's wrong with you. Can you tell me what happened?"

The man called the Pranksta Gayngsta swallowed as their eyes met. "Duane," he choked out. "My name is Duane."

"Duane," she repeated softly. "Could you tell me what happened?"

Duane's eyes went for Push and Wrath at once. "It started, I guess, after you turned me over to the cops," he said breathlessly. "Somebody showed up wearing a police uniform and told me I was about to be double-crossed."

Neither man spoke. "Double-crossed?" Scarlet Queen asked instead, curiously.

"Yeah," Duane grunted out while Wiccan Witch continued her examination. "There was this deal, see? The guy I used to work for, Dr.

Stephens? I married his daughter. Only he didn't think I was good enough. When I tried going into—" Duane winced, seemingly at nothing, before continuing, "…tried going into business for myself, he set out to ruin me. After I lost everything, somebody came to see me about doing a job for them."

Duane gasped. "They said they were with this big company that wanted to see Stephens take a fall. At the time, I knew it smelled bad, but we were almost broke, and the chance to give that bastard a black eye was too sweet for me to pass up."

Duane paused a moment, struggling to breathe. "They had it all planned out for me," he forced out. "They wanted to make it look like a super-criminal was targeting Stephens, like those guys from down in New Orleans several years ago. I had this background in theater, see, so they'd supply me with everything I needed and a new identity. In return, I'd get a full criminal defense when the time came. Plus, I was supposed to keep this journal of everything I'd done. Once I got arrested, it would be shipped to a publishing company so that my wife and kids would receive all the royalties."

Scarlet Queen looked skeptical. "They wanted you to pose as a supervillain?"

"Yeah," he grunted. "Only, I get word they're gonna double-cross me. The guy was somebody I didn't recognize, not the same ones I'd talked to when everything was being set up. He's brought a uniform for me to wear and slips me out, then tells me to head south to a town called Shove Point. There's a car waiting for me with a full tank of gas."

"What happened next?" Wrath asked coldly. "Why Shove Point, of all places?"

Duane winced. "Fuck, I don't know, man. None of this shit has made any sense to me. I considered running on through, but the car broke down the minute I got into town. It had this GPS thing hooked into it, so maybe somebody was tracking me. I had nowhere else to go and nothing left, so I found a bar and got shit-faced. Then the cops throw me in the tank and you three show up to drag me back. You saw the pale guy on top of the sheriff's department, right? He catches up to me and drags me off, wanting to know what happened to the arrangement."

Wrath and Push both frowned at the same time. "So Sloth was sent here to collect you?" Push asked, thinking fast.

"Yeah." Duane nodded as another pain spasm hit him. "That's him."

By now, Scratch and Trixter had rejoined the group. "The—" Wrath began before stopping himself short. "The... issue we discussed earlier about the Association," he said. "Suppose the one who set this whole thing up was that."

"Why send Sloth here after him, though?" Scratch pointed out. "Why break him out in the first place?"

"Later," Push said. "Go on, Duane."

"That Sloth had me chained up in this old farm house," Duane told them. "Not sure where it was. I had to track through the woods so he didn't find me, but he would leave me there a lot. I think he was looking for something. Anyway, he had these canisters with him. The other morning, he comes back pissed as hell and shoots me up with one of them while holding me down, saying he's gonna take care of something for good. Then he leaves, and I start feeling like I've gotta throw up. The sores started after that, and the cold chills."

"How did you escape?" Scratch asked.

Duane stared feebly down at the floor. "The chain broke," he mumbled

"As sick as you look?" Wrath asked. "You stay chained up while perfectly healthy, but then it breaks after you get sick."

Duane said nothing. "He's not lying," Wiccan Witch said, looking around the room. "Not about being sick at least, but I still have no clue as to what's wrong with him. Whatever Sloth injected into his body, it's doing a number on him. He belongs in a hospital."

"No hospital," Duane begged, rising sharply. "He'll find me there."

"The closest one is here in town," Push insisted, folding his arms. "Besides, it's only until we can airlift you back to Grand Rapids to stand trial. I'll call the sheriff's department, though they may not be eager to help."

"One of us can stand guard," Scratch said, looking to Push. "If Sloth tries something, we can radio for help."

"Whatever, man," Duane whimpered. "Just make it stop hurting, okay? I feel like I'm being torn apart from the inside."

Wiccan Witch moved aside so Professor Trixter could have a look, but Trixter was in no shape to tell them anything more, save that someone should call an ambulance and keep the Pranksta separated from the rest of the group until then. Nobody had a problem agreeing to this, and a few minutes later, the ambulance was pulling into their driveway. Apparently, Wiccan Witch had thought ahead and made the call while Trixter was looking the man over. By this time, Duane was huddled on the couch whimpering and sweating bullets. In his condition, Push couldn't help but feel sorry for him.

Upon entering, the paramedics took one look at the Pranksta and blanched. Push thought both men were going to bolt for a second. One mumbled under his breath something about getting a stretcher before leaving through the front door again. Push watched them go and joined Scratch and Wrath by the door to the kitchen.

"What's the plan?" Wrath asked, looking between Scratch and Push as the EMTs brought the stretcher in.

"You two go with him," Scratch suggested, watching the men work. "If Sloth shows up, you'll have the best chance of taking him down. I'm going to ask the girls if they would mind helping me track down that pod."

Push nodded. "That sounds good," he agreed. "If Sloth shows his face at the hospital, we'll radio for backup."

"Good," his lover said, looking stern as he turned toward Wrath. "Um, what the fuck do you think Sloth put into this guy?"

Wrath shook his head. "No clue," he said. "This wasn't Sloth's style back in the day."

"Do you think he'll come after this guy while he's in the hospital?" Push asked.

Wrath frowned. "Honestly, I'm counting on it. Sloth never did much without a reason. He may have let Duane escape on purpose, but I'm having trouble convincing myself of that right now. If any of you manage to hunt down that pod while we're guarding Sloth, we may get him right where we want him."

"Split his focus," said Push, coming to the same conclusion.

"What if he was just poisoning Duane?" Scarlet Queen asked, coming up from behind. "This could be his way of taking the guy out."

"Takes too long," Wrath dismissed at once. "And it left the door wide open for him to escape. Plus, Sloth wouldn't have wasted his time with poison. Even he wasn't too lazy to break someone's neck, if it needed doing."

"Then he did this for some other reason?" Scarlet Queen frowned hard as she thought that over. "Why, though?"

"To infect us?" Wiccan Witch offered worriedly. "We don't know that whatever Sloth gave him isn't contagious."

Wrath still didn't look convinced. "Maybe," he said thoughtfully, "but I still say this isn't his style."

"We'll ask Sloth soon enough," Push said. "With Trixter's help, you guys should have an easier time tracking down that pod."

"Isn't he going to be too busy finding out how to shut off those nanomachines?" she wondered.

Professor Trixter, it turned out, was on board. "I've run some projections through my palmtop computer," he said, turning in his chair to face them in the doorway to his work room. "Going on what I've observed about the nanobots' behavioral patterns so far, I overshot some on my initial guess. It should take another day or so for them to fully recover and start rebuilding. Also, my drive is running calculations for a computer virus to shut the hive off completely. It'll be a while before that's finished, but that's still enough time to give you guys a hand.

"Also," he added, holding up a petri dish full of the alien slime sample. "I took a look at this earlier while I was waiting on some calculations of mine to finish. I'll need to do lots more tests to be sure, but there's something fucked up about your 'aliens'."

"Like what?" Wrath asked.

"Later," Trixter said, turning away to pick something up off the desk. "When I know for sure. Meanwhile, I had some spare time, so I took the liberty of finishing the upgrades to some new equipment for everybody."

Push felt his eyes go wide. "You've been building new equipment for us in here while you were studying alien glop, observing how the nanomachines work, and figuring out how to shut them off permanently?"

"I'm just good like that," Trixter replied dismissively.

"I'll say," Scarlet Queen said, clearly impressed.

"I was looking over this alien blaster you guys had," he said, holding it up for them to see. "The thing is, this was made using Earth tech. If I'm wrong about our aliens, then they must be scavengers, because this thing was put together using basic technology found on this planet. It's pretty sophisticated, don't get me wrong, but still Earth-based. I adapted what I learned into some of the gear I'd been planning to make for you guys."

"What sort of gear?" Scarlet Queen asked, interested, while Push just shook his head in amazement.

Trixter put the alien blaster down on the desk before lifting up something else. "A new cue stick for our pool shark," he said, making Scratch frown uncomfortably. "You can still use this to shoot those trick billiards of yours, but this also fires a laser blast from the tip."

Trixter flipped the thicker metallic cue stick over in his hands as he spoke. "The grip has a vibrational shock emitter built into it," he explained, "that works like one of Push's telekinetic force bubbles. It can knock someone away from you, but it's not as powerful as the original. Also, it has a built-in grappling hook with flexi-wire, meaning you don't have to carry so many of them in your coat anymore."

"Cool," said Scratch, accepting his present gratefully.

"I got you a new pair of goggles," Trixter said to Push next, holding them up. "And a new telescopic bo. You told me about the older model breaking on you a while back, so I thought of a way to make it ten times more durable. I just haven't had the time until today to finish it."

"Wow," Push said, accepting both.

"For Scarlet Queen," Trixter presented, as the brunette stepped forward eagerly. "A new wrist crossbow and truncheon. The crossbow is a laser blaster now, similar to the alien one, and the club works like a Taser when you depress a switch near the bottom."

Scarlet Queen grinned as she snatched her new toys out of his hands. "I'm going to have fun with these," she declared.

"Lemme see!" Wiccan Witch said excitedly from behind them. Wrath moved along with the others so she could enter the room. "What did you make for me?"

"I'm still working on yours," Trixter replied. "It isn't easy building weapons around someone whose shtick includes talking to ghosts and predicting the future."

Wiccan Witch stuck her bottom lip out for a second, then went serious. "The ambulance is getting ready to leave," she told them. "Wrath, if you and Push are going with them, you need to get a move on now. The medic team is already suited up."

"We're gone," Push said at once. "Thanks for your help, guys."

"Get going," Scarlet Queen told him. "We're happy to, if only for the chance to fight aliens."

"And see what's so special about this pod business," Trixter added.

Push turned toward the door after Wrath, who was already moving down the hall, stopping as he felt Scratch's hand close around his forearm.

"Wait," Scratch said, pulling him back to him.

Push's eyes widened as Scratch's mouth closed over his for a brief but passionate kiss that left his toes curling inside his boots. "Be safe," Scratch said before letting him go.

Professor Trixter's eyes doubled in size as he cocked an eyebrow at them. "We'll explain later," Scratch told him calmly.

The stunned look didn't leave Trixter's face as both girls snickered. "This I can't wait to hear," he declared, before looking past Scratch at Push. "What you doing turning one of the Association's biggest horndogs into a fudge packer?"

Though in a rush, Push accepted the teasing for what it was. "Don't look at me," he replied, stopping as he headed out the door once again. "He came to my room begging for it. I guess if you can have black powers, I get to have queer powers. Straight men can't resist."

"No one is safe!" Wiccan Witch moaned in a ghostly voice. "The lesbian moon is upon us, Scarlet Queen! We must make out right now!"

Trixter turned his head toward them at once. "Don't let me stop you!" he said encouragingly as Scratch smiled. "Don't you wish you'd stayed straight long enough for this?"

"I'm gone," Push stated, walking away as Scarlet Queen and Wiccan Witch made loud, sucking kiss noises at one another.

Wrath was waiting at the end of the hall. "What's going on in there?" he wondered.

"Don't ask," Push replied as the laughter from the other room persisted.

CHAPTER
TEN

WICCAN WITCH had already explained the situation to the EMTs, but they still insisted on checking both of their identifications. Push and Wrath were then handed two hazmat suits to wear. The rest of the ambulance team was already suited up. Duane, the would-be Pranksta Gayngsta, had passed into a delirious fever. One of the trained medics was attempting to administer a sedative, but the moment the needle pierced the skin, it broke off.

The woman looked at each of them, stunned. "When did he first begin exhibiting these symptoms?" she asked them.

"He showed up that way," Push replied. "But probably for a few hours, at least, if his story is anything to go by."

The woman went quiet as she checked the arm with the broken needle sticking halfway out of it. "You guys are with the Association," a male EMT said. "What brings you all the way down here to Shove Point?"

"This guy," Push replied. "Initially, anyway. We're hunting another convict that's evaded capture for a while."

The woman was attempting to remove the needle from Duane's arm, which was proving difficult. The piece of metal appeared to be stuck somehow. The other EMT watched her for a moment as she gripped her patient's arm gingerly around the sores and tugged.

"I thought about joining once," the man said absentmindedly. "You think they'd take a small-town redneck from Arkansas?"

Push smiled. "We took him," he said, gesturing to Wrath sitting next to him. "I guess anything is possible."

The fellow's gaze fell on Wrath, who was scowling at Push. "You look familiar," he said thoughtfully, scratching what little beard he had. "My name's Matthew, by the way. What's yours?"

"Wrath," he replied. "And I know who you are."

Matthew frowned as Wrath leveled his gaze at the man coldly, but was saved from anything worse by the female EMT's cry.

"I don't believe this," she shouted, sounding close to panicking. "It's going into the arm!"

This got Matthew's attention. "What?" he wondered, moving in closer to see what the problem was.

"The needle," she insisted. "It's slipping further into his arm. I can't stop it!"

The female EMT let out a gasp as the broken hypodermic needle slipped out of her grip and into Duane's arm a second later.

No one moved.

"Holy shit," Matthew cried out. "What the fuck just happened?"

Both EMTs turned to face Push and Wrath. "Has anything like this happened before?" she demanded. "Before we showed up, I mean?"

"Not while we were watching him," Push replied at once, while Wrath stared at Duane's semilucid form thoughtfully.

They were coming up on the hospital now. It was one of the benefits of living in such a small town, Push supposed. A team was already waiting to help pull the stretcher out. Push whipped out his badge, nudging Wrath to do the same, before explaining the situation to the doctor in charge. The doctor appeared skeptical but didn't stop them as he and Wrath followed the team through the emergency entrance.

The medical team was chattering the whole time, working to figure out what was wrong with their newest patient.

"His eyes are… discolored," one said loudly.

Push spotted the reason for his falter at once. Duane's eyes had gone red, though not bloodshot. They were, in fact, a solid red color, bright like a neon sign and just short of glowing underneath the halogen bulbs. There was no sign of pupils or whites.

It gave him the creeps.

Both he and Wrath held back as the triage team lifted their patient onto a new stretcher. At this point, there was nothing for them to do there but watch and wait. Picking out a choice piece of wall, Push leaned back against it, satisfied it gave him a clear view of what was going on inside. Wrath picked a spot to his right and watched the scene unfold.

"I have a theory," he said quietly while the paramedics worked frantically. "It's a little out there, though."

Push glanced toward him. "Go ahead," he replied. "I'll hear you out."

Wrath hesitated a moment as he thought about how to put it. "It didn't dawn on me until we were in the ambulance," he began slowly. "When the needle went into his arm, the second time, I mean, I started thinking. What if what Sloth pumped into this guy was more of those nanomachines?"

Push frowned. "Okay," he admitted. "That is a little out there."

"His arm ate the needle," Wrath pointed out. "He's got symptoms no one can diagnose, and I don't know if you saw as they were wheeling him in here, but the man's eyes have gone red."

Remembering that made Push wince. "Yeah," he acknowledged. "I saw."

"And?"

Push chose what he had to say next carefully. "So, what is your theory exactly? That Sloth was hoping to turn Duane into some sort of killing machine?"

"Maybe."

The noise in the other room had shifted to a quieter yet much more intense level. "This isn't a SyFy Original Movie," Push said dismissively, more for his own comfort than anything. "Nanomachines can't do that sort of stuff. They're not even supposed to do what we saw them do earlier."

"And yet," Wrath countered, "the sun came up this morning to a giant robot battle."

Push tensed as the fresh memory in his mind came back with a vengeance. "I'd almost made myself believe that was a dream," he muttered before straightening against the wall. "About that, though…."

Push hesitated, only partly due to the number of people that were around. Wrath was a member of the Association now, yet he still made Push feel uneasy for some reason. This was the kind of thing he and Scratch did together, and talking with Wrath felt off. Taking a gamble, Push continued on anyway.

"The mole," he said more quietly, under the noise of the ER. "You really think the Pranksta Gayngsta was set up by them?"

"It was someone high up in the Association," Wrath replied, speaking low as Push did. "Someone who had access to where this Duane guy was being held, and someone with the knowledge of how to slip in unnoticed."

Push twisted his mouth in frustration. "I know," he said. "I didn't want to admit it, but that makes sense. Still, though, why go to the trouble of creating a super-criminal just so he'll get caught and then spring him free? The scenario fits in a weird sort of way, except for that last part. If someone was targeting Dr. Stephens but didn't want to get caught, sending in a third party works as a distraction."

Push swallowed as a nurse walked past. "But why set him free afterward?" he went on, as the room where Duane was being held bustled with activity. "That just opens the door for this guy to blab the whole scheme to the world. Strange as it sounds, everything adds up until that last part."

"Unless they were hoping he would start the scheme over somewhere else?" Wrath frowned as he thought this over. "No, that doesn't add up either. If we go with the idea that Sloth was the one feeding information to him during the warehouse brawl, then Duane was just the face of the operation."

"And right now, the theory goes that Sloth is working for the mole," Push continued, following the same line of thought. "So Duane was working for Sloth, who in turn is employed by our mole in the Association, which explains how Sloth was able to get his hands on the nanomachine project."

Push paused for a moment. "I still can't get over that."

Wrath looked at him. "Why not?" he asked plainly. "It can't be the weirdest thing you've ever encountered."

"Actually, it was," Push replied, laughing. "What, did the Deadly Seven go up against giant robots every other day of the week down in New Orleans?"

Wrath looked away. "We were a team of supervillains," he pointed out, folding both arms in front of his chest. "Each of us had unique abilities and powers. That's hardly a recipe for daily life."

Wrath hesitated a moment before looking back at Push. "And besides," he added, "you grew up with your abilities. You're telling me nothing unusual happened to you before you became a superhero?"

"Other than being gay?" Push countered. "It was pretty normal."

"You were lucky, then," Wrath said, his face turning sour. "Most people like us don't have that sort of luxury."

Something in his voice made Push look at Wrath differently. "I didn't say it was easy," he insisted, sounding a little angrier than he'd meant. "There were problems."

"I never said you didn't have them," Wrath interrupted, watching Duane's room closely. "You just didn't have the same type of problems most people like us do."

Push studied Wrath's face for a moment before speaking again. "What's that supposed to mean?" he pressed. "'People like us?'"

"People with powers." Wrath gave Push a look. "Unique abilities. There have been names for people like us since the very beginning. Different cultures called us by different titles: angels, demons, changelings, halflings. These days it's freak, mutant, or metahuman."

It sounded like Wrath was quoting someone. "Who told you all that?" Push wondered. "I went looking for information when I was a kid and couldn't find anything."

Wrath scoffed. "Of course you didn't," he said, still not looking at Push directly. "When people find out about us, it always ends badly, so we stick to the shadows. We hide in public, those of us that can, and put on the face of being just like everyone else. You, Scratch, and Wiccan Witch are some of the brave few to break that taboo."

"Scratch doesn't have powers," Push said automatically before something kicked in. "You mean the way his mind calculates angles?"

"He has an easier time of it," Wrath explained, as more personnel moved into Duane's room. "People are impressed by something like that, but it doesn't register as 'super' with them. Plus, he has to share the limelight with you, so it gets overshadowed a bit."

The ER hallway was getting crowded now. Another team was bringing in someone new on a gurney, and the two were forced to move further back so they could get through. This put their mark's room out of sight. Push strained to see inside, then gave up.

"What about Wiccan Witch?"

"She talks to ghosts," Wrath stated as if it were a fact. "And predicts the future through tarot cards. The cards are just a means of expressing her power, but most folks see that sort of thing as a parlor trick or a con. People turn their focus on us because we're the most obvious, but there are more out there."

Much as this wasn't the right time, Push couldn't help but find everything Wrath said fascinating. It had never occurred to him that Wrath might have information about his powers that he didn't have.

"Where did you learn all this?" Push felt himself tense but forced the next question out before he could change his mind. "How do you know so much?"

"I just know what someone told me a long time ago," Wrath answered. "And I'm hardly the first person you should ask about such things. I don't know what makes us what we are, if that was what you were thinking. The very, very few I've met who were 'different' in some way didn't know any more than me. They had their own hypothesis but were looking around in the dark."

Push considered this as another crowd moved through. "I guess I've always wondered in the back of my mind if I was the only one born this way," he said above the noise of footsteps echoing off the walls.

"Everyone wonders that at some point in their lives," Wrath replied, looking over at Push finally. "You were born gay with limited telekinesis. I was born a pyrokinetic with bisexuality. Neither is what you would call an ideal…."

Wrath went rigid all of a sudden. Push watched in surprise as his eyes nearly doubled in size from shock. Wrath's arms went from folded over his chest to clutching at his sides, as if in pain.

"What's wrong?" Push asked worriedly.

"This feeling," Wrath hissed softly, so quietly Push was forced to strain his ears to hear him. "I've felt this before."

"What?"

Push looked around, then placed a hand on Wrath's shoulder, which he quickly knocked away. "Don't touch me!" Wrath insisted, backing away from him. "Not yet. I have to find him."

"Who?" Push wondered.

Wrath was standing with his back bent slightly, hunched down like a lion getting ready to spring. "He's here," Wrath whispered, sweeping the corridor with his eyes. "I could feel him. It was just for a moment when the crowd passed by us, but there's no way it could have been anyone else. Envy is here."

Push watched as Wrath shut his eyes tightly, a feeling of absolute dread filling his insides as he gave Wrath room to work.

"It's gone," Wrath said, the anger thick in his voice. "At least for the moment. Chances are, he'll be back soon, though. Duane must be his target."

Several of the hospital's personnel were still lingering in the hallway. "Which one?" Push asked softly, watching each one closely as he felt his hands tingle. "Envy was the master of disguise, right?"

"Of a sort," Wrath said, doing the same. "Envy is a shape-shifter. Not to the extent like you see in the movies, but he had precise muscle control over his body. With enough effort, he could alter his appearance somewhat. He could be fatter, thinner, or somewhere in between, and shift his facial features. He and Lust were the top assassins out of the Seven. They were the ones Sloth sent out to do his killing for him."

"And Lust is the knife fighter, right?" Push pressed, keeping his eyes peeled with his back against the wall. "Superagility or something?"

"Hyperkinetic reflexes," Wrath corrected, "is what they called it. He's faster than the human eye can follow."

Nothing had happened. None of the hospital staff members in their line of sight were behaving strangely. "Any idea?" Push asked insistently.

"It's not them," Wrath said, sounding confident. "He must have moved on when he saw I was here. Chances are, though, if Sloth brought Envy in on the job, Lust is not far behind."

"Are you sure their target is Duane?" Push asked, keeping both hands up in case he needed to blast someone very quickly. "What if Sloth wanted us dead?"

"Doubtful," said Wrath, wearing a cocky smirk for a moment. "Even Sloth knows better than to underestimate me. I wouldn't hesitate to put those two creeps six feet under, Association or not."

"I still think—" Push started, but was cut off by a horrified scream from the room just down from them.

"There!" Wrath pointed. "That's the room where they brought Duane."

Push was already moving. It was only a few short steps, but for him, the trip might as well have taken an eternity. He hadn't noticed anyone going in there while they were on watch, yet Envy must have slipped through anyway. Push was cursing himself as he forced the door open to a room full of shocked nurses and one doctor, all of whom were standing far away from the body on the bed in the middle of the room.

It took a second for Push to register what it was he was seeing. As Wrath came up behind him, his brain struggled to take in what was in front of him. Without looking back, Push could feel Wrath recoiling from the sight.

There was a tangled mess of blood, wires, and bone. It was still alive, if the jerky movements were any indication. The metal wiring looked like it had sprung out of the body—and it was a body of some kind—in all directions. Flesh had been skinned away in numerous spots, but as Push looked on, it almost seemed as though it were being knitted slowly back into place.

"My God," he whispered.

"The hell?" Wrath echoed, grimacing. "What did Sloth do to him?"

The body on the cushioned slab jerked hard, and a choked gurgling sprung out of its throat. Push couldn't bring himself to call it Duane, even though that was who it must be. He forced himself to think of it as an "it," not a man, and not the person they'd spoken to at the house less than an hour ago. If he let himself think that, he'd probably be sick.

The metal wires were going back into what was left of its flesh now. The skin had gone positively obsidian. Red lines were appearing like cracks over it, but too straight and smooth to be that. The parts that weren't a solid, charred black appeared to be chrome and extended out of the flesh like bone appendages. Push took a step forward, intending in his stupor to get a closer look. From where he was, they almost looked metallic. Wrath grabbed him with one arm, though, and dragged him away from it.

"This isn't happening," someone whispered.

None of the nurses had spoken. The doctor wasn't even looking at it now. Push realized what a jolt it must have been for the man. Everything from his worst nightmares was being played out right in front of him. The thing on the table gurgled again as blood splashed out of it, landing on the floor in blotches. The transformation wasn't finished yet, but Push couldn't watch anymore.

"Everybody out," he ordered in a weak, broken voice. "Get out now."

The doctor gave him a look but didn't argue. Motioning at those nearest to him, he ran for the door and didn't look back. Push and Wrath both moved to the side so the room's occupants could clear out. The others were following along, practically on each other's heels. Once the room was empty save for the thing still wracked in agony, Push backed himself and Wrath out, closing the door behind him.

"What," a nurse tried, looking horribly pale. "What was that?"

"We don't know," Wrath told her before Push could bring himself to speak. "He was injected with something, but we're not sure of the details. For now, it would probably be better if no one went in there."

No one looked like they were about to argue. "I think it's safe to say the Pranksta Gayngsta's condition exceeds the capabilities of this facility," Wrath told Push, who shook his stupor off long enough to nod.

"Right," he replied, forcing his brain to think. "We need to get him out of town right now. The Association has a medical facility. They might be able to do something. I'll send a priority alert and get someone to chopper him out of here."

"Until then," the doctor said, looking grave, "I'm afraid this entire section of the hospital is under quarantine."

Push's eyes widened. "Why?"

"Because we don't know what we're dealing with," a nurse answered at once. "That man's symptoms, or whatever, are totally unidentifiable. For all we know, whatever he has is contagious."

"The last thing we need is to start an epidemic," the doctor finished. Push looked over and saw the badge clipped to his coat read "Hamilton."

"That means anyone who's had recent contact with this man will have to come under quarantine as well," Hamilton was saying now. "That includes everyone standing here, as well as anyone who was with you when that man showed up at your residence."

"The team in the ambulance who brought him in will have to be alerted also," said a different nurse. "I'll make the call."

"There might be a problem," Push warned. "There was an alert just before… the incident. We think there are two very dangerous men in this hospital right now."

"They can't be more dangerous than an unclassified disease threatening to break out and spread across town," Hamilton countered, sounding angry now.

"Don't count on it," Wrath told him calmly. "These two men were once members of the Deadly Seven. They are contract killers and notoriously bloodthirsty."

Push hadn't been expecting Hamilton or his staff members to know what Wrath was talking about, but the moment he mentioned "Deadly Seven" their eyes went wide.

"You're joking," a male nurse said almost pleadingly.

Wrath shook his head. "I wish I were," he said gravely. "Their code names were Lust and Envy. For all we know, one of you here is Envy in disguise."

Hamilton clearly didn't like the sound of that. "Regardless," Hamilton declared. "I'm putting the ER under quarantine right now. We can evacuate the rest of the hospital if necessary. That may be the best idea."

"Agreed," Wrath said before looking toward Push. "There will be fewer potential hostages that way and less ground to patrol."

"Except that the evacuation will leave them room to escape," Push countered, though he was already beginning to see Wrath's point.

Wrath stared hard at Push. "Even still," he said beseechingly. "It would be better to let them go now and begin a new search later than risk so many people."

Hamilton seemed to regard Wrath more favorably for a moment. "I'm going to lock down the ER doors," he said before walking away. "Once that's done, the staff can begin moving the rest of the building's patients out."

Push waited until Hamilton and the others had left before speaking. Sounds were still coming from the door behind them, but he forced himself to tune them out.

"Well?" he demanded urgently.

"None of them were Envy," Wrath insisted. "I was monitoring their emotions the whole time. Nothing about them reminded me of him."

"So he's somewhere else?" Push reached into his pocket for his Blackberry. "I'm going to call the others. This is bigger than Hamilton realizes."

"Are you going to tell them to come straight here?" Wrath asked as Push moved away slightly.

"No," Push said, as his phone rang. "If they're okay, I'm going to send them to look for Sloth. If they can find him, we might be able to negotiate something."

Wrath listened as Push sighed with relief at the sound of Scratch's voice. "I don't have much time," Push warned, holding the phone tightly to his ear as if hoping to absorb a part of Scratch into himself. "Whatever Sloth put inside Duane has done something horrible to him. The ER is going under quarantine, and the doctor is about to give the word to have the rest of the hospital evacuated. Wrath thinks that Envy and Lust are here."

"What?"

Scratch's voice came through the phone loud enough for Wrath to hear from farther back. "They're after Duane or the two of us," Push explained. "Right now, you and the others have got to find that pod. It may be our only bargaining chip."

"You're breaking up," Scratch warned as their connection began fading.

"I'm hanging up now," Push said. "I'll contact you later, if I can."

A second went by. Then Push blurted out, "I love you."

Wrath was watching Push as he put his phone away. "Have they found the pod yet?" he asked stiffly.

"Hopefully, they will soon," Push said, ignoring him for the most part as screams began drifting through the thick door where Duane was being kept. "We may be able to use whatever is inside of it to trick Sloth into calling off his goon squad and curing the Pranksta Gayngsta."

"Assuming Sloth even has a cure," Wrath reminded.

"Yeah," Push admitted, moving back a little as the screams grew louder. "I know."

It wasn't long before pandemonium was spreading. Push and Wrath had taken up a post near the sealed doors, standing guard outside Duane's room while simultaneously watching as patients were hurried out. Most looked less than thrilled at the rush. Some were attempting to resist, and security was forced to hold them back to keep them from forcing their way inside.

Somewhere a phone was ringing. A moment later, one of the aides stuck her head out of an opened door and looked toward them.

"Push?" she asked, her forehead wrinkling slightly in confusion.

"That's me," he said, holding his hand up.

"Telephone," she said, holding the receiver out for him. "It's Sheriff Black."

Black was yelling through the line before Push could hold it up to his ear. "...the fuck is wrong now?" the man demanded. "What's this about a plague and you being trapped on the other side of the quarantine line, huh?"

"Long story," Push said.

"The fuck you say!" Black hollered. "You people can't go more than a day without bringing some kind of disaster on my town."

Push couldn't find the words to argue with him. "I'll explain once I have something," he said, trying to remain calm. "Right now, we've got a patient who may or may not be turning into a nightmare of science and two killers who are on the loose."

"Killers?" Black paused at that. "Nobody told me anything about another escaped killer."

"Two killers," Push corrected. "And they never escaped. These two were associates of Sloth and evaded capture. We think he's called in reinforcements."

"Great," Black shouted loudly. "Just perfect. Now there are two more killers in my town."

"Looks that way," Push replied, smiling as he imagined the look on Black's face. "The good news is we've caught the Pranksta Gayngsta. He's the one we're locked inside the hospital with right now."

"What's he doing there?" Black wondered, his voice dropping an octave or two. "You boys work him over so bad he had to be put back together again?"

"We don't work like that," Push said. "We try not to, anyway, but no. He's the 'nightmare of science' I was talking about. We think Sloth injected him with something, and it's—"

Push was cut off by a grotesque sound coming from behind the door to Duane's room. Chills rolled down his spine, making him grip the receiver. It was like a mixture of a roar and a bloodcurdling scream.

"The hell was that?" Black wondered from the other end of the phone.

"Our nightmare of science," Wrath called out, placing a hand tentatively on the door handle. "I think whatever was happening to him, it's just about finished."

"Gotta go," Push said, already moving the phone away from his ear. "If we live through this, you can tell me all about how I ruined your town forever, afterward."

"If we live through this," Wrath echoed, an edge of poison to his voice. "Would it be all right if I burned the hair off his nuts?"

"Yes, it would," Push returned flatly. "Though I may change my mind later. Don't open the door until you're sure you are ready."

"I'm ready," Wrath assured him.

One hand gripped the handle while the other was holding up a ball of fire. "Do it," Push said, gathering a telekinetic bubble in his own palm. "Now!"

Wrath started to push the door in. He'd gotten it open maybe two inches wide when something slammed into it hard from the other side, forcing it closed. Right after, the wood splintered, forming what looked like claw indentations.

"I think this might be more of a problem than we thought," said Wrath as he backed away.

Chunks of the door shattered in pieces as what looked like a metal claw tore through. "Tell me I didn't see that," Push muttered as more of the door was torn away.

"I think our mark just went Terminator on us," Wrath said while the thing on the other side ripped at the door's hinges, tearing it loose. "Ideas?"

"Take him down," Push ordered.

"What?" Wrath gave him a look. "You're not going to give me a hard time about using excessive force on—"

"Do it!"

Push raised both hands as the thing staggered out into the hall. The sight of it made him freeze as it hesitated a moment, taking several deep breaths. Again, Push couldn't think of it as a person, as someone alive.

Its eyes glowed red, even in the brightly lit corridor. The hands were covered in some kind of silvery metal and shaped into lethal-looking claws. The skin that wasn't peeled away was as black as coal. Parts of what might have been bone were exposed to the surface, looking chipped in places, as though they were being broken away and repaired at the same time.

As it turned slightly, Push saw part of the spine exposed in back. Bile filled his mouth as his eyes remained rooted to the spot, unable to look away.

The smell reminded him of meat going bad.

"You!" it screamed, pointing a claw at them. "You were supposed to help me! Look at what he did, what it's doing to me!"

"Sloth," Push heard Wrath hiss out. "You unimaginable bastard."

"Why did you let this happen?" Duane was shouting still. "Why does it keep hurting?"

Push thought Duane was about to attack them, but the twisted man turned to the sealed ER doors and began hacking away at them. Glass and pieces of shrapnel flew as his claws sheared a hole in the door big enough to walk through.

"Why?" Duane howled. "Why hasn't it stopped hurting?"

Wrath looked at Push. "Do you want to tell him, or should I?"

"This isn't funny," Push countered angrily as Duane resumed his assault on his homemade exit.

"I never suggested it was," replied Wrath. "However, I think the good doctor's quarantine is over. Our mark is making his own exit, and security isn't going to be able to stop him."

The security guards, meanwhile, were watching from the other side, keeping a safe distance from Duane's claws and the door fragments flying in all directions. Alarms blared while none of the personnel made a move to stop him, which Push felt was the smartest thing they could have done.

"Duane, stop," he tried, yelling over the noise. "This isn't going to help anything."

"I think he's too busy going Adamantium Rage on the infrastructure to hear you," Wrath warned, lighting up his hands. "Reasoning may not be an option."

"I know," Push agreed sadly, watching as Duane tore away a large chunk of metal before stepping through the hole he'd finished making. "But we have to try."

"Try fast," Wrath said, following behind Push closely as he moved for the gaping wound in the building. "He's heading for the people."

Push thrust his palm out without hesitation and sent out a blast, striking Duane in the back before he could come close to one of the security guards, an overweight man who'd frozen up in terror. Duane staggered slightly but didn't appear too fazed.

"You can't hold back," Wrath warned, coming to a stop at Push's side. "He's not going to."

"I can handle this," Push snarled before giving Duane his full attention.

"Fine," said Wrath, taking a step backward. "We'll do this your way."

Push drew in a deep breath as Duane stared hard across the gap separating them. "We can help you, Duane," he tried, holding a hand out. "There's a medical branch of the Association that specializes in all sorts of cases. A chopper can airlift you out in less than an hour if you come with us, but this has to stop now. You're going to hurt someone if you don't reel yourself in."

Duane's red eyes narrowed as the skin surrounding the exposed bone on his face knitted closed. "Look at me," he demanded. "Look at me! I'm a monster."

"You're not a monster," Push made himself say, though he couldn't fight lowering his hand. "Not yet, anyway. These people didn't do anything to make you this way, so let them go. Once we get you out of here, the Association can analyze what's wrong with you and develop a cure."

"You mean put me in a cage!" Duane roared. "Right? I become one of the Association's freak shows. They put me on display as part of the tour."

"They can cure you," Push insisted. "Whatever Sloth did, they can reverse it."

"Bullshit!"

Duane swung his arms wildly, and this was all it took for the officers on scene to snap. One pulled a gun and fired while those closest to where Duane stood ran like scalded cats. The bullet lodged in Duane's side and stuck there, embedded only part of the way. Push watched as the bullet slowly soaked into the dark skin the same way the needle had in the ambulance.

Duane howled in pain again. "That's what it wants," he hissed through gritted teeth, leveling his eyes on the gun in the security guard's hands. "I need more!"

Duane was on the man before Push had time to react. Blood flew as the claws swiped the gun out of the officer's hands, leaving him bleeding and missing part of two fingers.

"Get out of here!" Push ordered, even as the man was already breaking into a run clutching his ruined, bleeding hand.

"More!"

Duane held the gun up to his chest clumsily. The claws that had been his fingers were ill-suited for holding a gun, though, and it took a moment for him to hold it properly. Push seized the chance to fire another telekinetic blast his way, knocking the firearm into a corner.

"No!" Duane cried out. "I need it!"

"Now?" Wrath asked.

"Just contain him," Push warned as Wrath surrounded Duane with a circle of fire before he could reach the gun.

Duane, however, dove right through the fire and managed to snatch the gun up off the floor. "Mine," he declared joyfully, aiming the gun at his chest.

"That didn't work so well," Wrath noted, gathering the fire up off the floor into his hands as the gun went off.

"Stop him!"

Duane was emptying the clip into his chest, crying out as each bullet pierced his skin. Wrath flung several fireballs across the room, snapping his fingers each time they came close to where Duane lay crouched on the floor, pumping his guts full of lead. The noise was distracting but did nothing to slow Duane down.

Slowly, he got to his feet, exposing his chest for Push to see. A dozen bullets were stuck in his chest and abdomen, sinking into the skin like droplets of water into a sponge. Duane gasped for air as the last of the bullets faded out of sight.

"Still hurts," he wheezed, looking around, for the moment not really seeing Wrath or Push standing nearby. "Still need more. Lots more!"

"More what?" Push pressed, hoping he could still reach the man. "Duane, tell us what it is you need."

"More metal," Wrath concluded, looking poised to attack. "If it is nanomachine technology altering his body internally, they must need metal to digest so they can reconstruct him. Thus far, they've had to make do with the iron in his bloodstream, but a human body can't survive without that, and there just isn't enough to keep him alive."

"That's insane," Push blurted out at once, trying to tune Wrath's voice out and focus on the problem at hand.

"Push," Wrath tried, sounding exasperated. "He's turning into a robot." Push looked at him. "Okay," Wrath replied. "A cyborg, then. Either way, something is altering his internal structure, and we've already dealt with giant robots today."

Push was finding it more and more difficult to dismiss the theory, though he hated saying so out loud.

"I know I'm not Scratch," Wrath finished stiffly. "But I'm the one that's here."

That jolted Push, and he looked over to where Wrath was watching him closely. "Hate me all you want," Wrath told him in a cold, flat tone. "But right now, we have a job to finish."

Duane chose that moment to rush them. Push caught the sudden movement out the corner of his eye, but not before Wrath did.

"Look out," Wrath shouted, but Push was already moving.

Leaping forward, he shoved Wrath aside as one of Duane's claws came whooshing down, clipping him on the right shoulder. Push winced but let the momentum carry them both into a roll. Duane was still coming for them, his claws glistening in the light. Push saw his own blood decorating the one Duane had caught him with and lashed out without thinking. The blast that flew from his hand rocketed out, catching Duane dead-center and sending him flying backward into a wall.

"Thanks," Wrath said softly as he got to his feet. "You didn't have to do that."

"Don't worry," replied Push dismissively as he accepted the hand up. "I probably owed you one. And just for the record, I don't hate you."

Wrath looked away and let go of Push's hand. "We'll just have to see," he said quietly before taking off. "He's going to get away. Come on!"

CHAPTER
ELEVEN

TRACKING Duane through the hospital was the easy part. The guy wasn't wasting time trying to conceal his trail. Two L-turns later down a long, twisting hallway and the two came across a set of claw marks raking sideways along the concrete brick wall. Beyond that was a door, or what might have been one not so long ago. Mostly, it was a mangled mess of glass and metal framing now. A few pieces of the framework looked to have been torn away by claws.

"He's already out of the building," Wrath said. "Finding him won't be easy."

"I'm more worried about what we do once we've caught up to him," Push said, running on ahead. "And who he might come across before then. I think it's safe to say he's not in his right mind."

"What gave you that idea?" Wrath quipped, following along behind.

Push dove through the opening, careful to avoid the sharp edges, and winced slightly as the injury on his back flared. Wrath caught up with him and ran alongside as they took off across the street, following the trail of destruction.

"You should have that looked at soon," Wrath told Push, nodding to the linear stripe of blood staining the back of his costume. "It could be worse than it looks."

"No time for that now," replied Push, turning the steam on.

There were screams coming from up ahead inside a home-style pizza parlor. The rear door to the place had been torn off, leaving little doubt as to where Duane was. Push charged forward and raced inside, passing one of the cooks lying wounded on the floor and another whose legs he had to jump over to keep going.

"Check them," Push instructed. "Then call an ambulance."

Wrath hesitated, spotting another worker who was hiding in the corner. "You," he barked, pulling her up by one arm. "If you're not injured, call the police and the hospital. Tell them to send an ambulance."

The woman was hyperventilating. "Hey!" Wrath shouted, snapping her out of it by igniting a fire in his hand inches from her face. "I need you to be strong. These people are going to die if you don't help." Some of the panic in her eyes cleared. "Good," he said, more gently as he let her go. "Find a cell phone. Then check to make sure they're all right. I've got to go help my partner."

The waitress was already pulling her cell phone out and dialing. Wrath checked both bodies on his way through, satisfied they were alive for now.

Push, meanwhile, was attempting to blast Duane into unconsciousness. Each telekinetic force blast knocked the budding cyborg backward, scattering the few remaining customers toward the exit doors. Several knives and forks were sticking out of his chest. It looked as though Duane had stabbed them there personally. Each one was working its way deeper into him, albeit more slowly than the bullets had.

"Duck!" Wrath called out as he rushed up behind Push.

Push dove down automatically, and Wrath blasted Duane with twin columns of fire from each hand. The cyborg had been about to get to his feet, and the flames blew him backward onto a table, scattering the empty plates and cups.

"They're alive for now," he told Push, who was rising. "One of the waitresses is calling for an ambulance."

"Good call," Push told him. "Now let's end this before anyone else gets hurt."

Duane was already getting up again. "He's tougher than he looks," Wrath mused. "I guess those nanomachines repair internal damage as it happens."

"Assuming that's what it is," Push countered, still skeptical. "I don't think holding back and trying to reason with him will work."

"Me either," Wrath said ruefully. "But neither of our attacks are doing much good."

"Right." Push flung Duane back into another table as the cyborg stood up again. "Ideas?"

"One," Wrath responded immediately. "If you're willing to try it."

Duane was on his feet again, his head tossed back in fury like some mechanical demon. "Telekinetic bomb," Wrath said. "Give it everything you've got. I'll hold him off."

"Are you sure you can?" Push asked, even as he brought his hands together to form the bomb.

Wrath unleashed a torrent of fire onto Duane, forcing him down again. "He's got nothing but rage and fury inside of him right now," Wrath told him, talking over the roar of the fire from his hands. "His mind is gone, so there's nothing but primal instinct. That's more than enough for me to draw power from."

Push nodded and closed both eyes to drown out the distractions. The adrenaline pumping through his bloodstream made focusing easy. With their lives on the line, it took mere moments for the bomb to take shape.

"Got it," Push said. "Now what?"

"Now this." Wrath lowered both arms and placed his hands around the invisible sphere Push had clutched in his palms. "Together."

As Wrath's hands came down, fire stretched from his fingers into the colorless sphere. The flames licked and danced at the air, gathering together. Sweat broke out across Wrath's face as he pumped in more of the anger flowing through him. Push could almost feel the rage coming off him now. They were so close, their noses practically touched. The rage made his skin crawl, and it felt like the orb was scalding him.

Wrath dodged to the side, his and Push's hands clutching the fire bomb. "Get ready," Wrath warned, as Push moved with him. "He's getting up."

"This is going to get messy," Push muttered, taking aim as Duane leveled his gaze at them. "Now?"

"Now!"

Wrath let go of the bomb as Push launched it through the air at Duane, who had already started charging for them. The moment he let go, Wrath grabbed him around the waist and dove behind the salad bar. Both men rolled, covering themselves in ranch dressing and bacon bits as the bomb hit its mark, blowing them farther away. The whole building shook, and windows shattered outward as Duane's body was blown through a wall by the combined power of a firestorm and telekinetic force.

The noise alone sounded like a jet engine taking off during a thunderstorm.

Tables and chairs were thrown everywhere as Wrath and Push covered their heads. As dust and shredded pieces of lettuce settled on top of them, Push realized Wrath had somehow rolled underneath him. Rising slightly, he looked down to find Wrath staring at him with a bemused sort of look.

"Okay," Wrath said between coughs. "So, maybe you don't hate me?"

"I never hated you," Push insisted, feeling a lump form in his throat. "I thought you hated me. What gave you that idea, anyway?"

"I'm an ex-con," Wrath stated at once.

Their eyes met, and Push felt a chill roll over him. Goose bumps formed underneath his clothes. He tried to move then, but his arms wouldn't cooperate.

"You're not an ex-con anymore," Push told him, despite the sudden unease creeping through his body. "Today, you're a hero."

Wrath glanced around at the state of the pizza parlor from his vantage point beneath Push's smaller form. "I think the owners of this place might disagree with that," he noted.

Sirens were already blaring in the distance. "We should get up," Push said, still not moving. "Make sure the ones in the rear of the building are all right. The blast might have done them more damage."

"Right." Wrath didn't move either. "About that. It was the only thing I could think of at the time that might slow him down."

Thinking of the maniac cyborg was finally enough to make Push move. "Looks like he's down for the count," he said, after peering over what remained of the salad bar.

Duane's body was lying halfway outside the building through a hole he'd made in the wall upon impact. The cyborg was stretched out unconscious across a bed made out of debris. From the looks of things, he was completely out of it.

"It was a good idea," Push added, turning back to Wrath, "just so you know, but I'm not in any hurry to try that again."

"Of course not." Wrath's words carried an edge now as he got up off the floor. "Why would you?"

An ambulance pulled up across the street before Push could ask what was wrong. "Are we staying?" Wrath asked. "Because something tells me Sheriff Black isn't going to like this."

"He'll have to deal," Push replied. "And we don't flee crime scenes. Remember that."

"If you say so." Wrath kept both eyes on the EMTs as they came through. "But I have the feeling this might have been one time when we should have."

The squad cars were rolling into the parking lot now. Push moved forward to point the EMTs to where the injured were. The whole time, an ill feeling grew inside of him. From the sour expressions on the officers waiting outside, Wrath had been right again.

THE EMTs were able to bandage the wound on Push's back. The cut was deep, but still within the superficial range, so he wouldn't need stitches. The woman bandaging him warned him to take it easy before moving on to the more serious patients. Wrath had some minor bruises and initially refused to let any of the paramedics so much as touch him. It was only when Push insisted he allow them to look him over that the man conceded.

The people that had been in the back of the pizza parlor when Duane raided the place were in far worse shape. Luckily, it was a short trip to the hospital, and from the sound of things, the paramedics were optimistic. Once he was sure that had been handled, Push turned his attention toward Wrath, who had taken a seat near the corner of the rear of the ambulance. Push watched as Wrath remained perfectly still the whole time the paramedic looked him over. Push saw it was Matthew, the guy who'd ridden with them to the hospital earlier, doctoring Wrath up. Wrath was practically seething the whole time the paramedic checked him over.

Tentatively, Push placed a hand on Wrath's shoulder. Wrath jumped slightly but relaxed a little once he saw who was touching him.

"No one here's going to hurt you," Matthew assured Wrath before looking past him to where Push was sitting. "Is he always like this?"

"I remember a slightly different opinion," Wrath said warningly, wincing as Matthew's fingers brushed a particularly bad bruise. "I see you haven't lost your delicate touch."

Push frowned right along with Matthew as he slowly drew his hand back. "Have we met before?" Matthew asked, looking confused.

"I doubt you remember," Wrath said. "No one else seems to."

Matthew looked over to Push again, clearly hoping for help, but Push wasn't about to bring up the fact Wrath had a history with Shove Point. For the most part, it wasn't any of his business. Also, he was sure Wrath would try to roast him alive.

Push waited until Matthew was gone. "What's your deal with that guy?" he asked, keeping his voice down so they weren't overheard.

Wrath kept his eyes focused on the chaos in the parking lot. "We used to be friends," he said after a moment. "For a while, anyway."

"What happened?"

The look on Wrath's face soured further.

"Did he find out about your powers?" Push asked. "Or was it something else?"

"He didn't find out," Wrath told him, still not meeting his gaze. "He didn't have to. There were enough stories all over town about me. We met the summer before third grade. Matthew's family had just moved here because of his dad's job, and they were renting a house not far from where I lived."

Wrath paused for a moment, swallowing what seemed to be a lump in his throat. "For a while, it seemed like things might get better. Then school started, and he decided I was too much of a liability. You couldn't be friends with me and hang with the cool kids, so I had to go. A week after the school year began, he jumped me on the playground at recess to show who he was loyal to."

Push looked back over his shoulder. Matthew was lurking in the front of the ambulance now, shifting some equipment. By Push's summation, however, he was eavesdropping.

"I hate this town," Wrath said with a great deal of venom. "If this place got wiped off the map, it wouldn't make me cry."

Off in the distance, a team wearing hazmat suits were loading Duane in a truck to be placed under private quarantine. A chopper had been called to airlift him upstate to a laboratory so he could be examined, but wouldn't show up for several hours. In the meantime, the locals weren't taking any chances. Push had overheard one saying how a special unit of the hospital was being set aside for Duane and no one else. It looked as though they were willing to believe he wasn't contagious, at least for now, but the risk was still high enough to keep him away from the other patients.

Of course, the fact that the man had torn through two separate sets of doors and attacked several people had something to do with it as well.

"I never liked any of the places where I grew up either," Push told Wrath, looking back at him. "Sometimes, we weren't there long enough for the dust to settle. Every so often, I would make friends, but it didn't seem worth the effort to try, since I knew we'd only end up leaving them behind. I always thought when I grew up I'd pick a spot where I felt at home and never go farther than a couple of blocks. Now I work for a group that sends me all over the country. Having an apartment almost doesn't feel worth the trouble."

Quiet settled between them for a moment. "It was different in New Orleans," Wrath began slowly. "Even though I knew what I was doing was wrong, that felt like a fair trade-off for not coming back here. We were criminals, but I had acquaintances, people who were willing to speak to me. There were people I trusted, at least somewhat, I guess, and not everyone in the Deadly Seven was like Sloth. The thing I hated about it falling apart in the end was having all of that go away. I knew we were done, even if we managed to get away.

"I wish I could go back there, but odds are, someone would be waiting to put a bullet in my skull. The crime families we dominated have long memories, but it's the town I miss more than anything. There was always something to do. New Orleans is a city that knows how to party."

Wrath finally looked toward Push. "The gay community has a powerful underground there," he said. "It was while I was in New Orleans I started to realize I was bi. Being there helped coming to grips with that a lot. I can't picture undergoing that transition in this place."

Push looked around at what he could see of the town from squatting in the ambulance and felt an ironic smile tug at his lips. Before he could comment on that, two officers were spotted in the distance, headed their way. Wrath noticed at the same time, and Push could practically see the heat come off him in waves.

"Calm down," he said warily. "Whatever it is, we'll handle it."

Wrath caught the plural term and glanced at him. "'We', huh?" he asked, looking uneasy. "You sure about that?"

Push thought for a moment as the cops came nearer. "Yeah," he stated firmly before they were close enough to hear. "I'm sure."

Neither officer was one Push recognized, which felt a little odd considering how small Shove Point was. Both were looking back and forth between him and Wrath as though watching something disgusting take place. Once they were close enough to be heard, the two stopped short.

"You're the fella called Push?" the shorter of the two with the beard asked. "We're Officers Lott and Wand. We've got a message for you."

"Okay," Push said, sensing the hostility behind their calm exterior.

"Sheriff Black told us to inform you that you and your Association members," the taller, clean-shaven one called Wand picked up, adding a great deal of disdain to the word *Association*, "have until sunrise tomorrow to vacate this town."

Push didn't respond.

"The owner of this here establishment has agreed not to press charges for the damages," Officer Lott went on, his drawl getting much thicker. "Or for the assault on his employees, but the sheriff says this town has seen just about enough 'heroics' to last a lifetime."

"If you refuse," Officer Wand added, "Black will see to it you all are hauled before a state judge and deemed a threat to local safety. Is that clear?"

"Perfectly," Push replied, not losing his calm. "Is there anything else?"

"That'll be all," said Lott, giving Push a nod. "Now why don't you boys move along and leave that ambulance for somebody that really needs it."

Push motioned for Wrath to follow. Surprisingly, Wrath stood without argument. Once they were far enough away, Push got out his phone to call Scratch.

"You took that well," Wrath noted. "I'm under the impression we're not really leaving?"

Push snorted. "It isn't the first time the local cops got their shorts in a knot because of the Association's involvement," he said, pausing before pushing Scratch's number. "Of course, things aren't usually this intense. I don't blame Black for being upset, but he couldn't force us to leave if he was the Arkansas governor's secret bunk mate. The Association has enough lawyers backing it to tie the whole thing up in litigation until this case is solved."

Wrath frowned. "That doesn't sound very heroic," he mused, keeping in step with Push. "Although it's probably very effective."

"It's been done before," Push informed, bringing the phone up to his ear. "Black's just making hollow threats. We'll get it sorted out. Finding Sloth is our priority."

Scratch's phone rang several times before switching over to voice mail. Push left a message, then turned to Wrath as he hung up.

"He must be in a dead zone," he said, putting the phone away. "I only got his voice mail. It looks like we're walking home."

"It isn't that far," Wrath told him, pointing at a side road across the street. "I know a shortcut, assuming the roads here haven't changed. We'll get to base faster if we go that way."

Push sighed long and hard as they made their way across the road. "This will be fun," he uttered dryly, once they reached the other side. "It doesn't help that I haven't been jogging lately. I guess now's as good a time as any to get caught up."

"They hardly ever let me out of my cell when I was in prison," Wrath said. "When that happened, I made the most out of it."

"Can you keep up?"

Wrath caught the smug glint in Push's eye and rose to the challenge. "I'll be waiting on the couch for your lazy ass when you finally get home," he declared cockily.

"You wish," Push said, laughing as he picked up speed.

Both broke into a run, keeping pace with one another as they took off down the road. The area Wrath led Push to resembled a historical district. Some of the houses were in better shape than others, and the streets were in need of repair. Push set all of this aside as Wrath gained a foot or so on him and focused on the task at hand.

Soon, they were running neck and neck. Push kept matching his pace to keep Wrath in his stride, but it wasn't easy. Just when it looked as though Wrath was beginning to tire, he would pour on the steam. More than once, Push felt himself getting winded and had to dig deep to keep up. It was hard not to try and break on ahead, since Wrath knew the way home, so Push kept an eye out for anything familiar as they raced down the side streets together.

Before long, they were getting close to the neighborhood where Wrath's old house was. By this point, Push had given up trying to beat him. They had kept pace with each other for a while now, enough that it almost felt natural.

Against his better judgment, Push found himself glancing toward Wrath every couple of steps. Sweat had soaked through the man's shirt, leaving it stuck to the surface of his body like a second skin. Each time Push looked his way, Wrath's face was screwed up in concentration, as though something heavy lingered in his mind.

To his surprise, Push felt himself growing hard. His dick flopped uncomfortably in his sweat-soaked boxers as they raced along together, before growing to full mast. A blush crept up his face, though with the heat coming off him, Push doubted Wrath would notice. Wrath didn't seem to be concerned with him anyway, which was one small thing to be thankful for. Seizing this small bit of good luck, Push tried to focus on anything around him that might help bring his cock back down to a manageable and less noticeable state.

Unfortunately, the area near their rented base was full of trees, which only served to fuel Push's imagination. Push drowned them out and stared hard at the manicured lawns, taking in the perfectly trimmed grass. Each time that seemed to work, though, he would catch himself looking toward Wrath, and his cock would jump in response. It was becoming painful now, begging for attention.

Instead, Push turned his thoughts toward Scratch, thinking it would be better to get aroused over his new boyfriend than his teammate. Push thought of Scratch's face, of the fact that they were an item now, and how overjoyed he was. For a moment, this seemed to work. His cock stayed hard the whole time and didn't soften in protest as Push thought back to earlier in the day when Scratch had grinned broadly from between his legs. He could feel his heart really pounding now as he wondered just how far Scratch was willing to take their relationship.

Satisfied, Push looked at Wrath again, confident that whatever had taken hold of his libido was no match for his feelings toward Scratch. Wrath was still staring down the road, breathing heavily as they turned onto the street where their temporary home was. The shirt was sticking closer to his body than ever. Push saw how the muscles in the man's arms moved like liquid iron underneath, and wondered how they would look bare. Suddenly, he was thinking back to the hotel room in Grand Rapids when Wrath had come out of the shower wearing nothing but a towel. Water had clung to Wrath's body then the way sweat was sticking to it now.

Push looked down, unsure of why, exactly, and saw a massive lump in the front of Wrath's pants. There was no question he was erect. The thick sausage hung to the left, straining against the material. If Wrath noticed, he gave no discernible sign, but Push found he couldn't turn away. In a flash, he was imagining the thick tube working its way past his lips and into his throat.

Shutting his eyes, Push forced the image away as he slowed his pace slightly, letting a gap form between them. By the time he got to the front door, Wrath already had it unlocked and was holding it open. Push ran past without a word and made a beeline for his room. Once there, he stripped down and dashed for the shower, praying all the while that cold water was the only thing needed.

The water hit his skin like ice, washing away the guilt sticking to him along with the grime. Push turned around several times, letting the spray hit him on all sides.

Still, his erection stubbornly persisted.

Frustrated, Push grasped himself and began stroking roughly back and forth, hoping to get himself off quickly. Determined, he pictured Scratch once more, remembered how it had felt touching his skin, having Scratch look at him like a man starved.

Remembering how it had felt when Scratch told Push he loved him.

Push made a noise somewhere begin a grunt and a gasp as his balls emptied themselves all over the side of the shower wall. His climax had come sudden and fast but intense. Push was left with a ringing in his ears as he struggled to regain control of himself. The cold water was making his skin shrivel up, so he turned it off before stepping out onto the mat. A knock came at the door as he was drying himself. Without thinking about it, Push knew who it was.

"What?" he asked, sounding mad. "Sorry," he tried again. "Who is it?"

"It's Wrath," came the reply. "You'd better get out here. There's something on the news you want to see."

Push made sure he was dry before wrapping the towel around his waist. The last thing he wanted was for Wrath to see him like this, but he hadn't brought anything with him to change into.

Wrath was looking grim when he opened the bathroom door. "See for yourself," he said, pointing to the TV, which had already been turned on and was broadcasting a news report.

"What…?" Push started, but cut himself off as the burning building on-screen registered with him.

"Officials continue to struggle to contain the fire," the reporter said as the bulletin at the bottom of the screen flashed. "For those just tuning in, behind me is the building where the Real-Life Superhero Association's main office is located here in Chicago. Reports are coming in all across the country. It seems that Association bases from Miami to New York City and even all the way out in San Francisco have come under bombing attacks." Push felt the blood rush from his face. "We're also getting reports that say even smaller Association offices were attacked," the reporter continued. "Hundreds of staff and personnel are reported either missing or dead, though we haven't gotten a confirmed count just yet. So far, authorities are keeping the channels of communication open in case this is the work of a terrorist group, but thus far, no one has stepped forward to claim responsibility or make demands. Heroes who are members of the Association are advised to remain calm and report in."

Wrath was watching as Push sat down on the foot of the bed. "Push?" he asked, as Push's eyes stayed glued to the TV set.

"It's the mole," Push said slowly, as if in a trance. "We were right all along."

"Push," Wrath said, sounding worried now. "Breathe, Push. It looks like you're going to pass out."

"I'm fine," Push told him, though he himself didn't believe it. "I'm…."

The camera suddenly gave a close-up of the Association building as flames exploded out of one side, licking hungrily at the air.

"Someone just sent us a message," he told Wrath, still watching the screen.

"I think you're right," Wrath said, taking a seat next to him. "But was the mole really behind this or someone else?"

"It doesn't matter," Push said, conviction gripping his heart. "I'm going to call Scratch and the others. If they haven't heard yet, they need to know. We have to regroup and compare notes."

"At least it can't get worse," Wrath said, retrieving Push's phone.

Push stared at Wrath as he accepted the phone from him. "Don't count on it," Push warned. "Remember, this was just the message. The worst is still on its way."

SLOTH looked at the two, keeping his eyes level with Envy more than Lust. "Well?" he asked impatiently.

"Just like you said," Envy answered in a smooth, liquid tone. "The nanomachines did their job, though it looks like the lack of iron in his body was making the transformation difficult. Still, I'm sure they'll compensate in some way."

Envy was stripping out of the doctor's coat as he spoke. "Funny," he continued. "I didn't expect either of them to buy that quarantine story I spun."

"It doesn't matter," Sloth insisted, thinking hard. "A little extra mayhem will keep the cops and those so-called heroes on their toes. The important thing is that you still have the Hamilton disguise available to use later on."

"It's a wonder it worked at all," said Envy, sneering. "That hospital is so small, an extra face should have stuck out like a sore thumb. I guess it says a lot for the health care in this rathole."

"As long as Wrath didn't give you away, we're good," Sloth told him, smiling now. "Since he didn't blow your cover, we can take that to mean he's on board with us."

"Maybe," Envy warned, turning away slightly. "The kid's grown up a lot since the last time I saw him. I don't suspect he's lost those so-called empathic abilities, but it's been a long time since we were around one another. I overheard him telling the other one that he sensed my presence."

Sloth thought this over.

"Maybe I've gotten better at masking my emotions?" Envy suggested, enjoying the conflicted look on Sloth's face as he sat down in the beat-up old chair. "After all, it was because of the brat that I thought of training myself to do that in the first place."

"Whatever," Sloth grunted, staring down at the desk in front of him. "For now, we move forward with the plan. Having Wrath is a necessity for the plan to work, but for now, we won't worry about it. Getting that damned pod back is the important thing."

Lust, meanwhile, was still standing in the same spot, pecking away at his oversized upper front teeth with one of his knives.

"Stop that," Sloth barked. "The noise is giving me gooseflesh."

"When do we get to wreak some havoc?" Lust demanded. "You told me this job would be fun. So far, it's been a huge snore. I wanna go out and make some children cry."

Envy snorted. "You sound like a bad comic book villain," he said, then ducked as the knife flew at his head, sticking in the wall behind him.

"Knock it off, you two," Sloth ordered wearily. "If you need something to do, why don't the both of you go out and find that pod for me."

"Isn't that supposed to be your job?"

Sloth glared hard at Envy. "My job is to explain to our... superiors," he said derisively, "why the pod hasn't been found yet. If you'd rather do that, be my guest. I'm sure they'd be real understanding."

Lust snorted. "I'm going," he said, already making his way toward the door. "It might be fun if some of those heroes get in my way."

"Keep the body count to a minimum," Sloth warned. "We don't need to draw too much attention to ourselves."

Envy was already getting up to follow Lust. "I'll go with him," Envy said, rolling his eyes. "You know he can't focus on more than one thing at a time, and any sudden impulses will take precedence without me there."

Sloth waited until he was sure the two of them were gone before pulling out the laptop. It took several minutes for the signal to relay through more than one satellite. During that time, his fingers drummed impatiently on the desk's surface. The old farmhouse was a derelict waste, but it offered some privacy. It still amazed him he was able to jury-rig a connection as far out as the property was and with just the equipment he had on hand.

The communication screen was a solid black, just like before. "What have you to report?" the distorted voice demanded. "Have you located the pod yet?"

"Two of my new associates are out looking," Sloth assured, clasping his hands together nervously. "They don't know the true nature of the pod, so it won't be an issue. The heroes are still distracted for now. Your prodigy looks to be coping well with the new gig."

"Find the pod," the voice said flatly, "and you will be handsomely rewarded. Perhaps even returned to active status. Fail, and—"

A loud pop came from the laptop speakers as the voice was abruptly cut off. Sloth frowned as words appeared in the screen window that had been blank moments before.

"The connection has been lost or terminated. Please wait while we reestablish your link."

Sloth refreshed the page several times, only to receive the same message over and over again. There didn't appear to be anything wrong with the hardware. Sloth checked the connection wires again, just to be on the safe side.

"The hell just happened?" he wondered, staring down at the screen. "It's like they just vanished."

EPILOGUE

Hero Gaiden

Night Sparrow

Anchorage, Alaska—1994

NIGHT SPARROW ducked as the punk heading toward him swung a fist, missing by a wide margin. Taking the initiative, Night Sparrow sprang up, flipping the grimy-looking bum over the side of the boat. The haunting sound of a gun cocking made him turn. Up on the yacht's balcony, Mr. Ludlow was aiming a gun down at his forehead as he grinned smugly.

"You know," he mused loudly. "I kept thinking the other one would show up if I held out long enough, but it looks like he's cut you from the purse strings."

Ludlow's voice echoed across the surface of Bootlegger's Cove, getting lost in the soft churning of the water.

Night Sparrow raised both hands in surrender as something behind the smuggler kingpin caught his eye. "Look behind you," he recommended.

"I wasn't born yesterday," Ludlow said, scowling. "You think I'm going to fall for that?"

"Not really," Night Sparrow said, smiling now. "But you're about to wish you had."

Ludlow didn't have time to turn. The blow to the back of the head knocked him over the side railing to the lower deck with a noisy crunch. The gun he'd been pointing at Night Sparrow clattered several feet away. Night Sparrow collected it as Snow Owl swooped down nearby.

"Stupid," she criticized, glaring hard at the side of his head. "He would have killed you if I hadn't showed up."

"Those are the breaks," Night Sparrow replied calmly, pinching the gun's barrel between his two gloved fingers. "This would be the gun he murdered the sergeant with. I was hoping he would fire it at least once at me, but the police should still be able to match the bullet in here with the one they took out of that cop's body."

"Wonderful." Snow Owl looked relieved as sirens filled the air. "That puts Midnight Owl and all of us in the clear."

With a nod, Night Sparrow placed the gun near Ludlow's unconscious body. From the looks of things, he wouldn't be going anywhere without a stretcher, assuming he managed to regain consciousness. Night Sparrow rather liked the idea of the man's last conscious moments of freedom being filled with pain. It was never something he'd have said to Snow Owl's face, though, knowing her, she probably could have guessed.

"Don't ever say I didn't get you anything," he told her, rising back up. "The chief can officially call off his manhunt now. You'd better go before the squad gets here, though, just to be on the safe side."

Snow Owl didn't move. "Stay," she blurted suddenly, giving him a pained expression. "This doesn't have to be the end. I know things were bad, but Midnight Owl only told you to stay away so you wouldn't get mixed up in all of this."

Night Sparrow smiled sadly. "I already knew that," he told her, watching as the strobe lights drew closer to the dock area. "I knew it when he first told me. I just wasn't happy about it. He still expected me to fall in line behind him without a word of protest."

"He doesn't want you making a mistake," Snow Owl insisted. "You know how he feels about the Association."

"It's different now," Night Sparrow told her, a little harder than he'd meant to. "They aren't just a bunch of weirdoes in bad costumes anymore. The Association is changing, getting bigger and doing more. They have a training program now. They're working with the police to solve cases."

"And you want to be a part of that?"

Night Sparrow scowled at the underlying tone in her voice. "I just want to be a part of something bigger," he mumbled.

Snow Owl turned her head away in a huff. "Fine," she bit back. "I'm sorry Midnight Owl and I weren't 'big' enough for you."

"Don't be stupid," he hissed, feeling angry for all the wrong reasons. "I wasn't going to stay here forever. I couldn't!"

"Why not?" she asked flatly, turning back to him. "What is it with you and Midnight Owl? You've both been weird around one another for a long time."

Night Sparrow felt a lump form in his throat. "Did he ever tell you?" he asked instead, hoping to change the subject. "Why he hates the Association so much, I mean? Has he ever explained to you why?"

Snow Owl didn't reply. Night Sparrow watched as she walked back toward the shadows hanging over the rear end of Ludlow's yacht. He knew without looking she would be gone. Disappearing that way had always been a specialty of hers.

HE MADE it home in record time. The fight on the yacht against Ludlow's top men had been more than enough for one night's work. Night Sparrow suspected he would be feeling the aches and pains from it for days. The flight he'd booked wasn't a red eye, but close enough he needed to get a decent night's sleep. There were also one or two things he hadn't packed yet. Most of his stuff had been sold already. The packet from the Association had specifically said he was allowed one suitcase and nothing more, so Night Sparrow was determined to bring only the essentials.

He'd narrowed it down to a few keepsakes, some clothes, toiletries, and the photograph that had once adorned his dresser.

Night Sparrow had nearly left it behind. It had been placed gently on top of his clothes first, then taken out, tucked away in the suitcase's side out of sight, yanked out again, and set facedown on top of the dresser. He hadn't thrown it away, thankfully. The three faces contained inside the simple, cheap frame had once represented the happiest time of his life.

To be fair, they were still the most important things to him, and the sheet had said he should only bring that.

Now, Night Sparrow picked the frame up tentatively and held it in his hand for a moment. An image of himself with Midnight Owl and Snow Owl in their civilian identities stared back. It was taken the night they'd gone to a film festival together. That had been the night Snow Owl introduced him to the glory that was *Casablanca*.

"If you don't get on that plane," he whispered to himself while holding the picture against his heart. "You'll regret it. Maybe not today and maybe not tomorrow...."

Night Sparrow couldn't bring himself to finish. Letting out a raspy sigh, he placed the frame facedown on top of his clothes where he was sure it wouldn't be damaged. Thinking on it further, he decided to wrap it inside one of his shirts and then sandwich it between several layers of clothing. This way, it was sure to survive the trip to Chicago. Now that it was out of sight, though, his body was starting to tremble.

"Here's looking at you, kid."

The voice startled him, but Night Sparrow knew who it was before he finished turning. Midnight Owl, better known as Professor Oakstone to his college students, stood in the door to his room, watching Night Sparrow with a neutral expression. Night Sparrow had been around the older man long enough to know this meant he was thinking hard about something. Oakstone did his best to conceal his emotions, while Night Sparrow wore his heart on his sleeve every day.

"I'm not a kid anymore," he answered defiantly. "I haven't been in years."

Oakstone looked off to the side at the spot where the picture had stood on the dresser. "I know," he replied quietly.

"You could've fooled me."

He didn't want to be angry now, not on his last night in Anchorage, but that seemed better than saying what was on the tip of his tongue.

"Just leave," Night Sparrow ordered, giving his back to the man who'd trained him. "We both know how this fight will end, so please just get out before one of us says something we'll regret even more."

"I didn't come here to fight," Oakstone said, his voice getting slightly gruff now, meaning he was holding back tears.

Night Sparrow could read him like a book, except where it counted most. "Why, then?" the young man choked out, keeping his face hidden.

Oakstone paused a foot or so from where Night Sparrow stood. "I don't want you to go," he whispered softly. "I came to ask if you would stay."

Anger bubbled inside of him. "You don't want me joining the Association, you mean," he countered, gathering all the rage he could before whirling around to face the man. "You know, I might not have been so pissed if you'd just told me all those years ago why you hate the Association so much. I get you just don't like them, but this goes way beyond that."

Night Sparrow took in a shaky breath as Oakstone stared blankly at him. "Something happened between those guys and you, though, and we both know it. You'll deny it until the sun freezes over, but there's a history there. Right now, I wish you'd fess up to it so I'd have a better idea of what I'm jumping into."

Oakstone winced at his words. "I can't."

Night Sparrow scowled, the anger inside seeping away to reveal the bitterness underneath. "Just like you couldn't say something else," he challenged in a much quieter, more confrontational tone. "I guess you never did care, huh?"

"No," Oakstone insisted, his eyes burrowing into Night Sparrow now. "I can't tell you."

It seemed like the man was trying to convey something, but the message was lost to him. "What?" Night Sparrow insisted. "Because I can't deal with it? Because you've done something so horrible I'd never be able to forgive you?"

The pain in his mentor's eyes was excruciating. "Haven't you learned anything about me at all?" Night Sparrow demanded. "When have you ever done anything to me I couldn't forgive? I've given you everything, yet you keep holding me at arm's length. If I could forgive that, if I could forgive you sending me away after...."

The rest of the sentence locked up in Night Sparrow's throat, though it was all too apparent Midnight Owl knew what he'd been about to say.

"I could forgive anything," he finished softly.

Midnight Owl nodded. "I know," he whispered, moving in closer now. "I've always known, and that's why I could never tell you. I don't deserve to be forgiven."

Night Sparrow lowered his head for a moment, unable to bear seeing the raw agony in his friend's face anymore. Finally, after several deep breaths, he managed to look up again.

"I already forgave you," he said, fighting back tears now. "I forgave you a long time ago. Whatever happened, it never mattered to me. Because, no matter how horrible it was, I've always loved you."

IT HAD been a mistake.

That was how Midnight Owl had put it the morning they'd woken up in bed together. The night before, they'd finally wrapped up Alastor Ludlow's smuggling operation. Ludlow and Midnight Owl had been bitter enemies for years, long before Night Sparrow or Snow Owl came along. The three had decided to celebrate and gone out for drinks. Being that he was finally twenty-one, Night Sparrow had been all for it.

After a long night of closing several bars, Snow Owl had gone home, leaving Night Sparrow and Midnight Owl to go back to their shared apartment for a nightcap.

Then it had happened.

Snow Owl and he had been dating for a while, with "dating" being the operative term. She had been the first real relationship for him and the one Night Sparrow had seriously considered settling down with. She'd known all about his past long before things had gotten serious, about the drug addiction he'd developed to cope with the abusive stepfather and alcoholic mother, and about him running away from home at the tender age of thirteen. She had understood too, understood him in a way most people never had. It was mainly why he'd assumed they had a future together.

Of course, there was that one thing he'd never told her about.

Midnight Owl had been his mentor, the one who'd found him slowly freezing to death in an alley. Midnight Owl had taken him in, trained him, and offered him a purpose, a goal he could aspire to. Night Sparrow hadn't much cared for the name initially, but time saw it grow on him. As Oakstone, Midnight Owl made sure Night Sparrow was well educated, knowing everything from complex math to computer science, and even classical music. By the time Night Sparrow was ready to enter college, he had become a veritable Renaissance man.

He'd also fallen for the man who'd saved him from himself.

In the beginning, it had seemed like a childish form of hero worship combined with having a father figure at long last. When he'd first become aware of it, Night Sparrow had done a little private research on the side. All the books he'd checked out suggested he was simply projecting a sense of adulation onto the person responsible for taking care of him. That had made sense, at least for the most part, yet it hadn't stopped there.

Outwardly, of course, everything appeared fine. By the time Night Sparrow had graduated summa cum laude, the world seemed to be his oyster. He was in love with a wonderful woman, had a promising career ahead of him in computer software design, and was keeping the criminal element at bay alongside his comrades.

Underneath it all, though, his emotional state was a nightmare. By that time, Night Sparrow could no longer deny what he was feeling. A year after he and Midnight Owl slept together, he was on the verge of a breakdown. No matter how hard he fought it, Night Sparrow hadn't been able to block out his feelings for the man, and he couldn't face Snow Owl anymore with the obvious lie standing between them.

In the end, Night Sparrow had broken off his engagement with her, leaving Snow Owl confused and hurt. He'd moved into his own little apartment and started a solo career, both as a web designer and a crime fighter.

And night after night, he'd passed out from exhaustion with the faces of the two people he loved the most drifting in and out of his mind.

Midnight Owl had never liked the Real-Life Superhero Association. For years, Night Sparrow hadn't given much thought to it. Now, though, he knew there had to be something there. Midnight Owl had far too much hate inside of him for the place, and that was too much negative attention to focus toward anything without it being personal. Night Sparrow had known right off the bat that joining would break his mentor's heart, and some sick part of him had rejoiced in the fact. It had felt good to hurt the man who'd rejected him, who'd refused to return his feelings despite them both knowing it was impractical.

Midnight Owl was, after all, old enough to be Night Sparrow's father. However, none of that mattered now. None of that was circulating through Night Sparrow's brain.

Now....

Now, he and Midnight Owl were kissing each other as they shucked their clothes to the floor. Now, Night Sparrow was feeling the thick carpet of hair covering Oakstone's chest and stomach as his mentor yanked his naked body close to deepen their kiss.

Now, more than anything, Night Sparrow wanted to stay.

"I shouldn't…," Midnight Owl started to say between kisses. "We—"

"Shut up!" Night Sparrow interrupted fiercely. "Just shut up and fuck me, please!"

Night Sparrow ate at his mentor's mouth like he was starved. "No," Midnight Owl insisted, forcing him back. "Not like that."

Night Sparrow watched, confused and more than slightly frustrated, as his mentor moved past him to stretch out atop the bed. The sheets were already gone. Midnight Owl was lying on his back with both legs spread wide, yet it still took a second for Night Sparrow to pick up on what he meant.

Midnight Owl nodded as the light dawned in Night Sparrow's eyes. "Do it," he whispered, holding his legs back. "It should have always been this way."

There was something to be said for preparation. Though he hadn't thought much of it at the time, Night Sparrow had nonetheless enough foresight to stuff a box of condoms and lube in an easy-to-reach corner of his suitcase. It took almost no time for him to prep them both. He'd expected Midnight Owl to offer more resistance, but the man only grunted when the bulbous head of Night Sparrow's dick broke past his sphincter. After that, it was smooth sailing.

It was glorious.

Night Sparrow kept his eyes locked on Midnight Owl's face as he moved in and out. There was no time for technique or finesse. Both of them needed it and needed it fast and hard. Midnight Owl's eyes glazed over as Night Sparrow picked up the pace. He could feel his cock brushing back and forth over his mentor's prostate. Midnight Owl's salt-and-pepper hair was soaked with sweat when Night Sparrow finally came, firing off like a cannon. His own dick launched three shots of cum up into the air in an arc, splashing his chest and soaking into the thick fur there.

Night Sparrow collapsed on top of him, spent, but nowhere near ready for it to be over.

"Don't even think about moving," he warned, an edge of violence in his voice as he pulled out to dispose of the condom.

Midnight Owl folded both of his tree trunk arms back behind his head in a seemingly casual gesture. "Do you see me moving?" he asked, almost tauntingly.

Night Sparrow dropped the rubber into a nearby wastebasket, then turned to stare at his mentor. His eyes drank in the sight of the man he'd loved for years, probably since he was a teenager. Slowly, as though afraid he might evaporate, Night Sparrow moved toward the bed and climbed on top, stretching his body out over Midnight Owl's.

"What now?" he asked, afraid of the answer.

Midnight Owl shrugged again nonchalantly. "Whatever you want," he replied in a falsely calm voice. "We've got all night."

Night Sparrow smiled in spite of his irritation. "Yeah," he said. "And don't think for a second you're getting off that easy."

IT WAS late.

Or rather, he was. Night Sparrow checked his pockets one last time to ensure he had left nothing vital behind. His plane ticket was folded in an envelope inside his jacket pocket. The suitcase was waiting for him by the front door. Outside, the sun was beginning to rise over Anchorage.

He'd been going through the motions of this for the last half hour. There was something he was forgetting, yet even as he searched, Night Sparrow knew he wouldn't find it. "It" was currently stretched out across his bare mattress, lightly snoring and naked as a jaybird. Night Sparrow finally couldn't stand it anymore and made himself face one of the two loves of his life he was leaving behind. As he watched Midnight Owl sleep, it dawned on him he'd never said good-bye properly to Snow Owl. For all he knew, she might have slammed the door in his face. It probably said something that Midnight Owl was the one stretched out comfortably in front of him at the moment, yet as

Night Sparrow searched his heart, he couldn't find anything that suggested one was significantly less than the other.

Different perhaps, in their own unique ways, but the love was equally there. In the end, he hadn't been able to choose. That was the real reason why he was leaving. The realization slammed into him hard. He was running because he couldn't be both, couldn't have both.

And somehow, he felt they deserved better.

Tears were streaming down his face. Night Sparrow tried to breathe through his nose, but it had become clogged tighter than an expressway at noon. In films, people always cried with dignity, their faces barely moving. His was screwed up and swollen like an allergic reaction.

The noise of his sobbing should have woken Midnight Owl, but the man never moved. Gathering himself up, Night Sparrow walked toward the door, forcing himself not to look back. The suitcase was still there, a mark of how much his life was about to change. Supposedly, Chicago was going through a cold spell at the moment. For Night Sparrow, winter had already come.

The bastard hadn't even tried to stop him. He'd been lying in bed awake the whole time and never said a word to him. Night Sparrow wanted to hate the man, but it was love burning through him as he stood in the doorway of his home, looking over it for the last time.

"I love you, Richard Oakstone!" he shouted, the words bursting out of him like water from a broken dam.

There was so much more he wanted to say, but that was it. In the end, those had been the words he'd wanted to say for years, and now he had. A strange sense of peace settled the cataclysm raging inside his chest. It felt horrible and out of place next to the other emotions, but Night Sparrow locked onto it with everything he had. It gave him the strength to pick up his suitcase and close the door behind him.

He needed to hurry. The Association was waiting, after all, and he was already running the risk of missing his flight.

J.L. O'FAOLAIN was born the youngest, with four older sisters, in the backwoods of the Deep South. Those that have braved getting to know him have attributed this to being the root of his growing insanity. A teased bibliophile in his youth, O'Faolain spent his years prior to getting published as a cook, laundry man, delivery boy, grease monkey, and retail stocker. He has a plethora of skills and abilities, none of which would work well on a job application. In his spare time, O'Faolain enjoys weightlifting, philosophy, deconstruction, reading, writing, porn, and the Internet in general. Aside from becoming a successfully published author, he would very much like to pilot a giant robot while Two-Mix's "Rhythm Emotion" is playing in the background. Either that, or travel the world in a dirigible. In short, the general consensus by all, including himself, is that he is a mighty strange fellow.

Section Thirteen from J.L. O'FAOLAIN

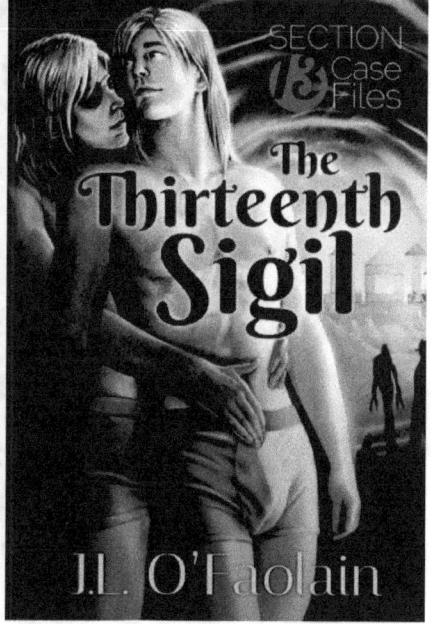

http://www.dreamspinnerpress.com